Martin Rowson is an award-winning political cartoonist whose work appears regularly in the *Guardian*, the *Independent on Sunday*, the *Daily Mirror*, the *Scotsman*, *Tribune*, *Index on Censorship* and *Granta*. His previous publications include comic-book adaptations of *The Waste Land* and *Tristram Shandy*. He lives with his wife and their two teenage children in south-east London. He enjoys red wine and the company of agents.

By the same author

Scenes from the Lives of the Great Socialists
Lower Than Vermin: An Anatomy of Thatcher's Britain
The Waste Land
The Nodland Express (with Anna Clarke)
The Life and Opinions of Tristram Shandy, Gentleman
The Sweet Smell of Psychosis (with Will Self)
Imperial Exits (with Julius Cicatrix)
Purple Homicide (with John Sweeney)
Mugshots

Snatches

Martin Rowson

JONATHAN CAPE
LONDON

Published by Jonathan Cape 2006

2 4 6 8 10 9 7 5 3 1

Text and illustrations copyright © Martin Rowson 2006

First published in Great Britain in 2006 by
Jonathan Cape
Random House, 20 Vauxhall Bridge Road,
London SW1V 2SA

Random House Australia (Pty) Limited
20 Alfred Street, Milsons Point, Sydney,
New South Wales 2061, Australia

Random House New Zealand Limited
18 Poland Road, Glenfield,
Auckland 10, New Zealand

Random House South Africa (Pty) Limited
Isle of Houghton, Corner of Boundary Road & Carse O'Gowrie,
Houghton 2198, South Africa

The Random House Group Limited Reg. No. 954009
www.randomhouse.co.uk

A CIP catalogue record for this book is available from the British Library

ISBN 0-224-07604-3
ISBN 978-0-224-07604-3

Papers used by Random House are natural,
recyclable products made from wood grown in sustainable
forests; the manufacturing processes conform to the
environmental regulations of the country of origin

Typeset by Palimpsest Book Production Limited,
Polmont, Stirlingshire
Printed and bound in Great Britain by
Mackays of Chatham PLC

For Anna, Fred and Rose, and in
loving memory of Annie, Butti, Russell, Jon,
Giles, Ossie and Jos, most of whom would,
I hope, have enjoyed the following . . .

'For what man in the natural state or course of thinking, did ever conceive it in his power to reduce the notions of all mankind exactly to the same length, and breadth, and height as his own?'

Jonathan Swift, 'A Digression on Madness',
in *Tale of a Tub*

'A failure of correspondence between subjective and objective is, generally speaking, the fountain-source of the comic as also the tragic in both life and art. The sphere of politics less than any other is exempted from the action of this law. People or parties are heroic or comic not in themselves but in their relation to circumstances.'

Leon Trotsky

Adam and Eve

Lucy strode across the hard ground before, briefly, traversing a small patch of mud which squidged softly between the long toes of her bare feet. The tickly ooze made her giggle, and then she marched off westward, grinning broadly into the setting sun.

The day, which had been hot, was cooling now it moved towards its close, eased that way by the gentle breeze blowing through the valley and Lucy's hair, ever so slightly disturbing the bits of leaf and flower she'd forgotten were still caught there. Distant animals gave hesitant voice to greet the easterly wind bringing the night. Lucy, now not just pleased but close to joyous, hooted in reply. This was, without doubt, the happiest day of her young life, and when she could clearly make out the darker outcrop of rock jutting from the verdant valley floor she broke into a run, laughing wildly even as she tripped and tumbled, as she often did, pounding across the countryside, each time righting herself and belting forward with a push from her calloused knuckles.

Soon she'd reached the rocks, and screamed with delight when she saw him, squatting on his haunches on a rock about twelve feet above her head, and squinting into the setting sun. He turned his head when he heard her, screamed himself and pounced off the rock to where Lucy stood, grabbing her in his arms and kissing her passionately on her open, gasping mouth. Their tongues writhed together, intermingling their spit and panting breath as he held her tightly in his strong

1

and hairy arms and she pressed herself against him, feeling that strange something melt inside which only melts, though you hardly know it, when you're in love.

He finally drew back from the embrace, breathing heavily, and held her at arm's length just to look at her. The sun, now very low and very red, glimmered in her eyes. They both smiled, then grinned, then grinned more broadly, idiotically, exposing the teeth at the edges of their upturned mouths, before they kissed again. Oh, how she loved him, Lucy thought, how she adored his firm body and funny, puzzled look and even the strange and different smells emanating from the various soft crevices about his body which her short fingers now gently probed. And oh! How she yearned to spend tonight and every night here beneath the stars, him holding her and her holding him in each other's hairy arms, their muzzles locked together in an endless kiss, and neither of them caring that they didn't know each other's names, backgrounds, origins or even, in these changeable times, species. They were young and in love, which is all that really matters.

Soon, as the moon rose and the stars shone bright, they made love on a narrow ledge among the rocks, in the gentle way they liked. Far off and closer by, envious lionesses roared and early elephants trumpeted and monogamous jackals yelped and the whole of animal creation chorused Lucy and her lover as they climaxed and came, over and over again, the warm juices of their love spilling and sticking to their furry loins, legs and bellies until, exhausted and happier than they could have thought possible, they fell asleep, still clinging together on their narrow, rocky, sticky, stinky bower of bliss about five foot three inches above the Rift Valley.

It was around twenty minutes before dawn that they fell.

Eden

By the time the sun had been up for a couple of hours, and was rising higher and higher into the equatorial sky, Lucy's lover left, loping off across the savannah to who knows where. He'd licked her muzzle and groomed her pelt at the nape of the neck, in the way he knew she loved, and left her to sit sunning herself, leaning against the warming rock. As she watched him go, she smiled and smiled and smiled.

The serpent, coiled up in a crevice close by, opened first one eye and then the other and slithered over to Lucy, where he coiled up again between her splayed legs. She smiled down at the narrow creature, her australopithecine heart still overbrimming with unconditional love for the whole of creation.

'Well,' said the snake, nestling closer to the inside of her left thigh, 'you certainly look pleased with yourself.'

'Hmmmmm,' Lucy hummed, still grinning, and playing with her hair.

'It won't do, you know.'

'Mmmmmmmmmmm.'

'It's going to get worse after this. It's downhill all the way from here on in. You realise that we're all doomed.'

Lucy picked at a scab on her right elbow, not really listening. Snakes were all like this, full of gloom, doom and their own self-importance.

'Soon will come a time when the threads of life that connect us living creatures will be broken. Different species will no longer be able to speak to each other as we do now. The bonds that unite us will be severed and a terrible time will come, when creature will turn on creature. No longer will the edible give themselves from love to those who eat them, but from fear and terror. No longer will the eaters consume their friends with blissful gratitude. All will be sundered. We will become mere beasts, your kind most of all.'

'Yeah. Right.' Lucy wiggled a bit as the snake nestled closer in.

'My kind can see all this, for we have, in this golden age, the gift of foresight and prophecy. I can see right now the fruit of last night's love growing inside you. You and lover-boy have produced something new, something different. You have a monster inside you, Lucy, a new kind of creature. I can see hundreds and thousands and millions of years into the future, and I can see what it and its kind will turn into. They will seek only to destroy all our friends, they will be driven by greed and fear and hatred, and they will despoil this beautiful world of ours, and make things far far worse whenever they pause, reflect on the ruination and try to make things, as they see it, better.' The snake slithered in even closer.

'Jesus Christ!' Lucy yelped.

'Who?' the snake asked, distracted for a second from his oration.

'What are you up to down there?'

'But while your unborn child, subdividing away in there' – the snake paused to lick whatever it was he had instead of lips – 'shows every prospect of becoming the very devil, I know a way of turning it into an angel. All it lacks, the tiny but defining factor that will and can change all our destinies, is compassion. Just that feeble spark that permits us all to see the bigger picture. Call it empathy if you like, that intangible thing which, it so happens, my species has in spades, and which I can give

6

your little unborn baby and all the creatures after its kind that will succeed it. I can save us all, Lucy. Just let me inside you, there's a poppet. Simply a little nip from my fangs and everything will be fine, as good as it is now, and soon even better. Then we can all live happily ever after. Just . . . let . . . me . . . in . . .'

'Cor! What a perv!' Lucy giggled as the snake pushed his head forward. 'Ooo! Hmmm . . . Ooo, that's . . . mmmmm . . .'

What the snake said next was, obviously, rather muffled, including his hoarse squawk as Lucy instinctively and involuntarily started to squeeze.

The Apotheosis of Saint Lucy

Rocking on thin haunches as if about to leap up to Heaven, Saint Simeon Stylites wiped his long and dripping nose on the sleeve of his hair shirt, peered into the Wilderness through his senile yellow eyes and, rising slowly, stiffly and loudly from his crouching position, shuffled about his platform. His lips fluttered in prayer as he clasped his hands round a jagged lump of rock, specks and patches of skin dropping into his beard and mouth. The rheumy eyes watered as he stared fixedly into the spinning and crossing circles in the heart of the rising sun, bisected by a thin skirt of cloud just above the horizon. The fleshless legs that had lately borne manacles, heavy chains and primitive barbed wire smarted as his knees struck the floor of the platform and crunched on the litter of sharp little pebbles, bones and ossified turds that covered it, and his throat, lined with gritty phlegm, rasped. He spat over the parapet and sixty feet below and several seconds later, the desert hissed briefly in reply. Saint Simeon Stylites, his loins tightening at the chance remembrance of a fifteen-year-old thought, ground his unforgiving fist into his wayward groin, and then clutched the rock tighter, smiling as the blood began to dribble between his fingers and drip onto his sacred thighs, meandering thereafter down to the floor to cloy as it mingled with the dusty rubbish round his knees. And indeed, the saint concluded in his blessed head teetering on top of his weak old spine, surely I am the holiest man alive.

* * *

Below, meanwhile, in the cool shadows just before dawn, the first pilgrims took up their places for the day ahead and Saint Daniel Stylites, a disciple of Saint Simeon's on holiday from his hermitage in the rocks outside Constantinople, was chatting to a Nubian centurion.

'Oh yes,' he said, looking up at the platform and smiling contentedly, 'I've been coming here regularly for the last, let's see, fourteen years, is it? Or is it fifteen? Good heavens! But I must say he's ailing noticeably. Terrible shame, really, when you think about all the marvellous things he did when he was younger. Do you know that he once fasted for three whole years? Not a drop of water, not a bite to eat. Wonderful really when you think about it.'

Above them the saint could just be seen stumbling at the edge of his platform, and for a second Saint Daniel thought of jumping up and down and waving. Then he remembered his companion and his dignity, though not necessarily in that order, and cocked his head and smiled benignly instead.

The Nubian clicked his tongue. 'You think he'll be dead before Christmas? Bloody tragic, that. I'm told the Emperor was planning to come and see him.'

'The Emperor, eh?'

'That's right. This new one we just got.'

'Yeah,' interrupted an Italian tourist who, like Saint Daniel and the Nubian, held out his arms in the shape of Christ crucified and squinted through the rays of the sun rising out of Persia at the old man on top of his pillar. 'Another Egyptian wide boy. The things they lumber us with from Byzantium.' Saint Daniel looked sideways at the tourist and sniffed loudly. The sun rose higher over the edge of the World, obliterating the shadows as it went.

They stood in silence for a while amid the bustle of

pilgrims around the column's base, each left to his own prayers or thoughts. Saint Daniel thought about his old friend who'd fled the World and its temptations, and thought with fond recollection of Simeon's rejection of its greatest perils and his remarkable demonstrations of faith performed in his efforts to come to terms with the Living God: the chains wound tightly round his scrotum and linked to heavy weights dangling from the edge of his plinth; the ever growing height of the pillar as he removed himself further and further away from the perfidious ways of womankind; the turmoils and battles for his soul as sultry succubi disported themselves in the guise of pilgrims in the surrounding deserts and sought to pull him down to Damnation with their caresses.

A reflex grunt of disgust disturbed Daniel's thoughts. It was now nearing noon, and most of the pilgrims were already at lunch in the white convent down the valley. Just a few of the specially pious or especially curious stood, arms extended cruciform, in the heat of the Syrian desert. Saint Daniel blew out of the corners of his mouth at the tiny flies buzzing round his eyes, as scorpions scurried across the hot bright sand.

'Come here often?' the Italian tourist asked.

'Oh yes, fourteenth year. They really are terribly good about it down at the convent, you know. All these people descending on them all year round and never a word of complaint.'

The Italian mumbled something in Latin which Saint Daniel chose to ignore.

'Yes, they all know me down there, but then I am what you might call something of a regular.' Saint Daniel chortled to himself and adopted a blank expression which seemed to tell of some inner peace, as if his soul had settled down to rest amidst the turmoil of this

Temporal Battlefield. 'Well, lunch time I think,' he said, patting his stomach, and he trudged off down the valley across the broken stones that littered the ground.

After lunch, having fallen asleep in a grove of ancient olive trees several hundred yards behind the convent, Saint Daniel was disturbed. Having been lulled to sleep by the monotones of the cicadas, he now awoke to the sound of his own name being repeated in a harsh whisper. He opened an eye and saw one of the Brothers from the convent, who he couldn't remember having seen before. Opening the other eye, he focused on the monk who was, he reckoned, about fourteen years old and, by the look of him, a Greek. 'What is it?' croaked Saint Daniel. 'What do you want?'

'Father Daniel, you must help me!'

The saint grimaced. 'Look, I'm awfully tired. What is it? I can't really hear a confession out here, you know.'

'Father Daniel!' The monk stared at him with the look of certain madness. 'Father Daniel, I can't hear anything!'

'Well, I'm sorry, but . . .' The saint checked himself and was about to shout the same words again when he was hushed by loud, nasal whimpers as the monk pawed violently at his robes.

'No, no! In here! In here!' The young monk banged his temples with both his fists until his ears began to bleed. Then he told Saint Daniel the wildest story he'd ever heard.

Many years ago – the year Daniel had first come on pilgrimage to Syria, in fact – when Simeon was in his prime and his pillar was only forty feet high, a naive local Arab girl had scaled the column one night, thinking to join the lonely holy man on top in prayer to his potent djinn. Simeon had been scourging himself at the time, and tied up in chains he hadn't noticed the girl pull

12

herself up over the edge of his platform because of the noise of clanking. But when he did, and saw her smiling at him and brushing the muck from her clothes, he let out a dreadful scream that startled even the jackals cringing among the rocks. Before she even had a chance to say hello, the saint jumped on her, tripping over his chains and bringing them both crashing to the filthy floor. Her cries were drowned out by his, as he alternately throttled her and called her Satan, then raped and buggered her, calling her Gabriel, before he grabbed her round the waist and hurled her off his pillar.

Later some monks chased away the jackals with their torches and carried the mad girl they'd found being eaten by the beasts to their convent to see if she'd live, doing their best to ignore her crazy stories. Shortly afterwards Simeon started work on heightening his column.

Daniel remembered this. He also remembered how grumpy the saint had been during the construction, throwing rocks and rubbish at any pilgrim who came within range, and spending the nights preaching vile apocalyptic sermons to the jackals sitting attentively round the base of the pillar. But he'd never heard of any girl rescued from the desert night, nor indeed of any motherless child being reared at the convent. The mad monk's eyes blazed with either rage or fervour, and he went on with his story.

When he was born his mother had stared at him, screamed and run off into Syria. Thus abandoned, he'd been brought up in seclusion by a gossipy old nun who told him contradictory tales of his origins. Yes, he was the diabolical issue of a union between his succubus whore mother and the jackal god of the pagan Egyptians; he was holy Simeon's holy son, brought down to earth on a cushion carried by angels; he was hellspawn conceived in Simeon's battle with Satan, born with no skin to a camel and with eagle's claws instead of hands and feet; he'd been wrested from the slavering maw of a she-jackal loping off to her den with him held in her jaws by the scruff of his neck. His father was, variously, Simeon, Satan, Jesus, Caesar, an Ethiopian eunuch, the sun itself and the dust of the desert; his mother, alternatively, had been eaten finally by the jackals, had become a pagan empress of terrific cruelty in the East, had been changed into a goblin and swallowed up by a hellhole or had assumed the Kingdom of Heaven in a chariot of fire. But whatever his origins, and whoever his parents, the monk knew this: as he'd grown, and the nun told him thousands upon thousands of stories, she'd mingled them with tales of how Simeon, the holiest man alive, spent every day in earnest conversation with the Living God, which was why he'd built his pillar to get closer and closer to Heaven, as he was getting a bit hard of hearing these days. Oh yes, the nun added, she and everyone else on God's good Earth had been spoken to by God, and He said the nicest things too.

But as the monk tried to sleep at night, listening to the songs of the cicadas and hearing the sands shift and the rocks crunch as they settled down round Hell, he'd never heard a word from God.

'Never! And now there's the dreams and the blood, Father Daniel! And I can't sleep because of the noise of the pilgrims breathing and the monks praying and the jackals and everything and the pounding in my head and my hair and my fingernails growing and . . . and . . .' The monk was grinding his teeth and rolling his eyes. 'I can't hear God! What does He say? Why won't He speak to me like He does to everyone else? And why haven't I got . . . why haven't I got a . . .' But unable to continue, the monk collapsed in sobs into Saint Daniel's coarse shirt.

*   *   *

'Hi!' Saint Daniel called to the Nubian after evensong. 'Extraordinary thing happened to me this afternoon,' he gasped as he hurried to catch up with the centurion. 'Most peculiar fellow came and told me he couldn't hear God. Now what do you make of that?'

The Nubian snorted. 'Bloody fool.'

'Well, that's what I thought too, and a lunatic as well. And you know what? He claimed he was Simeon's son too! Now, I've known Simeon long enough to know that he's . . .' Then Daniel half heard the Italian mumble something obscene in his vile Latin drawl, and was about to admonish him when a long, loud wail broke through the night.

Up on top of the pillar, with the Great Wilderness dimly lit by distant stars, Saint Simeon Stylites lay dead on the floor of his platform covered with dust, sand and garbage. His broken body gave off a slight yellow glow and a powerful stench, his hair shirt was alive with bugs, rigid with age and in tatters, his beard stiff with sweat, saliva and grease. The young monk stood over him, trembling with fear. The old man's gums had snapped shut and his jaw had then fallen down to his deflated chest as he'd stared into the Wilderness; there was a gleam in his clouded eye and a smile turning up the edges of his loose mouth, just as if he'd heard nothing the young monk had said to him. Then the saint had tried to point to something, but when the monk looked round there was nothing there. The saint had mumbled words which the monk couldn't understand, and had paid no attention when he'd pulled up his habit to show his father the pubescent female body God had cursed him with. Then Saint Simeon Stylites had given up the ghost. The monk fell to his knees and threw himself across the saint's body, the enormity of the World closing

15

down on him. And yet still he heard no God. As he looked at the cohorts of pilgrims that came and went each day, he'd hear everything: court gossip, the moans of beggars and cripples, the tourists' gasps and chitchat. Thousands, and thousands of thousands, came: on crutches, in litters, with diamonds on every finger, with no toes at all, with powdered or painted or oiled or pitted or disintegrating faces, in the middle of which were the always open mouths from which issued a Pandemonium that filled the skies and enveloped the globe, loading the air to the point of explosion and bashing on the doors of Heaven and Hell alike. And the monk heard nothing through the babel, and began to sob again, his beardless lower lip, set low down in his girlish face, trembling between gasps. Then, slowly, he looked up, and listened to something he'd never heard before. And, more curiously, to nothing else. On top of a pillar some sixty feet from base to summit, in the middle of an empty waste in a barbaric age a small girl, who believed what she was told and so thought herself a freak on more levels than she could count, heard the word of God come tumbling at her through thousands of miles across the Wilderness.

And the word was 'Jump'.

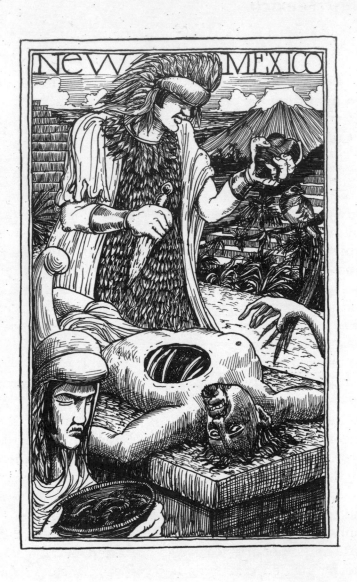

New Mexico

'Well?' The albino's red eyes flashed in reply to the thin red light from the setting sun and he counted on up to fifteen. 'Hard day?'

Cortés, you see, came early. That, or the beginning of the World came late. Either way, the conquistador, working to a different timetable, gave the matter little thought and instead screamed blue murder as the attendant priests bolted the crystal skull over his hairy face, counting aloud as they did so. The screams were drowned by the noise of chanting and music while Moctezuma, smiling idiotically at the bound and masked Spaniard, patted his arm and cooed at him. The attendant priests, eyes averted from the God King, smeared narcotic potions of ash and spumen over Cortés's heaving chest and then Moctezuma lowered the onyx knife to the prescribed place a fraction above Cortés's left nipple, drove it in and sliced out a perfect circle in the flesh. The attendant priests danced and chanted. Other priests continued counting as they smeared the blood in geometric patterns on Cortés's torso. Absurd equations flashed through Moctezuma's mind, addled by the peyote he chewed frantically and the hallucinogenic greasepaint covering his face, limbs and torso. A sacred oil of mescal was poured over his hands as he snapped apart Cortés's ribs and severed the aorta and other arteries in a single, rapid, circular slash and he giggled crazily as he held up the vanquished conquistador's black and still beating heart high above his head, silhouetted against the rising sun over the roaring Mexican nation. Then, suddenly, Moctezuma lost count.

Cortés, as I said, came early. The sheaf was not complete. Quetzalcoatl was not yet expected. The end of the World, moreover, was by no means due.

Down in the plaza below the Great Pyramid youths swung in an unwinding motion from lianas tied to their feet, marking out in their revolutions the exactitudes of the Aztec calendar. Feathered headdresses bobbed among the crowd between huddles of priests adding, subtracting, dividing and multiplying back to the moment of Creation and then back again to now. Old women made signs in the air with their hands, while the priests around Moctezuma counted up to fifteen, then up to fifteen again in a ceaseless round. The remaining blood in Cortés's heart beat out over Moctezuma's cheeks and mingled with the greasepaint, exacerbating its effect.

Cortés had come early. The reports of the invaders failed to alarm the priests busy over their sums. The Spanish envoy had been laughed at and then sacrificed, thus ensuring the easy victory the following dawn when Cortés's army had been ambushed, disarmed and captured. And Moctezuma now laughed out loud, lurched sideways and tossed Cortés's heart over the edge of the pyramid as he was guided to the altar where the Tlaxcalan chief, Cortés's ally and co-celebrant in the continuing act of devotion, lay bound.

Later, however, the Aztec was troubled. Back in the palace in the late afternoon he splashed his sleeve stirring gold dust and marijuana shavings into his coffee, and shouted at the feathered lackey who cringed and backed away, eyes averted according to custom. How could he be sure, despite all the calculations, that this absurd army of pale monkeys had not, after all, been a foretaste of things to come? The Fire Era, although not over, was close to its end and so, therefore, were History, Time and the World itself. Moctezuma wondered, with a tightening feeling in his chest, whether his calculations had been as exact as his fellow gods'. Worse still, the victory sacrifices had, exceptionally, taken place on the eleventh day of the week – with the Tlaxcalans included, the invading army had numbered nearly 2000, and today they'd only got as far as the self-proclaimed Bishop of Mexico – even though the stability of the whole Empire depended on the strict observation of religious precedent and the liturgical calendar. Perplexed, Moctezuma decided to go for a walk round his zoo.

The sun edged towards the horizon of jungle at the eastern edge of the plateau and the creatures in the zoo prepared, in the ways individual to their species, for the night. Several slaves who tended the animals scampered from sight as Moctezuma passed between the cages and paddocks, clicking his tongue at the lonely tapir in the cage next to the puma devouring the scraps of Cortés's empty-chested corpse. He dug out a length of sugar cane for the deer from the sun, but Cortés's white mare spurned the gift and trotted proudly away in her enclosure. Moctezuma sighed and hurried past the cage housing the remainder of the Spanish priests who, naked and gasping in the thin air, were praying fervently and ignoring their Aztec counterparts who sought an understanding of minds over the nature of sacrifice and the supporting, emblematic functions of cannibalism and sodomy. The Aztec priests bowed their heads and shielded their eyes when they saw Moctezuma, and bowed lower towards his retreating back while the King groaned and squinted at the sun, deep red and ready to set, in order to calculate the time of day.

21

There is no room for variables, he concluded in dismay as he hurried on. The sacrifices should have waited two days. Everything is set down in an absolute pattern: the sun rises, reaches its zenith, then moves interminably onwards to sink under the World as its protector Blue Hummingbird moves from the realm of the Living to that of the Dead, giving up his place as he goes to Tezcatlipoca, god of night, who emerges from below the firmament to take possession of Heaven until he, in his turn, hands everything back to the Hummingbird. And, just as night follows day, so too could he, Moctezuma, never consider (as he was tempted to do at the moment) throwing away his Kingship, Divinity or any of the other forces and factors that governed his life to the winds now blowing over the disc of the World. For these too were controlled, by the sublime mathematics of Tlaloc, by the multiplicity of Earth goddesses, tree spirits and swamp gnomes, and sped on their way through the air high above the now dark sand and shrubbery and creeping forest to the distant waters, just as they ever had, ever did, and ever will. And on their way the winds ruffled Moctezuma's hair as they must, so that he was required, in an action determined before the commencement of time, to pass an inevitably heavily ringed hand through the locks to separate them out again.

The numbers were added up, taken away, divided and multiplied as he walked among the animals howling at the rising moon to his favourite part of his zoo where, in larger cages hung with baskets of jungle flowers, a troop of human freaks sat drooling and rolling their eyes and lolling about in floppy, deformed acrobatics, back and forth against the bars.

'Hard day?' the albino repeated.

Except, thought Moctezuma, there always seemed to

be departures from the invariable course of History, and he hardly knew, looking at the freaks, what function it served for children to be born with their heads growing between their shoulders, or too tall, or as midgets, maniacs or idiots, or llama-necked geeks or rhea-toed spazzes or tapir-nosed monstrosities, or else doomed to hop through life on a single, centrally placed leg. For although the astrologers drew up unconvincing tables that sought to explain the temporal aberrances at the moment of conception that resulted in these misconceptions, Moctezuma still could not understand the purpose of these half-people who, after all, had no part to play in his total society: they couldn't be slaves, or warriors, or priests, and it would be almost sacrilegious to permit them to meet the public-spirited demands of citizenship, apart from being unnecessarily cruel, by being sacrificed with the regularity he'd have liked. Moctezuma frowned as the albino said, 'Hard day?' a third time, and proceeded to feed brazil nuts to an imbecile hanging from the bars. The albino smiled to himself in the gloaming and scratched some figures in the sand with a piece of balsa wood, calculating back to the Creation and then back again to now.

'Hard day?'

'Hmmm.' Moctezuma answered half-heartedly the fourth time of asking, more concerned with poking the idiot and trying to count to fifteen.

'Heard you.'

'Hmmm.'

A red sliver of the sun disappeared below the treeline and the freaks and animals began to howl and whimper and hoot.

'Noisy.'

'Yes,' said the King. 'Yes, it was.' And he sighed again and turned to the albino. The latter's red eyes dulled

23

with the dusk. Macaws cawed. Savage beasts pawed the ground and yelped.

'Oh fuck it!' Moctezuma shouted suddenly. The crazy boy shrieked and scampered away. 'Fuck it, fuck it, fuck it!'

'Er, sorry?'

'Oh God,' the Aztec groaned, shaking his head in his hands. 'It's all so fucking complicated! It's not as if I didn't try to tell them. I mean, rules are rules. How am I expected to tell everyone that the World might end tomorrow?'

The albino made an unseen gesture in the twilight. Moths collided noisily, giddy in the high altitude, but Moctezuma ignored them.

'And what with all this going on even I've started to have my doubts. I mean, God help us, does any of it actually *mean* anything?'

'Well . . .'

'I mean, just think what I have to put up with. What's it to me whether thirteen days in one week add up to fifty-two somewhere else? Life goes on, doesn't it? And then there's all my bloody generals moaning at me day in day out to tell them whether twenty Cholulans are as good as fifteen Tlaxcalans for the sacrifices, and how many have to be killed in battle, and how many sacrificed, and whether this attack today is propitious from an astrological point of view when we had a retreat last week when some idiot saw a toucan up a gum tree the previous Thursday. And snakes! Jesus! Do you know how much of my time is taken up with snakes? They're fucking everywhere! And then there's all this crap about this Coctés or whatever his name was. Half the bloody priesthood tell me he's Quetzalcoatl, while the other half bore me stiff with endless recitations of the calendar saying he can't possibly have been old Death and

24

Feathers. If even they don't know, how the hell am I meant to?'

Moctezuma paused to breathe heavily, but the adrenalin was pumping hard and his heartbeat quickened.

'I mean! It's not even as if we're in the middle of a series of bad years or anything. These are good years, I tell them, bloody good years! So the hunting's bad, but the crops are good and all the signs are that everything's fucking dandy for the foreseeable future, so don't worry about a thing. And then these ignorant pricks come along and tell me they've seen an axolotl riding on the back of a coyote and oh dearie me, that's all their calculations up the bloody spout, sorry and all that but there you go. But then the other lot say, that was no axolotl, no no no, that was a *fish*! Quetzalcoatl can't come now, no way, José! But then I say, look, it's years before the Big Q's due anyway, so *what* are you *talking* about, and then this pale bastard Cortés turns up and the first lot say told you so at the first pink face they see while the second bunch start monkeying about with the creed, the liturgy and everything else they can lay their hands on. And suddenly I just don't know any more. I mean, if they want a white man to be Quetzy, why don't they pick on *you*, for Christ's sake?' The albino raised his pale eyebrows, unseen. 'I mean, I don't know if Cortés was Quetzacoatl or not, do I? The calendar says no, the omens say yes, and now I don't know whether we've done something unbelievably awful by topping him and this really is the end of the World or if I've done the right thing and it's business as usual. I mean, these Spaniards claim that they killed their god years ago and now they eat him in a biscuit or something. Well, if that's possible, anything is. Isn't it? I just don't know any more.'

And, just as abruptly as he began, Moctezuma stopped, and the silence was broken only by his heavy sobs, the distant noises of the jungle and a low gurgle from the frightened freaks.

After a while smoothing his white hair, the albino clears his throat and speaks.

'Why bother?'

'Sorry?' Moctezuma is brought back from his miserable reveries with a start.

'Um. I said, er, why bother?'

'What do you mean?'

'Well, er, it's just a thought, of course, but it has occurred to me – and I have a lot to think about, stuck out here, very grateful though I am, of course, for your hospitality and everything and, er . . . anyway, it occurred to me' – the albino coughs and laughs nervously – 'that these sacrifices are really a bit of a waste of time. What I mean, er, is that, while it's quite obvious that they do an enormous amount of good, naturally, has it never struck you that we've had enough of them? That is, that the gods are now fully appeased and that the sun will rise tomorrow come what may, even without all these slaves being sacrificed?'

'What do you mean?' Moctezuma's eyes narrow in the darkness, and the albino, gaining confidence, expands on his theme.

'Well, take your problem: was he, or wasn't he? Quetzalcoatl, I mean. Now, I'd say not, but that's just my opinion. But I wonder, does it really matter either way? I mean, if he was Quetz, you've at least stopped him destroying the World, eh? But that's not really my point. The whole Quetzalcoatl cult, if you think about it, isn't really doing Mexico any favours, is it? I mean, as the observance of the cult is currently administered, it really is the most terrible waste of resources, let alone the psycho-cultural implications of predicating your entire society on the principle that some malign honky is expected to turn up at any minute to destroy the World. Talk about inferiority complexes! This is such a vapid cliché of bleeding heart post-colonialism that it's almost a joke! Look at it this way. With all these sacrifices you're using up considerable manpower resources from both sides. On the one hand half the army has no other function than to capture savages for sacrifice, while you can add to that all these thousands of priests, protecting their own vested interests and doing nothing more than constantly counting and recounting the number of days since Creation and until the Apocalypse. And on the other hand there are these thousands of slaves, using up precious resources in being housed and fed, and to what end? To be killed. Just think about it. Our methods of warfare are, to say the least, hardly the most efficient, with this imperative to take prisoners who are going to be killed anyway, but then you compound it by having all these prisoners languishing away in gaol, often for months on end, getting fatter and fatter, when it's not their bellies you're interested in, but their hearts and minds. As for the priesthood, they're merely another of the forces of conservatism that are holding the Empire back, alternatively counting and then panicking whenever they come across something they imagine might be a bad omen. It's obviously just a self-perpetuating oligarchical racket to maintain jobs for the boys!

'Might it not, therefore, be simpler to let the army get on with what it should be doing best, which is having proper battles, conquering our enemies and neighbours and expanding the Empire? Then you can set all the priests and slaves to work in the fields. Dare I say it, it might even be an idea, when there's a drought, rather than butchering thousands of people till it rains to get them to dig some irrigation ditches instead.

'What I'm saying really is this. In terms of military strategy and the economy, the system as it stands is wasteful in the extreme. In simple human terms, I might add, our religious and cultural practices do nothing to enhance the quality and standing of our civilisation. After all, these Spaniards may look ridiculous to us with their biscuit god, but hasn't it occurred to you how ridiculous – indeed, how barbaric – we might look to them? Of course, we all know about cultural diversity, but diversity can only go so far. In short, is eccentricity for its own sake justifiable at the end of the day? When an alternative presents itself, shouldn't we embrace change, rather than sticking with the status quo just because? Let's not do what we've always done just because we've always done it, but instead do *what works*. In the light of what I've said, it strikes me that our whole way of life – religious, economic, military and cultural – is almost completely indefensible. Therefore, accepting that our present devotional practices are wasteful economically, obstructive strategically, peculiar culturally and very probably totally irrelevant to the workings of the real World, I modestly propose that you abandon them forthwith. And while we're about it we can cease these interminable bloody calculations of the calendar and start counting this Spanish money stuff instead!'

Moctezuma was really rather startled when the pale sophist concluded his speech. But, as he valued the albino's counsel on many things, he had listened attentively. A quick straw poll of the other incarcerated freaks revealed that they entirely agreed with their eloquent fellow, so Moctezuma decided to act on the albino's suggestions. Thus was a new age of secular pragmatism born, with one last great festival of sacrifice which saw off the entire priesthood and, out of respect, the albino himself. And as superstition and the terrors of the night receded, the armies of the Aztec Empire won greater, bloodier and more glorious victories than ever before, the Empire expanded at an unprecedented rate, the economy boomed and hope for the brightest of futures warmed every now inviolate breast. Everything was reasonable, decent, fair and thoroughly sensible, the expeditionary force for the invasion of Europe was nearly ready and, of course, when Popocatepetl indignantly exploded soon thereafter the entire civilisation was completely destroyed.

THE DILEMMA OF DON JUAN
DE ESCALANTE

The Dilemma of Don Juan de Escalante

In mid-spring 1521 by the Christian calendar, Juan de Escalante, commander of the Spanish coastal base of Vera Cruz, was beginning to get worried. Cortés and his army, which consisted of most of the conquistadors, had set off for the interior in August two years previously and, save for the occasional rumour, he hadn't heard anything of them since. Now, his spirits dejected, he began with half a mind to pay these rumours greater attention. Could it be possible that 400 men, their horses and their artillery had all been devoured by monstrously large jaguars as some of the Indians claimed? Or perhaps they'd been struck down and destroyed by the same disgusting and unique disease that had decimated de Escalante's own meagre force. He picked agitatedly at the scab at the corner of his mouth. However, whatever Cortés's problems, and whatever his fate, he, Juan de Escalante, had problems of his own. The native women he had received as nominal gifts from the local chiefs had learned Spanish with surprising ease and now nagged him all the day long; of the 150 or so troops left him by Cortés, the sick had all died and then been dug up and eaten by the Indians, so that all corpses now had to be burnt immediately after death which, because the already drunken physician had enthusiastically embraced the efficacy of the abundant natural pharmacopoeia and thus often made mistakes, had led to ugly scenes with the men; of the living, half the troops had contracted the same filthy disease that was even now eating away at de Escalante's bones, while the rest

31

commuted between Vera Cruz and Zempoala where they lived, quite openly and beyond discipline, with their new Indian families; worst of all, de Escalante's own chaplain and confessor was in ecumenical cahoots with the local shamans and was modifying Christian dogma in a blatantly heretical way, on top of developing an inappropriate taste for the ancient sodomitic rituals of the local Amerindians. De Escalante thanked God that at least he'd put a stop to the human sacrifices, or at least as far as he could tell. It was all very distressing.

Things wouldn't have been quite so bad if Cortés hadn't scuppered all their ships on landing and then taken all the shipwrights with him into the interior. This had seemed like a good idea at the time, as at least it had pacified the more hot-headed conquistadors. But now, nearly two years later, it meant that they had no means of contact with civilisation. It was unlikely that either Garey in Jamaica or Velázquez in Cuba would bother to find out what had happened to their old rival Cortés, and so de Escalante was rapidly coming to the conclusion that he was doomed.

'Bugger the man,' Juan hissed between his rotting teeth. It was clearly all Cortés's fault that he was soon going to die in this godforsaken dump, and then in all likelihood end up as someone's dinner, and he decided venomously that whatever fate had befallen the arrogant bastard was fully deserved. However, it wasn't just Cortés he hadn't heard from. There had been no news of any kind from the interior: no deserters, no Aztec tax collectors, no rampaging armies collecting sacrificial victims, no cannibal raids. Not a sausage, in fact. Perhaps he really ought to do something.

A month and a half later de Escalante and the remnants of his task force arrived in Mexico. They presented an unassuming embassy for Emperor Charles V and the Church of Christ. Of the forty men pressed into coming, only nine remained and three of these had become insane with fever and, haunted by the unquiet ghosts of the Aztecs, had been bound in chains for their own protection. Their eyes rolled round in their burning sockets and they gibbered quietly as they followed their five comrades bearing de Escalante's litter across the vulcan landscape. The lava was still warm, and the Zempoalan guide and interpreter, Cuitlahuac, hopped gingerly over the crenellations in his bare feet, mumbling snatches of popular songs to himself as he went. Eventually they stopped.

'Well, boss,' said Cuitlahuac, leaning into the litter, 'this is the place.'

De Escalante lifted himself feebly into a sitting position and peered out into the desolation. 'Wherezhur city, Cutluck?'

'Damned if I know, squire. That bloody mountain must've blown 'imself up. This is the place all right.'

Some wayward spittle dribbled by one of the deranged soldiers landed with a sizzle on the ground as de Escalante was lifted from his bier. Unsteadily he stood and, witnessed by the last of the conquistadors, took Mexico for Christ and Spain, briefly swearing an oath before collapsing, breathless, back into the litter. Cuitlahuac kicked idly at a pumice stone as he squinted through the thin, still air at the sun, still weak and shrouded by the settling clouds of volcanic dust. A distant rumble brought furtive glances from the five sane soldiers as they squatted on their haunches and tried to breathe in that high and blighted place, and they started to prepare the litter for retreat. The poor loonies began to rattle their chains and howl in anguish as the rumbles grew louder and the earth began to shudder beneath their feet, and in their haste to escape the scene no one noticed the giant shards of gold begin to push their way through the clinker.

Inside SAINT LUCIAN's

Inside Saint Lucian's

Crespolini ducked out of the unforgiving Roman sunshine into the dimness of the Church of Saint Lucian, and for several seconds stood in what seemed to be total darkness. As his eyes grew accustomed to the gloom, it was stutteringly intruded on here and there by the increasingly discernible racks of offertory candles and, at the very edge of his vision, small, backlit geometrical yet beautiful patterns. The silence, after the cacophonous catastrophes of the streets outside was, in a way, more disabling than his temporary blindness, and waiting for the rest of his senses to return, Crespolini breathed in the smells of the place, jumbled up but each distinctive: the incense, obviously; the beeswax; the bittersweet smell of fresh plaster and drying oil paint; the absence (equally discernible) of a usual churchy mustiness; and, informing all, the unmistakable and constant stench of death and human corruption.

The sharp, echoing sound of a tool of some undisclosed type having been dropped, maybe accidentally, from the top of the scaffolding at the east end of the building and hitting the marble floor thirty feet beneath made his ears prick up with a start. Although his sight was now improving, after that it took a further moment or two for Crespolini to recover his nerves. He sniffed, raising and lowering his eyebrows in a rapid, private admonition to get a grip. This place always gave him the creeps, but he had to pull himself together, get on with the job and take in the scene before him as he'd been trained to do.

The church itself was relatively new, built on the site of another church dating from the twelfth century which, in its turn, was built around, over or onto the foundations of previous churches and, before them, pagan temples all the way back to the days of Imperial Rome. God only knew what they'd got up to, and in whose name, back then. The church's current dedicatee, however, was Saint Lucian, a deacon, or a soldier or a proconsul martyred for his faith during the Maximian persecution. Although, according to some, it was actually named (or renamed) after another Lucian, or Lucius, or Lucy or Lucia (the saint's gender was now forgotten), a figure about whom absolutely nothing was known but who had enjoyed a fleeting cultus in the Holy Land during a period which happened to coincide with the Second Crusade. His or her defining ambiguity provided the possibilities of a devotional palimpsest which proved irresistible to a small band of the crusaders, naturally attracted to anything which mirrored or even might, by association, sanction the ambiguity of their actions. Those who returned in pilgrimage to Rome repaid the apparent protection Lucius (or Lucy, or Lucian) had afforded them with this church. Or the last one, or the one before that.

To be honest Crespolini didn't care. Facts were his job, not speculation, and he quickly scanned the body of the church, noting the two or three old women fussing around the various altars and side chapels, the priests and Brothers about their business and the artist and artisans working on the fresco, one of whom had, maybe not accidentally, dropped the unknown tool. Satisfied that he could let things here wait, he nodded briefly towards the altar and strode off to the crypt.

It was closed to tourists today, several of whom glowered at him malignantly as he nodded to the civilian policeman granting him ingress.

A part of him could understand their disappointment. They'd come to see the church's famous ossuarial sculptures, the stacks of skulls and bits of bone of dead members of the order, arranged in beautiful patterns by their successors. These memento mori, although not precisely Crespolini's cup of tea, had been a particular joy to the last pontiff, who was now, as these things invariably turned out, enjoying a cultus of his own. That Pope had encouraged other churches to establish their own installations in imitation, and it was even said that the flying cupids, being the complete skeletons of stillborn babies, were his idea and that he'd retrospectively baptised several boxes of bones before they'd been articulated by the lay Brothers whose job it was to add to the display in the most artistic fashion they could conceive or accomplish. The current Pope, Crespolini's boss and patron, was more impatient with these exercises in *vanitas*, for a whole lot of different reasons (and the rumours, as only Roman rumours can, abounded as to precisely why). Still, His Holiness was shrewd enough to see the importance of the Lucian displays for the tourist trade, so he let them alone.

As Crespolini descended into the crypt, the staircase lined with skulls and other bones wired together, he passed up any moral or aesthetic judgement, ignoring them just like he'd ignore any other kind of interior decor which was immaterial to the particular case he was on, and untempted to be as dismissive as his more fashionable colleagues in the Curia. Both in line with what they perceived, judiciously, as papal whim, and because of other political and social factors, this season it was wise to talk enthusiastically about the latest wax sculptures of the grislier martyrdoms Salvia had commissioned in Venice and which arrived in Rome earlier that year. But although Crespolini couldn't be bothered to pay much attention to fashion, he was notorious in certain circles for both his cold ambition and his ruthless eye for detail.

It was that which made him notice, and note, the fresh plaster in the crypt, newly painted white, before surrendering himself to overwhelming irritation when he saw a largish group of men huddled together in the middle of the room, several of whom turned round as he entered. A few of the Swiss Guards stiffened, not sure, with this new arrival, what to do or to whom to defer. A youngish man broke away from the group to greet him.

'Ah, Monsignor!'

'Inquisitor,' Crespolini grunted. Shit! he thought, smiling at Iniezione from the Holy Office of the Inquisition. What's he doing here? Why wasn't he told these bastards would be on the case as well?

'What a delight!' Iniezione was smiling beautifully. 'Although I was unaware that the Curia was interested in something as mundane as this little, ah, nonsense.'

'Well, Inquisitor,' Crespolini continued smiling back, confused, 'you know the Curia is interested in everything.'

Iniezione's smile trembled slightly at the universal implications of Crespolini's concluding word, then he smiled even more beautifully. 'Of course, of course! As are we all.'

Their little joust concluded, Iniezione beckoned Crespolini into the huddle across the crypt, and carried on smiling as he made the customary introductions. Crespolini noted how very white, very sound and very sharp his teeth were. That was something he could see to later. Right now he was rapidly calculating the interplay of rival, conflicting and mutually hostile jurisdictions gathered unexpectedly in this low place. There was him, bloody Iniezione from the Inquisition (why?), Schlefen from the Swiss Guard, the Father Abbot of the Carmelite order (obviously) whose church this was and whose name he'd forgotten as soon as he'd heard it, Gordo the Jesuit (again, why?) and some little shit from the College of Cardinals, whom he could safely ignore. Crespolini's irritation was compounded when he noted how they'd all come mob-handed, with secretaries, chaplains, bodyguards and other lackeys, although he could, and would, play his solitary status as a signal of the greater authority he'd had invested in him. They all knew he was a loner by temperament. Now they could pretend that they thought he was one by delegated authority as well.

The Father Abbot looked at Crespolini nervously, and Crespolini toyed for a moment with the idea of winking at the old bastard, just to compound his discomfort, but decided against it. He saw he was going to have to play this one straight and keep his penchant for fun and games in check for later on when things got really nasty.

Meanwhile, Iniezione had resumed his conversation with Schlefen, the kind of fat, stupid German Swiss who did well in the Guards, and who owed Crespolini no more love than the rest of them.

'So, just to make sure we're all in the picture' – here Iniezione simpered towards Crespolini, who smirked back – 'we're talking now about five of the lay Brothers having disappeared, it would seem from what the Father Abbot says, into thin air.'

'Six, Inquisitor,' the German said with a pout.

'Six! Heavens, Father Abbot! This is beginning to look like carelessness!' No one laughed, but Iniezione kept on smiling. 'And obviously you've checked the usual places.'

'Obviously. Done the brothels, and chased leads in

Florence, Paris, Geneva and even Constantinople.' The German said this to impress the others with the breadth of his network of intelligence and detection, and awe them with the terrible extent of his reach. Needless to say, no one was either impressed or, for that matter, awestruck.

'Mexico? Lima?'

'No time to get there. Anyway, we're not looking at abscondment. This is murder.'

'Well, I think we must be the judge of that.' Iniezione beamed, making it quite clear that his use of the plural pronoun excluded all of them except himself. Gordo the Jesuit snorted his disgust and clattered the rapier at his belt.

'This is all rubbish. This kind of thing is happening all the time, and it's never any big deal. Anyone can disappear in this city, or end up as catamites in Naples or whoremongers in Amsterdam or London, or whatever it is that tickles a Carmelite's fancy these days.' The Jesuit literally spat the last words, significantly, Crespolini noted, at Iniezione and not at the Father Abbot. That little hatred was worth knowing about.

'But my dear Gordo' – the Inquisitor paused for a moment to lick a gob of the Spaniard's spittle from the corner of his mouth – 'you must appreciate that there are other forces at play here. For example, my team has already gathered a great deal of evidence of a cell of Epicureans . . .'

Crespolini switched off. He was bored with all this shit. True, there was something fishy here, something beyond simple abscondment, which was how the Curia had come to hear of it, and why it appeared he'd been sent over to check things out, but at the moment he could do without all this endless wrangling between departments, the constant one-upmanship, the ceaseless needling. In all likelihood six bodies would eventually wash up in the Tiber, and they'd find out it was money or love or the petty rivalries that informed every last aspect of life in Rome. Sickening, but not that important. But he was much more nauseated by the Inquisition's latest obsession with the so-called Epicurean heresy which, if it existed at all, had all the hallmarks of one of the Holy Office's gaudier set-up jobs. Set 'em up, knock 'em down, burn the bastards along with anyone else who's causing trouble you can catch in the net, and everyone keeps in line. They all knew the drill and, as it tended to work quite well, tolerated it. But this latest Epicurean stuff was the worst kind of self-serving paranoid bullshit. He'd even heard rumours of pastry cooks being tortured in Tuscany, for Christ's sake!

Iniezione was still talking about heresy when Crespolini's unfocused gaze was suddenly caught by something at the other end of the crypt.

'With the greatest of respect!' Gordo was now shouting at the Inquisitor. 'I see no connection at all. If there's buggery, burn 'em, pure and simple. If there's anything else, we'll get the fuckers, but why muddy the waters? So Schlefen says there's no trace of these six idiots anywhere, which we must accept' – Gordo looked round them all to show that he didn't accept a word of it – 'but without bodies you have nothing: no evidence, no motive, nothing! This is all just a complete waste of time engineered by empire-building jobsworths!'

Oops, thought Crespolini, suddenly re-engaged by the squabbling prelates around him.

There followed a terrible silence for several seconds as each of them quickly calculated if Gordo had gone too far, although the Spaniard himself seemed unaware of what danger he'd placed himself in. But if such was the case Iniezione, who finally broke the silence, rescued him by revealing that he'd calculated the balances of power with reckless haste.

'Are you condoning heresy then?'

Double oops.

The words were, for him, chosen extremely foolishly. Bluntness in a Jesuit was a forgivable foible, just, but not in an Inquisitor.

And Iniezione knew as well as any of them that what he'd just said was as good as lighting a bonfire beneath a man with friends and protectors as powerful as Gordo's. Worse, the Inquisitor instinctively and immediately recognised the deadly mistake he'd just made, and had no idea, perversely for a man of his experience and training, how to unmake it. The renewed silence, previously terrible, worsened in its murderous intensity, and it slithered and seeped among the group of the still living and between the bones of the dead.

It gave him no pleasure rescuing Iniezione from the pit he'd dug himself due to his own carelessness and ambition but, Crespolini decided in those few, long seconds in which not a single one of the living souls there seemed to dare to breathe, an escalation of the turf war between the Inquisition and the Jesuits would, viewed dispassionately, do him no more good than it would harm. When he finally spoke he was certain he could hear Iniezione's fine white teeth chatter in his skull as he exhaled.

'How tall were the missing monks?'

One of Gordo's chaplains guffawed for an instant but then shut up. Schlefen, the slowest of them all, blustered, 'What? What's that got to do with anything? As it happens they were all exactly six foot tall. All of them from the north, though I don't see . . .'

The rest of them, however, were now looking where

Crespolini's eyes led them, to the end wall of the crypt and the rather beautiful and perfectly symmetrical dodecahedron of clean, white human femurs hanging on the freshly painted white wall. Then they all looked back at the Father Abbot, whose skull appeared to bulge beneath his ashen face. He was dead from Crespolini's stiletto before he'd gone a yard.

Of course they screwed it up. The rain didn't help, but what did they expect? As the bonfires went out a third time, with all the condemned Carmelites in their paper mitres clearly fully conscious, Crespolini caught a look of undisguised joy on the faces of Gordo and his gang of Jesuits and almost felt sorry for Iniezione, who kept on smiling, although his eyes betrayed something which Crespolini judged to be halfway between total panic and complete terror. Naturally, when he'd reported back His Holiness had laughed till he'd choked, which was how it seemed things were being run now. Not that that was any of Crespolini's business.

A short while later, busy tying up the paperwork on what appeared to be a routine case involving an English Protestant married to a widowed Jewess who'd sold sausages during Lent to one of his undercover agents, Crespolini was annoyed to receive an unannounced visit from Iniezione.

The Inquisitor walked in without knocking, which was the kind of thing guaranteed to irritate Crespolini even more than seeing an Inquisitor, so he neither offered his guest a chair nor did he look up from the papers on his desk.

'Look, you'll get him soon enough when we've finished with the wife and due process has been gone through.'

'Um, it wasn't about that actually.'

45

Crespolini finally raised his head, surprised by Iniezione's atypically hesitant and, he might almost have said, abject tone. The Inquisitor wasn't, for once, even pretending to smile. Sensing an advantage, Crespolini indicated a chair opposite his desk. Iniezione fell into it with a deep sigh. More puzzled than anything else, Crespolini waited for him to speak.

'Silvio.' Crespolini didn't like people he didn't like using his Christian name, especially an arsehole from the Holy Office who was about as far away from being a friend as it was possible to be for someone who had no friends anyway. He started grinding his teeth as he waited for Iniezione to get to the point.

'Silvio, I know you weren't happy about how that Lucian business turned out, and I can't really blame you from your point of view.'

Crespolini said nothing.

'You think it should have been a civil matter, or at least open and shut. Well, I can see that, but I don't want any bad feelings between us' – Crespolini tensed his shoulders beneath his cassock and started absent-mindedly fingering some rosary beads on the desktop – 'but there are things going on you probably don't know about. Probably shouldn't know about . . .'

Oh Christ, thought Crespolini, save us the sob story. Iniezione paused and shrugged beneath his soutane, staring for a moment at one of his rings. Feeling increasingly embarrassed, Crespolini threw Iniezione another lifeline with which, he hoped to God, the dumb fuck would be smart enough to save himself.

'Look, Inquisitor, the case is closed. Let's not discuss it further.'

Iniezione looked up into Crespolini's eyes, and he realised that the Inquisitor wouldn't or couldn't let it go. A wave of tiredness swept over him as Iniezione went on.

'I can't do that, Silvio. To you it looked like murder, pure and simple, albeit with a more . . . aesthetic motive than most.' Iniezione half smiled, for the first time during the interview, at his feeble conceit. Crespolini could almost see his mind polishing it up for later use. 'And you not unreasonably question why any of us, perhaps the Holy Office most of all, should have got involved in such a mundane if bizarre case. But . . .'

Iniezione paused again, and looked as if he was having difficulty swallowing something particularly sharp yet glutinous. 'But we had to act as we did. It's not just the clear evidence we had of Epicureanism we found in the kitchens – they had five copies of de Sacchi's banned *Platine de honesta voluptate et valetudine* hidden in the vestry as well, and then there are the confessions we got under torture . . .'

Crespolini snuffled dismissively, and Iniezione's eyes flashed.

'That's right.' Crespolini saw he was losing it. 'Just dismiss all the hard work we do to protect us all! I know some of you people don't even believe in the Epicurean heresy. You just think we've made it up! But we've got thousands of pieces of evidence, from way back when de Sacchi was Vatican librarian and published that poisonous cookbook of his to what's going on right now, all around us! Do you know . . . have you any idea what these people get up to? The way they've shat on scripture in promulgating their vile errors? How they connive at new, horrible ways of cooking the Blessed Sacrament? I tell you, we've found wine lists! Wine lists! They're turning the Blood of the Lamb, the sacred blood of Our Saviour who died for our sins, into a fucking wine tasting!'

To his amazement Crespolini saw that Iniezione was actually crying, and he was aware, to his consternation, that his embarrassment was turning, uncontrollably, into pity. While he waited for the Inquisitor to compose himself, Crespolini breathed deeply, and then said, 'Look, I don't for a moment discount the importance of your work. It's just in this case . . .'

Before he could continue Iniezione leaned forward to silence him with a raised finger, glancing behind him to make sure they weren't overheard, although of course they would have been. 'It's worse. We're pretty certain that the Father Abbot was . . .' he swallowed hard again '. . . eating the bodies, you know, the flesh after it had been taken from the bones they used for the . . . ah . . . installations. Cooking it. In all sorts of . . . fancy ways.' The Inquisitor looked as if he might be sick, and swallowed something nasty once more.

Crespolini didn't let on that he'd already heard this rumour, as had most of the rest of Rome, and discounted it. His men had traced the monks' extraneous meat to a butcher in the Via Magistrale who, usefully enough, had supplied the kitchens of both the Holy Office and the Jesuits, information which he was keeping to himself for the time being.

'But it's even worse than that. Do you know who the Abbot you . . . conveniently . . . despatched actually was?' Iniezione leaned even closer. 'His Holiness's "nephew"!' As Iniezione hissed the words Crespolini almost laughed out loud, and gnawed furiously at the inside of his cheeks to keep a straight face. What was it about Iniezione that was so ludicrous? His misplaced zealotry? His ignorance? His prudishness in using that clichéd old euphemism with such a sense of outrage and shock? Or his unforgivable stupidity at not realising that Crespolini's sole reason for visiting the church that day was to ensure the outcome that eventually though fortuitously came to pass? What was exasperating was that all the other stuff, the murders and the bone sculptures, while providing the perfect pretext for the inevitable act, had also thrown up all this other nonsense and confusion. A smokescreen is useful, but not when the smoke starts drifting and the fire shows every indication of getting completely out of control. He had to put a stop to all this, and fast. But first he had to let Iniezione uncoil just a few more feet of rope to make sure he hanged himself once and for all. Figuratively speaking, of course.

The Inquisitor's face was still close to the edge of Crespolini's desk, his words still an urgent whisper. 'The heresy is important, of course. And very real, don't be in any doubt of that. But Silvio, believe me when I say that I acted as I did in order to protect His Holiness. And, of course . . .' a final pause '. . . you.'

Bingo! Crespolini could have hugged himself, and then kissed Iniezione. But instead he lowered his eyes and took his time before speaking.

'Sergio.' The Inquisitor looked almost pathetically grateful for the proffered intimacy. 'Obviously I've heard the rumours, and if you acted as you did for the reasons you've stated, I'm touched. Clearly any perceived . . . mistakes that may have happened in dealing with this case will be . . . dealt with in a spirit of understanding, cooperation and . . . forgiveness.' That was good. Very good. 'My problem is that you're right. This case does go further, further than maybe even you can guess at.' He let that sink in, and mentally licked his finger to mark up another point to himself. 'We know about the Epicureans, of course, but there is growing evidence that they are just a front, if you see what I mean.' Iniezione's brows furrowed. 'No no, I don't for a moment under-value your work in uncovering their activities, but those activities, we believe, are intended to distract from what's really going on. You remember the man doing the frescoes at Saint Jude's last year . . .'

'The one we got for satanism with sodomy taken into consideration?'

'That's right. Anyway, that case wasn't as simple as it seemed. Just think about it. What were the Carmelites doing? Who was that painter's original patron? What is Rome famous for throughout the world? Where does the money go? *Where does the money go*, Sergio?'

'You mean . . . ?'

'Think about it for a moment, Sergio,' and Crespolini paused to dart his eyes to left and right as he leaned closer. Iniezione did the same, now entirely captivated by Crespolini's little pantomime, and luckily didn't spot the two spyholes, with the eyes behind them, that Crespolini was checking. His next words were barely audible, and trained ears pricked behind the panelling. 'What does any of it actually mean?'

'What?'

Crespolini glanced to left and right again. 'Look, Sergio, have you thought about this at all? What the actual purpose of all this so-called art is? Take a look at the frescoes they're doing in that new Jesuit church. Now don't tell me that that Mannerist monstrosity Gordo's commissioned . . .'

'You mean "The Immaculate Conception" thing . . .'

'Sshhhh! Yes.' Crespolini hunkered down closer.

'But everyone says . . .'

'You and I know what everyone says. That's why we're here. But have you looked closely at the . . . handling of the robes? The way he's painted them, it looks like . . .'

'Yes, an unmade bed. I've heard that. Does it mean something else? Have I missed something?'

Crespolini almost snarled. 'That's the point, Sergio. It

doesn't mean anything. You could walk across a lake of these people's conceptions and you wouldn't get your feet wet. All that . . . stuff at Saint Lucian's. Does that honestly make you think . . . anything?'

Iniezione looked round nervously. His words were hardly breathed at all. 'But His late Holiness . . .'

'*Exactly.*'

'I'm no expert, Silvio.'

'It doesn't matter. You and I know, and so does everyone else, that it's all just . . .'

Neither of them needed to finish the sentence, which trailed off into the heavy air.

Iniezione leaned back, gnawed his lower lip as he stared at nothing, then opened his mouth to speak before thinking better of it. A comforting silence hovered between them, finally broken by Crespolini, still hissing in a whisper, 'Remember those bones, Sergio.' He then raised his eyebrows, shrugged and sat back in his chair. The silence resumed, until Iniezione leaned forward again.

'But where do I . . . ? I should start with the man at Lucian's, right?'

Crespolini pursed his lips and with a wave of his flattened hand, palm down, indicated that this was already dealt with. Finally, and in a louder voice, he said, 'You follow the money, Sergio. Start with the Jesuits.'

Iniezione really looked like he was going to start crying again, although Crespolini couldn't immediately gauge whether this was from fear or gratitude. He was beginning to feel embarrassed again, so he quickly showed Iniezione to the door, ushering him out with a friendly rub on the back before returning to the papers on his desk, where he ticked off the Inquisitor's name and that of the Spanish Jesuit on the long list in front of him. Crespolini stretched, yawned, smiled and yearned, inarticulately, for a cigarette, yet to be invented. Distantly, the screams of some artisans and other riff-raff mingled with those of other malefactors, and the bones of the dead, in the vaults of Saint Lucian's (or Lucius's, or Lucy's) and elsewhere throughout Rome and the Christian world, settled inaudibly into beautiful patterns of dust.

Family

Did you know that the word caviar comes from the Turkish? God knows what the original word means, but it's interesting, isn't it, what these words mean and where they come from and all that. I suppose, if you had a mind to, you could trace back every word I say to some other word in some other language that might mean something completely different. Fascinating. But you're not listening, are you? Oh Mother, you can't understand half of what I'm saying.

If anything at all, if it comes to that. But if you could . . . My God! It would amaze you, you know, it really would, my story. All the stuff that's happened to me, to your little boy, all my adventures and everything. Make your hair curl, if you had any. What the hell, I'll tell you anyway. I've got to tell someone. Don't bottle it up, speak my mind and all that.

I can't be quite sure about the beginning, although I picked his brains to find out how it all started, you know, how we first met, so at least we've got his side of it. Well, sort of. Him? Oh yes, poor old Schlefen, we can't forget him, he's central to the whole thing. A clever man, but limited, if you see what I mean. Their word for him would be 'bourgeois', which suits him to a tee. I hope you're impressed by all these smart words I've picked up, by the way. He was certainly fat.

And that's how we met. Him eating. That's what brought him and me together.

But concentrate. I've got to get this right so you'll understand it all. I'll tell it from the beginning, like he would.

55

It was Walpurgesnacht, not that that would mean anything to you, or to me either, naturally enough. Didn't mean much to him, either, beyond some loose ideas about spooks and ghosts and fear and stuff, and even those had been all messed up by the other stuff he'd picked up from Beardie and Specky. No, I'll get on to them later. More importantly, from his point of view anyway, it was his birthday. Mine too, I suppose. Yes. My birthday. How about that, then? Anyway, because it was his birthday . . . No, I know you can't understand all this at once, but just be patient . . . Because it was his birthday he'd decided to eat out for a change. All alone, he was, when he came into the restaurant. His wife . . . What? No, don't worry about that, it's not important . . . had died, yes, *died* in this epidemic the year before and his only child, this boy . . . Look, just let me tell the story, okay? . . . anyway, his only son had got himself killed in the war in Italy. Don't ask me, I'm just telling you his side of it. Anyway, he was used to being on his own, and didn't even like mixing with his own sort much. But this was a special occasion, right? So he goes to one of the three restaurants in Vienna, that's where this all happened, this restaurant in Vienna, to celebrate his birthday with a treat. Not much of a treat – I pick all this up later, you must understand, picking his brains – the place is full of English and riff-raff like Poles and Czechs and Hungarians and all, and there's a table of drunk English soldiers at the next table to him, right next to him, singing a song about a sturgeon. Right! Anyway, old Schlefen thinks, to hell with this, I'll show them, so he orders caviar as his friend Schmidt's told him there are only five jars of caviar left in Vienna and this restaurant's got all five!

What? Caviar? No, it's what I was talking about earlier. What is it? Well, I hardly like to say . . . Er, well,

it's sorted of salted fish, er, eggs you know. Yes, it's
pretty disgusting but they're like that, these people, eat
anything. Anyway, he orders the caviar, drinks champagne, thinks how this is like the old days as he smears
these little black eggs – I'm not upsetting you, am I? Just
telling you the way it was, that's all – anyway, smears
all this stuff on these bits of toast and starts munching
away, although of course they're so tiny, some of the
eggs get caught in his teeth, not that he notices, and
there's these English shouting and the champagne's
giving him a headache and he's swilling this champagne
and caviar and these crumbs from the toast round in his
mouth and this headache's become a migraine and he
can't even bear to open his eyes now and it's then, don't
ask me how, but then, that's when me and old Schlefen
get together!

Now, where was I? Of course, it's a million to one
chance – billion to one, trillion to one, more likely – no,
that's maths, counting, stuff you wouldn't understand
. . . anyway, it was a million to one us getting together
like that, Schlefen and me. You wouldn't have thought
it possible really, would you? But to be honest he didn't
pay me much attention at first, hardly seemed to be
aware of my existence. And, I'll admit, I was pretty
insignificant by his standards, and he had other things
on his mind. Like these migraines. Then, a bit later,
when I got to know him a bit better, growing on him so
to speak, there were the dreams. Very disturbing, he
found them. Well, I found them pretty worrying too, to
be honest, but for different reasons obviously.

Now it so happens that there was this woman, what
was her name? Adele? Charlotte? Anyway, a widow I
think she must have been, who was after Schlefen at
that time with an eye to marriage. Oh yes, they're like
that, you know. Seems he still had a bit of money or

property or something, hadn't done too badly out of this big war they'd all had – don't ask me to explain it – whereas she's lost the lot, all except her airs and graces, that is. I couldn't stand her, needless to say, and I dealt with her once and for all later on. But I'm getting ahead of myself. Anyway, before the war this old trout had been one of Freud's most fashionable patients. Yes. Freud. Old Beardie. Frightful man, didn't have a clue what he was on about if you ask me. But to get back to the story. One night Schlefen tells his lady friend about these nightmares he's been having – we're having, I might say – so she suggests he consult old Beardie, who's in as much need of cash as everyone else in Vienna round then, so this is what he does. And Freud gets him in his surgery or whatever, shoes off, socks up on the sofa and it's 'Tell me about your dreams, Herr Schlefen.'

And of course Schlefen doesn't know where to begin. Terrible dreams they are, started just after his last birthday. 'Tell me, tell me,' implores Beardie, pacing round the room and waving his cigar all over the place (God, those cigars were the worst! I was having enough trouble breathing already, without all that shit floating around the place – but I'm getting off the point again). The dreams, yes. Hadn't been too bad at first, although worrying enough. 'My teeth, Herr Doktor, I dreamed my teeth were growing up into my skull, the roots growing up into my brain,' says Schlefen, coughing through the clouds of smoke. Old Beardie raises his eyebrows at this, writes something down and then asks Schlefen what else. So then Herr S. tells him about the dreams he's been having for the last few weeks. That's right, same dream every night. Well, almost, with a few differences every night.

And it's like this, right? He's swimming in this huge pool or ocean. He thinks to begin with that maybe he sees his wife and son – the dead ones, you remember – drowning nearby and he tries to rescue them but ends up starting to eat their bodies. Pretty gross, eh? Anyway, recently they haven't been there, not that he's alone, mind. This sea's teeming, with millions and millions of Schlefens. Everywhere he turns, other people just like him. Identical. As like as two peas in a pod, all round him. Schlefen's sweating now (and I'm getting pretty hot too, as you can imagine), becoming really agitated. These dreams really terrify him, right? So Freud sucks on his stinky cigar, sticks his lower lip out, paces round a bit more and says come back next week.

Well, all this time I was learning a few things, quite a few things. It wasn't easy, naturally, but I was growing, you know, almost spiritual it was, all the time. Finding my feet, so to speak. Seeing things through Schlefen's eyes, the way he saw things. And, you know, he was coming round to my point of view too, which is pretty flattering if you think about it. Anyway, this makes the weekly session with Beardie more interesting every time, as Schlefen and I make our own contributions, confusing old Freudie like nobody's business.

'These dreams about the sea,' Freud says one afternoon, gobbing in a corner as he says so, 'you don't seem to find them so traumatic any more.'

'No, not really,' says Schlefen, though he can't say why. Freud grimaces and sniffs, and tries another tack he's used before. 'What about your mother?'

'Sorry? I don't see the relevance. My mother means nothing to me. Why should she? I'm not even sure I know what you mean.' Well, he was certainly getting round to my way of thinking, although he might have gone a bit far with that last crack. Anyway, Freud sniffs at this, excuses himself and leaves the room for a bit, so I occupy the time doing some exercises, staring at

Schlefen's outstretched arms and feet. And this is when Freud brings his friend Specky into it all, Jung I think his name was, po-faced, stuck-up, you know the type. Of course while Freud was getting all wound up about Schlefen's attitude to his mum (I met her once, shrivelled old bag, no wonder Schlefen wasn't getting excited), anyway this Jung was cockahoop, raving on about Schlefen's dream being the expression of the collectivist folk something or other. Can't remember, and it doesn't matter anyway. That was the trouble with these people, always trying to explain things, couldn't leave anything well alone.

It was soon after this that I convinced Schlefen to stop seeing Freud, even though Beardie said his condition was getting worse and it was essential to continue the therapy. Well, I wasn't having any of that, spending the best part of the day lying flat on my back playing stupid word games. I mean, I was just finding out all these words for the first time, you know, actually articulating now and again. 'Little fishes, yum yum yum,' Schlefen would find himself saying in the middle of the street, and be worrying about it for the rest of the afternoon. And of course I was exerting more and more influence over him, although he didn't realise it at the time. I even managed to convince him to sleep in the bath and spend all day down by the river.

It wasn't all perfect, of course. There was still the lady friend who was flapping around all the time trying to persuade Schlefen to start acting more normally, like sleeping in a bed again, not sticking his head in fountains in the parks, and then she tried taking him out for a meal, incidentally in *that* restaurant, and ordered him caviar, which used to be his favourite food in all the world, right? And you know what? He pukes it up right in her face! Laugh? You bet I did! Then, as she's still shrieking 'Otto! Otto!' and she's screaming, 'What's got into you? Oh God, oh God!', I turn round and fix her with my eyes. Well, that shuts her up, then I grab hold of her and drag her out of the restaurant, and everyone's staring at this fat old man and scrawny old woman running out, knocking over tables and everything, and I drag her down to the river, right? The Danube, they call it. Anyway, she's screaming away saying 'Otto! Otto!' – Schlefen had this other name, you know – but then she looks into my eyes and, you know, I think she realised what was going on. Well, I certainly looked like Schlefen, but maybe it was the eyes. Cold, 'a cold fish' she used to call him, you know, as a kind of tease. Maybe that's what she saw, saw it wasn't Schlefen at all any more. I didn't give her long to think about it, though, and pulled her into the river with me.

Of course, from my point of view I had no option, did I? I'm still not entirely sure how it all worked out, but I presume, if my head had grown inside his, with my brain and mind and stuff intermeshing with his, then the rest of me was growing in the rest of him. But what about the lungs? That's the bit I don't quite understand. Anyway, I knew that by this time it was bloody murder trying to breathe out of the water, so I was all for getting back in quick as I could. But I suppose there was enough of Schlefen left in me to want to take her with him. Me. Us. A last bid to proclaim his precious individuality or something. Strange if you think about it, the way these people set so much store by themselves as separate individuals and all that. Doesn't really make sense, does it? Well, anyway, he wouldn't let go of her, although as far as I was concerned she was just slowing me down as I swam downriver. She was dead soon enough, and by the time we reached the sea I'd taken over more or less completely, and although he was still hanging on to her like grim death, I'd eaten most of her by then.

So, anyway, here I am. What? You don't remember me at all? No, I don't suppose there's any reason why you should. Of course I hadn't got my hopes up of some big deal reunion, no, no, it doesn't matter. I'm not upset. No, no, I reckon I do look a bit weird for a sturgeon, though I should have sloughed most of Schlefen off soon enough, that's what seems to be happening anyway. What? Oh, sorry about that, there must be a vestige of him left somewhere. I keep screaming like that, out of the blue. How he does it underwater I don't know, it's like the lungs bit. A mystery. Yes, it is kind of spooky, yes, but I reckon it should pass. What's that? Why have I come to see you? Well, it's what that man Freud was saying, you know, what I was telling you. I mean, you are my mother, aren't you. Mother?

The Last Train from Madrid

The Contessa awoke slowly, lulled conscious by the punctuating clicks of the train's wheels passing agonisingly slowly over the gaps in the track. The dream she'd been having, almost ever since boarding the last train for the north leaving Madrid, of herself being assiduously seduced by an androgynous doppelgänger of herself, dimmed. The old man by the window was growingly silhouetted by the coming dawn seething across the fleeting sierra.

'Going far?' he asked quietly. She ignored him, and what she guessed would be his scaly skin blotched with telltale signs of mortality, along with a lecherous glint in his dull, hooded, evil old eyes. Then, as the reassuring visions of self-seduction stutteringly started to return, she was fully awoken by the compartment light being turned on. A young Republican officer, of high rank and obvious good breeding, stood in the doorway.

'May I sit here?' he asked with a grandee's assurance, the redness of his tongue visible as he spoke. The Contessa mewed sourly, and he turned off the light and sat down opposite her. Outside, the immense empty plain was tinging orange as the sun, below the horizon, was mirrored from the sky, bringing into perceptibility occasional trees at different depths of perspective, moving at different speeds. The officer leaned across in the dark and placed his large hand on the Contessa's warm thigh. She responded with a breathy shudder as he moved his hand and, with his other arm, pulled her over to him. Their lips met, their mouths opened and

65

their moist tongues touched. Slowly, gently, they undressed each other, falling to the floor and moving their bodies together in the shadows. The Contessa drove her fingernails into the officer's firm buttocks as muscles tightened and the blood pumped in her head. She gasped and the back of her head vibrated, and slowly the flesh between her fingers became soft, then pliable, then runny. Turning on her back, she pulled him on top of her just in time to feel his tongue trickle down her throat and his forehead ooze warmly over hers and then dribble past her ears to the floor. Soon his body had almost completely melted, now pouring down her flanks and limbs in smooth, sensuous rivulets and, her eyes closed, panting in short gasps, she rubbed a lard-like remnant of his backbone into her white belly. Then she got on all fours, bent her head downwards and lapped up the pool of tepid liquid, tasting faintly of marzipan, until you couldn't tell if the dampness there came from the Contessa's drool or the officer's liquidation.

Bloated, she sat up, naked, in her seat, and took a compact from her clutch bag, in the process dropping her party card to the floor of the compartment.

'Going far?' asked the old man by the window, making the secret sign of the Falange with his fingers in the gloom. Enzymes squirted in her full tummy and, rather regretting that she hadn't booked a berth on a Pullman, she licked her teeth before answering.

66

Sod

(to be read aloud)

No no no yes awake yes waking up now yes fine yes
to continue without doubt had I started sweating
money when I was younger my life would have turned
out quite differently for a start I would never have
enjoyed the grinding poverty I would later recognise
as the badge of citizenship and a passport to the smarter
salons I doubt however whether riches would have
done my mother any good whatever other circumstances or alternatives or possibilities or probabilities
or hopes or dreams or nightmares may have presented
themselves the fact remains my uncle her brother had
been one of the boys yes those boys who went out
against Collins and for his and our pains ended up a
prisoner captured and chained to a hollow tree trunk
before the Free Staters chucked in a live grenade well
there it was my mother had had plenty of other brothers
some of whom had died on the Western Front another
was executed by firing squad no less after that business in 1916 and several more were killed by those
Black and Tans bastards but none of them really
counted with the ma and it was only the last brother
who did the trick for her encapsulating for her as he
was blown to bits all those gorgeous emotions of sacrifice betrayal blood brotherhood redemption land
martyrdom and mourning which left her breathless
and as it turned out speechless too perhaps the disquiet-
ing psychosexual dimensions of it all were more
obvious to her than they were to us which isn't saying

much and that was why she never uttered another
word of spoken language just sighing shrugging and
rolling her regretful revengeful reverent red Republican
eyes instead in my youth of course all of us were all
for that old stuff because to be frank there was nothing
else on offer it should be said however that my mother
took it all rather to extremes obviously with us all
caught in the contemptibly familiar web of poverty but
she doubly ensnared us yes in another clinging and
deadly web of her unassuageable grief while spinning
herself a further cocoon of glory out of her brother's
uncollectable end leaving herself snugly constrained
between those unbreakable threads of piety misery
immobility and silence oh the silence that silence was
sexual no erotic is more the word you know just as
much as it was palpable you could taste it in the air as
if with that one death she'd reached such heights or
depths the vertical moral scale remains as always open
to question of rapture that mere speech was no longer
necessary as no more need ever be said which was fine
for her but sheer hell for my father me and my brothers
I tell you that silence could tame wild beasts cow an
army or inspire it to commit ever more terrible atro-
cities and animal and soldier alike tried for the life of
him and anyone else in his way to work out what the
hell it was she actually wanted I was no different and
being none the wiser usually took her silence for
approval as I swallowed the lot the brotherhood the
betrayal blood land martyrdom and more blood as
unconsciously as I inhaled the incense candle smoke
and compost stench of the soil and as instinctively as
we all got misty-eyed about the bloody mist while we
were about it it was only later that I worked out that
the light that made the mists glow so beguilingly was
inevitably the light of the sun setting into the western

sea as the night came thundering out of England as I
say I don't think it would have made any difference at
all if my symptoms had presented themselves earlier
and this curious condition by which I perspire large
amounts of English coin at every turn had shown itself
soon after I was born true they say money can't buy
happiness they in this case being those without it who
are just fooling themselves and those with it who are
trying to fool everyone else into not wanting any as is
always the way but in my mother's case I believe
money back in those days would have made no material difference to either her circumstances or her
emotional condition in her mute poverty-racked misery
I never met a happier woman in my life her happiness
exclusively based upon her limitless capacity to make
her immediate family miserable in ways almost magical
in their Mystery but who knows with money it might
have been even worse

naturally as I loved my mother so I loved my dead
uncle her brother and took my turn in making my devotions to his sacred memory instructed in this with
pinpoint precision by my mother the movement of her
eyes the examination of her fingernails and the precise
way she'd sigh through her nose as I say I had I knew
a whole gang of other dead uncles just as much her
brothers but you'd never have killed a man to save their
memory not a single one and yet even as a tiny child
I'd have killed you without a second's thought for a
wrong word said about my last dead uncle or a right
word said wrong or possibly even a right word
pronounced properly meaning exactly what you and I
both wanted it to mean or even wanted it to mean even
if I suspected you of nothing at all and I'd have done it
for him silently blessed by my silent mother almost
unperceived in her benediction in our silent house where

the slightest lowering of an eyelid was as powerfully oratorical as any of the Big Boys cutting the blarney to send us small boys to death and glory with our brains in a whirl our hearts fit to bust and laughing at the sheer lunatic joy of it all but it was all like that then and that was the point though in our house of course we never laughed we all knew it the thing the point whatever you want to call it *was a laugh* those Free State boyos had laughed as they chucked that grenade under my uncle and my uncle had laughed as he'd been blown to Kingdom Come that was the point it was a laugh even while you did it to all those chaps for reasons you didn't even need to remember any more and that's the actual point despite what some of my smarter former colleagues from both my former disciplines now insist now they're all up at the Big House sipping sherry and eyeing up the old master's riding boots by the back door and wondering how many heads they can kick in for a laugh before they reach the car but ever since I began to sweat money I've personally put all that old stuff behind me although there's many that haven't as we know

not that I was much good at it in the first place you should understand I never got further than a wet night in the bracken with a handful of my brothers biological and otherwise all of us waiting to embrace the fate of my uncle in the vain hope this might result in some deathbed scene which included a single word of approbation from the ma but all I got out of it the man didn't turn up as someone else had got him down the road was bronchitis for my trouble and an end to that kind of game after I got in sodden freezing and wheezing my mother's eyes gleamed in the low light with a kind of unassailably miserable certainty as with not a word she tucked me in and it was my father who broke the news to me once I got better or as better as I'd ever get I wonder still how they reached a decision if they never spoke but then again as I was no good as a potential martyred corpse any more there was little other choice I remember that night and how I couldn't tell if it was the odour of sanctity rising up from my dead uncle's little shrine by the Sacred Heart in the parlour or the damp coming through the walls that made me feel so cosy in that high bed and as cosy as I knew the destiny the da had laid out for me would be although martyrdom I felt was by and large preferable but this wouldn't perhaps be all that bad

it's an old joke about how you know Jesus was Irish because he lived at home until he was thirty he thought his mother was a virgin and she thought he was God I'm told it works just as well with Jews and Eyeties though I got out just before I was thirty at which point I still didn't really know what a virgin was apart from looking drippy and miserable like the BVM like my ma and if she my mother thought I was God her devotions on my behalf were so quiet they were bloody inaudible apart that is from the deafening but hardly devout roar of that silence as I've said my father was and always had been in total awe of her single-mindedness of purpose in never divulging what her purpose might ever be and so skulked between the pub on the corner and the back kitchen like a monk pacing a cloister saying his rosary she was a Mystery and that was quite enough for him and my brothers and me venerated her with just as much fear as he did which left us with few reserves of fear for anything else back at school when the Brothers walloped me and my brothers statistically more frequently than they did anyone else I should add they clearly thought we were the bolshie little buggers we were because we were a clan of untameable and

73

inveterate Shinners like our dead and sainted uncle
which was why a session with the belt was always
followed by a manly cuddle of forgiveness and a pocket-
ful of gobstoppers if you get my drift to show us they
knew we were all good boys and good boys for blood
and land beneath it all and they never even guessed
that anything they could throw at us or threaten us with
up to and including Himself could ever be as truly
terrible as our ma sitting silently at the kitchen over
half a loaf of stale bread lit by a forty watt bulb and
slowly
    forlornly
turning her eyes to the window rattling under a fusil-
lade of raindrops from the west anyway I got out of
the family home as Dev got in and we all thought this
is it at last we are ourselves alone and the dead albeit
perforce in several parts will be interred in glory in the
pantheon or whatever and Ma might actually talk but
no so instead I rose to the occasion when it became
clear that the hour for holy streaks of misery was upon
us God I was one myself thin gaunt slightly rangy and
with those kind of narrow spectacles that can freeze
the water in fonts and turn your guts to jelly whenever the subject of the Bountiful Love of God comes
up in casual conversation but let's get on to when I
actually started sweating the money I'd moved to
Dublin when I left that silent bloody mausoleum at
home and was now in my fifth year at the Theological
College I had recently started hearing confessions at
Saint Lucian's for which I'd give them as much hell as
I had at my disposal although mostly I remained under
the guidance of Iniezione the renowned Jesuit penseur
broadcaster athlete and all that whose presence in
Dublin was an abiding and unfathomable Mystery he
and my mother would have got on like a house on fire

though he'd have done all the talking it was whispered that he'd refused any academic position in Italy because of the Duce but that was all my eye anyone who'd heard any of Iniezione's sermons or broadcasts would know he was no Red although his English was shaky to say the least and therefore permissive of a certain level of ambiguity let us say it was also whispered that he was in cahoots with Dev and the Boys in some way or other which was Far Too Mysterious for anyone to explain at all clearly all of that on top of all the other rumours helped maintain an atmosphere of highly charged excitement some of it perhaps slightly less than altogether wholesome shall we say all round him which of course did him nothing but good young nuns blushed at the sight of him old women collapsed clutching religious medals in joyous keening as he walked past old priests whose faces had been stuck for decades in expressions that could sour cream in a jug five streets away smiled like choirboys when he spoke to them and the Big Boys who everyone knew would have scooped out your eyeballs with a cold spoon if they thought you'd once crossed the road with insufficient patriotic fervour fawned over him with such unguarded adulation you'd never guess they'd ever broken their best friends' legs or burnt down more Georgian country houses than most of the citizens of North Dublin had had hot dinners and of course there was the other rumour about his frosty relations with Monsignor Sykes-Wolsey which only improved his reputation

Sykes-Wolsey oh yes Sykes-Wolsey we all knew that fellah knew he was one of the old Mob from the Big House my brothers biological and non-biological had gone to burn it to the ground after I'd run home to Mammy coughing sharp phlegm and sniffing with lost hope my martyrdom snatched from me by the dampness of the undergrowth they succeeded in burning down a barn before they scarpered another Sykes-Wolsey loosing off a firearm Crimean War vintage I'd hazard into the blazing night anyway the Sykes-Wolseys had stuck around although everyone knew they and their class had nothing left to do or even offer they looked picturesque I suppose though he had a cousin I think back in England a poet painter or some such messing with all that surrealism stuff you know a girl with no knickers and no head looking gormless next to a giant thimble ankle deep in a lake of mauve jam deep it was meant to be I suppose about as deep as the wax in your ears if you ask me anyway and they offered a wealth of material for a certain kind of writer the kind not yet quite respectable with the Boys now running the show those authors who knew better words wrote them best in a tongue no one in his right mind wanted to or could speak although perhaps my mother was mute in two languages who knows except of course the nice people like the Sykes-Wolseys and the others who if their homes weren't ash would put on old boots pluck a bloody harp and sing plaintively in the auld tongue but with vowel sounds that would have cracked the chapel window at Eton and killed ducks on the bloody Cam anyway some shut up shop and bequeathed the infant nation potential poignant and romantic ruins thank you very much while others skulked and sulked behind their charred country park walls in the converted abattoir block and the best or the worst or what you will with a passionate intensity that soiled doilies and might mean half a bob from a gloved hand for lads like me if we came on and glowed with the spirituality peculiar to the starving took to thinking about fairies up the Abbey and getting even mistier-eyed about the bloody mists than the rest of us Sykes-Wolsey though was worse than that he'd gone as they say the whole hog from high-riding on its back to wallowing in its sty with the rest of us that he'd ratted on his class his family and his religion although admittedly with every outward sign of success rendering himself through the rigorous application of nationalist piety even more desiccated bloodless and miserable than the native product he imitated cut no ice with us and made him no friends at all but Jaysus what did he expect his lot naturally down on their uppers but still trying to live the grand life round the embers of the family pile in the west the unscorched turrets making the hearts of men with smooth hands melt as they glowed through the mist in the sunset were frankly disgusted that he'd thrown in his lot with us while all we saw was another bloody Englishman with 800 years of our blood on his hands still despite our endeavours our struggles and his disguise telling us what to do however deeply his cheeks sunk in quietly he whispered or however often he delivered sermons in praise of General Franco although to be fair you couldn't fault the man for trying

which brings me to the first time I sweated money and when I first became aware that Sykes-Wolsey wasn't as otherworldly as he tried in his plaint to make us love him to make out although his skin stretched like papyrus over his domed skull you could hang a sparrow in the shade beneath his cheekbones and his Adam's apple was now protruding so far you'd think he was the genuine article after all he was in fact conscious to an also embarrassing degree for us of the fact that we hated his guts for what if not who he was although all of us hated him for that too to try to remedy this it's inevitable he just made things worse but although none of us could stand him it would have been unthinkable to turn down an invitation from someone as senior in the seminary as Sykes-Wolsey whenever he asked us round to tea a friend of mine at the time who later ended up badly tried to joke as we walked towards Sykes-Wolsey's lodgings suspiciously near TCD that at least we would be drinking the old coot out of house and home I glowered my disapproval at him and he said no more as we crossed the river leaving behind the smell of coal smoke and cooking Sykes-Wolsey's door was opened by a skeletal housekeeper just another hamfisted attempt to ingratiate himself with further evidence of how complete was his conversion to and wholehearted embracing of our ways the walking skeleton simpered at us as she showed us into Sykes-Wolsey's study where he stood in front of the fire nibbling at an Osbourne biscuit like a badly emaciated rat he looked up and welcomed the four of us indicating where we should sit before offering each of us a glass of stout God help us getting as close to a snarl as I dared I stated that tap water would suffice although I noticed that my friend the one who ended up badly fell for Sykes-Wolsey's bait as polite chitchat was clearly out of the question we sat in silence for a while as I became increasingly aware of my uncomfortably close proximity to the roaring fire which Sykes-Wolsey presumably required to warm his by the standards of his class and race scantily cloaked bones he was sitting opposite me just as close as I was to that fire but seemed almost to huddle trying to keep warm and I thought I heard his teeth chatter an instant as he tried as a conversational gambit to pick up where he'd left off in his last lecture about the Council of Ephesus with a feeble joke about the heretical Arians and Herr Hitler doing my best to show no emotion whatsoever in response to his overture I shifted for a moment in my seat rearranging my legs so as to remove them from the direct scalding glare of the fire when raising my left leg to cross it over my right I was surprised to feel a coin dribble down the inside of my trouser leg and land with a plop on the thin rug at my feet

Sykes-Wolsey paused as we looked first to the coin and then at each other

he then leaned down into the space between us picked up the coin it was a two bob bit and trousered it before wheezing at another of his own awful jokes naturally I was troubled by this so the next day I determined to visit the doctor an amiable Jew round the corner from my own lodgings up in the realm of coal smoke and cooking smells and far removed from the comfortable district where the odious Sykes-Wolsey tried to smarm to his students while at the same time robbing them in full view of at least three independent witnesses or four if you count the skeletal housekeeper who at the moment of the theft stuck her skull round the door to leer at Sykes-Wolsey with a rictus straight from the tomb but it wasn't the distress I'd suffered from the crime committed against me which drove me to see my physician to whom I now described the previous night's events while emphasising first my sobriety and second my agitation and my irritation at my host the doctor wrote down something on the pad before him and without looking up asked if the incident was isolated so I told him what had happened in his own waiting room only about three minutes previously that morning as every morning my own landlady had handed me a neatly ironed handkerchief for my breast pocket this was an indulgence of mine by which I signalled how I was getting ahead in life compared to how I used to be my mother having never even been on sighing acquaintance with a steam iron and our crumpledness as children only adding to our reputation as wild rebels anyway the point was that it was an unseasonably warm morning in spite of which the waiting room was heated perhaps overheated by a gas fire next to which I was compelled to sit courtesy of my cloth and at the insistence of the other waiting patients all of whom smiled at me as if I was some species of retarded crippled child I was soon sweating heavily so naturally pulled the handkerchief from my pocket to mop my brow I now showed the doctor what I'd wiped from my forehead resting in the middle of the hankie the creases ironed there by my landlady spreading out from it like a cross was a rather grubby English ten shilling note

the doctor whistled through his teeth in wonder and prescribed a course of chalk tablets to reduce the sweating

the chalk tablets did not work

by the end of that week in the course of my normal daily life I'd sweated twenty-seven pounds thirteen shillings and thruppence five shillings of which had poured from my sleeves in farthings as I rushed one afternoon for a tram and I had to abandon all plans of ever going to the Turkish baths again when without any intention on my part I handed the attendant an absurdly large tip in the used towel I chucked at him as I left after two weeks things became intolerable the slightest change in atmospheric pressure or even mood had catastrophically embarrassing consequences I raised my hat to a young woman on O'Connell Street and pennies tinkled to the ground from it as if I was some kind of madman the sun came out from behind a cloud and sixpences cascaded from my trouser cuffs like I was an ecclesiastical one-armed bandit the street urchins loved me of course but it wouldn't do for me to be seen pursued by a charivari of grubby children and as medical science clearly had no answers in desperation I went to see Iniezione as I think I may have said at this time Iniezione was at the height of his powers and his influence and although the way History turned out subsequently means that his reputation has been let us say somewhat revised while his memory is now reviled at this time he was an awesome and in many ways terrifying figure even I immunised against almost all forms of fear by my mother's terrible silence was more than a little scared when I knocked on the door of his office from behind the oak his deep voice boomed that I was to enter on doing so I was greeted by the sight of Iniezione standing in the middle of his room dressed only in a purple leotard and with a set of weights held high up above his head while with his eyes tight shut his lips fluttered obviously in prayer this was the kind of stunt for which he was famous and which recommended him so highly to both the people and the politicians he was A Man of Action a breed popular back then before most of us quite understood what their actions were going to be so I stood more in awe than embarrassment as he finished his prayer and then gently lowered the weights to their stand on the floor and if there was a definite squeak of embarrassment it arose from my impertinence at intruding on such a magnificent display of muscular piety with my petty personal problems rather than from any conscious prescience of what a ludicrous ham he truly was Iniezione still panting beamed at me and indicated I sit down on the sofa where he joined me okay, kid he smiled whas thar problem so doing my best to stop thinking how much he reminded me of Chico Marx I started to explain what had been happening to me and how for over two weeks now I appeared to have been sweating considerable sums of raw cash from my body to my great personal and vocational embarrassment and how I now sought his advice I'd made my little speech staring at my shoes as was appropriate to someone in my position but when I looked up I caught a quizzical look of amusement in his twinkling eye and so disguising my irritation as much as I was able I went over to the set of weights Iniezione had seemed to lift with such ease and which I after several moments' straining managed to budge a couple of inches from the floor a large white Bank of England five pound note now fluttered from the back of my neck and slowly wafted down to join the pile of silver on the thick carpet Iniezione sat staring at me for several minutes until he finally let out a long whistle jumped to his feet and started pacing the room in a manner briefly made famous by George Raft cast against type we thought in a Hollywood film briefly popular in the late thirties this he continued to do for several minutes pausing only to pick a bob from the floor which he handed back to me finally he stopped and turned to stare at me kid this iss weird he said onna the one han' this could be a miracle he pronounced the end of the word like clay I remember if you jus' think what you coulda do with this money from God all the charity he stopped furrowed his brow and clicked his tongue a few times before continuing but I fear iss not datta simple he stopped again and stared down at his plimsolls whistling noiselessly I shifted uneasily Mattyew Sees Twenny-four he suddenly bellowed and rushed towards me I jumped and thought for one mad moment that he was about to attack me he stopped just short and towering over me and with a face like thunder bellowed You Canno

Serva Two Massers iss God or Memmon no choice buddy I think about this very hard kid an iss clear to me that you got Memmon squirtins outa your body all damn day long

I started to cringe

Hey youra smart kid you know the Albigensian 'Eresy right I cringed even further thinking about the virulent Manichaean error successive French kings had suppressed in southern France throughout the fourteenth and fifteenth centuries these punks they say this worl' iss da realm of Rex Mundi right 'oo's the Devil Satan da Prince of Lies you get me an' as a consequence all physical matter iss eveel while all that iss good iss jus' pure spirit right an' is further maintain that these two iss in permanent an' unendin' struggle right now that's 'eresy pure an' simple but what I see when I see you sweatin' out Memmon in alla dis money iss jus' a corporeal demonstration of eveel comin' out of the flesh of Man which iss the same flesh as taken on by Our Lord Christ Almighty son whass this gonna imply about the 'Ypostatic Union to be honest iss obvious to me that your entire body is a living embodiment of 'eresy Jesus he meant it the thing about Iniezione that few people got when they just considered all the showbiz and the charm and which they forgot when considering his career later was that he may well have been a fascist crook but he also believed quite sincerely in the teachings of the Catholic Church on reflection I'm certain that he wanted genuinely to attack me there and then in his room and only stopped himself with a monumental effort of will I'm also certain that he deeply regretted and resented the decadent and lax times he found himself living in and would much preferred to have had me burnt at the stake in accordance with traditional canon law as it

83

was he had to content himself with my immediate expulsion from the college my removal from holy orders my excommunication from the Church and my banishment from his sight for ever at the time the last one was the most painful for I was as taken in as mesmerised into a kind of puppyish love for and awe of Iniezione and his easy white smile and jet black hair and loose soft eyes as everyone else and my exile from his electrifying presence compounded my already deep misery obviously my few friends had all abandoned me as soon as Iniezione withdrew his love and just as naturally my landlady threw me out onto the streets of North Dublin where it's said the natives eat their young with almost equal despatch but worse than all that I had to live and somehow come to terms with Iniezione's diagnosis of my curious affliction could it really be that Almighty God had created in miniature in microcosm within me the universal struggle between Good and Evil and moreover had purposefully cursed me by making my body personify this unending dualism in the most obviously heretical way imaginable not that I'd ever fallen for all that stuff it was just a laugh like the rest of it my five years training for holy orders was in no way compromised by my personal beliefs I hasten to add does after all a plumber have to believe in plumbing no that's not quite right all right what about a printer does he have to agree with everything he prints of course not all that said I found it hard to reconcile such divine inventiveness artifice and spite with the rather small-minded petty and prissy God on whose behalf I had been trained to intercede with humankind who was always on hand to make sure some dirty-minded fifteen-year-old girl from Howth minded her p's and q's at the peril of her immortal soul but was so busy keeping an eye on

84

whatever filthiness people got up to that He had no time to do a thing about War Injustice Famine Earthquakes and all the other pratfalls implicit in His Creation why then choose me to make some arcane theological point when surely He had Created the Universe in the first place solely in order to stop little boys fiddling with themselves and their mas taking a fancy to the milkman it was indeed a Mystery another one although this knowledge did nothing to ease the burdens it laid on my spirit I was preparing to take my final leave of Dublin and return with the heaviest of hearts to the horrible silence of my mother's house when I dropped in one last time at Saint Lucian's although I had no intention it goes without saying of praying though a sentimental part of me thought I might draw some comfort from contemplation in a familiar place where once I'd been happy standing in that small church and staring at the rather formless and ambiguous statue of the obscure saint to whom the place was dedicated I was suddenly conscious of a noise in the vestry and was about to investigate further when to my amazement the appalling Sykes-Wolsey strode through the vestry door and behind him seeking another exit I thought I actually glimpsed one of my own brothers

a long bag laden with some heavy piece of kit swung from Sykes-Wolsey's left hand we both double took at the unwelcome sight of each other although I was struck that he looked far guiltier than I felt then even more surprisingly he didn't walk straight past me cutting me dead like all the others but came over to wish me good luck trying to ingratiate himself to the end I thought uncharitably and then chided myself as I looked at his narrow haunted yearning bitter yellow face I held out a hand which he took in his knobbly mottled paw and as he did so I noticed quite how hairy a man he was and how shabby and soiled his clothes were we ended up shaking hands warmly with me overcome with a whole pile of mixed-up emotions the only clearly discernible one being how hideously conscious I was that this was probably the very last kind of human contact I'd ever have outside the morbid trappism of my family and so perhaps our hands were clasped together slightly longer than was entirely wise needless to say when I finally released his hand from mine I left about forty pounds in fivers stuck to his palm

for a horrified moment I thought he might think that I was trying to bribe my way back into the college instead that strange man merely thanked me put the money in his pocket and asked if I could spare him any more after we'd discussed my medical condition and his personal ambitions we ran together the distance to the bank his estranged family had used for centuries by which time I was able to open a current and savings account on very preferable terms and deposit in them a really quite significant sum of money the manager presented me with a chequebook my very first and even bowed his consent when I asked if I could write a cheque out there and then this I made out to Sykes-Wolsey in respect of his family's grand house which wasn't as badly burnt as some might have feared and all its estates in the west and which he now sold to me at a fair price he was the eldest son and despite his family's disapproval of his conversion to Catholicism and attempts at collaboration with the new masters they'd never quite given up hope and so never actually disowned or disinherited him by a stroke of the purest luck his father had died recently and it's said repulsively and as new head of the family he was finally at liberty to sell his family home to anyone who'd buy it allowing him to pursue his other interests with the funds realised although how far he got and how successful he was in his endeavours is something of a Mystery like the mysterious and not necessarily accidental explosion in the north that blew him into as many bits as surely my uncle was blown

anyway I bought Sykes-Wolsey's pile and kicked out his family including his poor white-haired horsefaced foulmouthed old mummy and a couple of spayed looking sisters and a chinless younger brother or two they'd been there since Cromwell's day we all appreciated the irony in that what a laugh they all buggered off back to England and soon inherited back all the money I'd paid Sykes-Wolsey when he died so prematurely unexpectedly and unfortunately considering his political and religious sensibilities which were at such variance to those of his family intestate I never thought about any of them again and instead for the first few years thanks to the sweat of my brow forgive me here I sat in splendid isolation not wanting for a thing getting immensely rich immensely fat and free from God History and my mother immensely happy and although some locals thought I treated the Sykes-Wolseys mean like and shabby had not my own brothers courted death or at least a heavy chill to free the land and was I not merely finishing the job by other and possibly better means I distributed land to the miserable sods for God's sake at reasonable terms but gratitude's always been at a premium among those who love their country enough to kill all or any of its inhabitants but this I will say back then there was more than one red-faced Protestant on a horse who'd nod politely and give me the time of day thank you very much I was cutting a fine and respectable figure in the country and still sweating the stuff faster than I could count it and those grand boys and girls they know which side their crustless white bread's buttered I tell you I even drained the bogs and got rid of the bloody mists and it was wine women and song in those days setting my cap at those haughty dogfaced girls and the one I chose grand family she came from like the rest a debutante she'd been would you believe quite gorgeous in a big-boned way and all of eight feet tall in her ostrich feather headdress at one of the grand balls I was getting invited to I even got to swill round the vintage brandy in bowls as big as your head with her brother the head of the family a gale howling at our backs in the big hall and dogs asleep or maybe even dying in front of a fireplace bigger than the house where I was born a fine clever man he was with letters as long as your arm after his name psychiatry he'd got into and I remember him telling me how he'd let the loonies out one Christmas to go home to their loved ones for want of a better term in fact of course they were the ones who'd driven them mad in the first place but he was like that full of progressive ideas you understand but you know what it'd quite ruined his Christmas the phone never stopped ringing with he's got his mother at knifepoint in the kitchen doctor what should we do I smiled at that back then and continued courting his magnificent giantess of a sister and complete happiness was just within my grasp but then

but then my mother and the da and the brothers turned up and I was finished

with court orders and masters of lunacy of a totally different stamp to my beloved's brother and her warned off and the dogs set on her

and restraints and the drugs to keep me quiet and the exercise machines and only woken up like now to do another turn on the treadmill and

and the ducts and tubes and

and my mother never stops talking these days counting up the money and on the telephone at my expense to her stockbroker and other fine gentlemen in every country in the world I know I know I'm no more a corporeal metaphor for that universal struggle between Good and Evil than the country round here's full of fairies souring the milk and bewitching the fine folk up at the Big House as once they did and what's she doing now it's inhuman

setting up shrines

nuns

tourists

gawping tourists behind the bars

another brief disembarkation from the charabanc for more bloody Yanks just another bit of misty-eyed mystical whimsical Oirish bollocks but I'd ask you this why is it do you think why every time I even move a muscle do I now sweat cheques written in a red spidery hand for many thousands of pounds drawn from a bank in Liechtenstein and made out to cash is that what you'd call normal and is it normal for a disabled person like me to be exploited like this for what's mine no I mean would an old woman sell her spastic child's shit and piss the way she sells what's mine of me from me and they say it all goes on cocoa for evil old pederast priests and more guns for the Boys and sannies for nuns for all I know I'm old I'm tired I'm more miserable than I ever was when I was poor will the woman live for ever will I never escape from her web of no no I'm not finished no not yet please please don't not yet no no no just a minute before you do that tell me tell me this in a lather of sweat and money just tell me no

89

no no don't no why of course you'd expect me in the circumstances no not to be at my freshest no a little high perhaps no but but why no why do I smell of *pastry*?

Men of Steel

Incidentally, due to the endemic corruption and incompetence which was also largely responsible for the imminent destruction of his home planet, the infant Kal-El left the surface of Krypton in his little spaceship twelve terrestrial hours later than planned. When it arrived on Earth, therefore, that planet had rotated on its axis through 180 degrees, and the craft landed not in the Midwest of the United States of America but in Soviet Central Asia.

The crashed pod and its alien passenger were discovered by a peasant called Vadim from a nearby collective farm, who reported back to the farm's political officer, who in turn reported up the chain of command. A division of Yagoda's Chekists soon arrived and arrested and then shot everyone in sight, although the strange baby at the centre of this new instance of fiendish sabotage proved impervious to all their efforts to liquidate him. Nervously, the Chekists on the ground reported back to their masters in Moscow, who ordered the infant to be placed in a special state orphanage, where he grew to adulthood and, in time, became a hero of Truth, Justice and the Soviet Way. However, Stalin, another man of steel, continued to view him with mounting suspicion.

Subsequently, dates for the achievement of several Five Year Plans were recalculated by Gosplan, and the Berlin Wall did not fall.

Joe

Josif Vissarionovich breathed an aerosol of phlegm and dying old man's bad breath out into the room, grey hairs from his moustache parting and floating for a second on exhalation, resting for another and waving back the other way as he breathed in noisily and with a distinct rattle.

Kuntsevo's cold. It's March already, but it's still cold. His blood is getting thin, like they're all saying? Huh. But he's an old man these days, seventy-four years old, with thirty-six years since the Revolution and, thirteen minus seven, that's six, carry one, five minus three equals two, twenty-six years since he's been the boss. He's always been good at sums, although recently he has tended to lose count. He felt the back of his head in the cold and banged his brown teeth together, although whether in an ague or because he was trying to speak they couldn't tell.

Lavrenty Beria smiled down at him and raised his long, straight glass as if he was making a toast. Lavrenty thinks I'm asleep, thought Josif Vissarionovich, looking thin looks at Beria, who looked away and said something to Malenkov. Lavrenty's telling Yegor that I'm asleep, thought Josif Vissarionovich, so they can talk about me behind my back. What are they saying? I can't hear them. Josif Vissarionovich parted his eyelids and squinted sideways into the big, cold room. Isn't that Molotov? Isn't Molotov an American spy? What's he doing here? thought Josif Vissarionovich. Is that a drink he's mixing?

And where were Khrushchev and Bulganin?

Nikita's all right. Nikita's down-to-earth, likes a joke, likes it when I take him off with a Ukrainian accent. And Nikolai's an upright, solid sort of fellow, does what he's told, no nonsense. Josif Vissarionovich wobbled some mucus at the back of his throat as he exhaled again.

Kuntsevo's cold.

But it is only March, and they were in the country. Was there snow on the ground? There might be pockets of fog around the wooden huts built in the hollows in the countryside surrounding his dacha, thought Josif Vissarionovich, if there isn't any snow. What time of day was it?

What day of the week was it? It's March already, and it's still cold. What's Beria doing here? Isn't he an English spy? Georgia's warmer than Russia in March, even Lavrenty can't cool it down, although both of them tend to like it hot. Lavrenty? Josif Vissarionovich gasped and Beria, Molotov and Malenkov turned round to look at him.

'What's he saying?'

'Search me, Yegor. He's delirious.'

'L-l-lavrenty, h-h-how much v-v-vermouth do you want in this Mmmmmartini?'

'Hmmm, Vyacheslav Mikhailovich?' Beria replied dreamily and whistled a few bars of Prokofiev's *Peter and the Wolf*.

What's Malenkov doing here? What's he up to? Does he think that because I let him read the general report at the Nineteenth Congress he's something special? thought Josif Vissarionovich. Lavrenty can still get rid of him, before I get rid of Lavrenty. What's Molotov doing here?

Kuntsevo's cold.

Not as cold as Siberia though, thought Josif Vissarionovich.

The politicals moaned and grouched about the ice outside and the cockroaches inside, while he was quite happy to go out to the bars in town with the criminal convicts and get so drunk they couldn't get out from under the table. They didn't feel the cold then, like they were men made out of steel. The rats among the political convicts once organised a comrades' court and put Josif Vissarionovich on trial for drinking with the criminal convicts, down-to-earth men, thought Josif Vissarionovich, with no bloody nonsense about convening committees in the tundra and putting comrades on trial on trumped-up charges, just a slug of vodka or two until you puked it all up over the permafrost. Well, he'd got even, thought Josif Vissarionovich as a draught touched his cheek and he shivered. Khrushchev and Bulganin came into the room. What's Khrushchev doing here?

Kuntsevo's cold.

Not as cold as the Kremlin, though, even in winter, thought Josif Vissarionovich, even in March. Vladimir Ilyich complained about the cold while he, Josif Vissarionovich, had stood at his side masterminding our victory in the Civil War. Why should it be any other way? Vladimir Ilyich had been ready to change Russia to fit History, so why shouldn't he, Josif Vissarionovich, be able to change History to suit himself? Vladimir Ilyich was a great man, concedes Josif Vissarionovich, even if a little too much given to thinking, like some kike. The so-called Lenin's testament said that Josif Vissarionovich was too rude. Well, maybe I am, thinks Josif Vissarionovich, but better to call a spade a spade and shock a few Jew ponces than lickspittle to all and sundry just so no one's offended! Christ! What's more offensive than a revolution? People can just like it or lump it. And if they lump it, that's their lookout. You can't make a revolution without . . . But Josif Vissarionovich lost the thought as

97

he suddenly coughed and retched for an instant, before subsiding back into his torpor. Malenkov slurped his egg-nog and smiled at Josif Vissarionovich. Khrushchev moved behind him.

Kuntsevo's cold.

It isn't just the cold that's wrong with the Kremlin, thought Josif Vissarionovich. A doctor was now taking his pulse. Who's he? What's he doing here? How did he get in? During the Civil War when we moved in the food was appalling and we complained about it too. Lev Davidovich in particular . . . Josif Vissarionovich swallowed some bitter bile with difficulty. Lev Davidovich particularly complained about the food. But he would do that, with his fine cosmopolitan ways, his nice Menshevik manners, while good old Lavrenty eats his greens with his fingers like an honest peasant from Asia. Doesn't he? Or is he a spy and saboteur? Josif Vissarionovich forgets, and then remembers and thinks to hell and back again with good manners and politeness and the whole fucking lot of it. Of course, Lev Davidovich was a Yid, which makes a difference. Like Yids are naturally fussy and poncey, it's in their natures to be. This doctor is saying something to Molotov, and I can't hear what it is, thought Josif Vissarionovich, so what's Molotov after anyway? Does he think he knows enough to get his way? He knows a sight too fucking much to stop him burning his fingers down to the fucking knuckle, by Christ! A vein throbbed in Josif Vissarionovich's ear. He'd better watch it if he thinks he knows enough!

The vein throbbed in Josif Vissarionovich's ear again so he tried to rub it against his pillow, and in so doing caught sight of another figure in the room, standing some distance from the bedside. Is that Bulganin, thought Josif Vissarionovich, slouching at the back as

98

usual? But Bulganin was standing over there by the cocktail cabinet, next to Malenkov, helping himself to a dry sherry and some peanuts. Molotov bent down over Josif Vissarionovich and pushed a spoon between his rubbery yet dry lips, which parted easily and although Josif Vissarionovich tried to grit his false teeth to stop the spoon getting any further, his jaw wouldn't respond to his orders and his mouth sagged open. Molotov gently caught the fluid that was dribbling down Josif Vissarionovich's chin, and put the spoon back in his mouth. Is this a Zionist plot? thought Josif Vissarionovich. Isn't Vyacheslav's wife a Jewess? But hadn't he, Josif Vissarionovich, made his own daughter Svetlana divorce her husband because he's a Jew? Has Malenkov forgotten how he got rid of his son-in-law for exactly the same reasons? Isn't it clear that there are forces within the state determined to destroy the state? Isn't Molotov a Jew? Who's this doctor? That isn't Bulganin, is it? Molotov looked up at Beria. Bulganin pouted beside Malenkov. Khrushchev moved in front of Malenkov.

Kuntsevo's cold. Outside, NKVD men in double-breasted overcoats stamped their boots on the gravel and blew into their gloved hands, and the white-haired, bearded man – that isn't Bulganin, so who the fuck is it? what's he doing here? – removes his pince-nez from his broad nose and breathes on the lenses, taking care in wiping them clean with a coloured handkerchief taken from his breast pocket. Josif Vissarionovich's eyelids fluttered as he strained his yellow eyeballs round in their sockets to look at this stranger and find out who he is. Molotov, meanwhile, fed some more of the liquid in the spoon to Josif Vissarionovich. Josif Vissarionovich racks his brains, already calcifying. He *knows* this bastard, but from where? From when? The glasses, the beard. Could it be that Jew brain doctor, whatsisname?

Freud? But why? He can't be in on the conspiracy too, can he? Josif Vissarionovich's finely trained mind is beginning to piece together the compelling evidence against Freud when the white-haired, bearded stranger walks straight through Beria and comes right up to Josif Vissarionovich's bedside. The spectre smiles down at him and Josif Vissarionovich finally makes the connection.

'Lev Davidovich,' Josif Vissarionovich breathes throatily. He opens his thin eyes wide, a whitish film already beginning to coat their defining yellowness. 'Lev Davidovich Bronstein!'

'Yeah yeah yeah. Hello, Josif Vissarionovich Dzhugashvili. And how are you yourself? But what's with all the standing on ceremony? I'm not going to rupture my tongue with your pig of a Georgian name just because you've decided to be all stand-offish after all this time.'

'Trotsky,' Josif Vissarionovich growls. 'I got rid of you years ago. You're dead.'

'You noticed? Nice of you to think of your old friends from time to time. I tell you, you gotta keep in with your old pals, you never know when you might need them.' Trotsky gestures at the members of the Praesidium around Josif Vissarionovich's bed. 'With this bunch of jokers around, you need all the friends you can get.'

Josif Vissarionovich lifts his head a fraction from his pillow. 'You are dead, aren't you?'

'What do you think?'

A fearful thought crosses Josif Vissarionovich's mind. His eyes move from one attending comrade to another. All are looking straight at him – Khrushchev, Beria, Molotov, Malenkov and Bulganin – but in a peculiar way, with the appearance of not particularly well-made waxworks. None of them seems to have noticed Trotsky, who is still smiling down at Josif Vissarionovich.

'I knew it!' gasps Josif Vissarionovich, more in desperation than discovery. 'It *is* a plot. A Zionist plot you have masterminded to kill me, in league with these arselicking bastards! Jewish cunt!' he snarls, and as his head falls back onto the pillow he spits an ochre bolus at Trotsky's smiling face. Trotsky ducks, however, and the spittle lands in Bulganin's trimmed goatee, where it runs down the grey hairs and forms a patch of filthy dampness on his dull and ill-fitting business suit.

'God, you're always so paranoid! I've been dead for thirteen years already, or had you forgotten?'

'No, not forgotten.' Josif Vissarionovich nods his head slightly. 'So why the social call, Trotsky?' Josif Vissarionovich's way with snide sarcasm hasn't quite deserted him yet.

'Always you got to have reasons! Just like you're so suspicious all the time!'

'But you are dead, aren't you?'

'Oh yes, Josif Vissarionovich, you can be sure of that. As dead as you'll be in half an hour's time or less.' Trotsky looks at his watch as he says these last words.

'What?'

'You mean you don't know? Molotov's been feeding you poison from that dry Martini for the last ten minutes. But hey! It comes to us all in the end.' Trotsky looks wistful, then smiles again.

Josif Vissarionovich grits his teeth and screws his eyes up in an expression of crushing realisation. 'Molotov!' he hisses. 'And what about the others?'

'Oh, they're all in on it, but for different reasons, obviously.'

'Bastards! Who's behind it? The Jews?'

'What's this thing you got against Jews already? You

think this bunch of goyim would do something useful? Be reasonable, Josif Vissarionovich! They wouldn't kick their own granny in the teeth if they knew it was her birthday! But tell me, what's this beef you got against Jews?'

'Oh, nothing, Lev Davidovich, nothing at all. It's just that you can't trust just anybody these days.'

'That's very true, Josif Vissarionovich. Not that there's anybody much left to trust.'

Josif Vissarionovich narrows his eyes. 'What do you mean by that, Trotsky?'

'Oh, nothing much. But hey, you know, I hear these things. Who was it now? Mikhail Ivanovich was talking to me the other day . . . you remember, Josif Vissariono-vich, come on! Mikhail Ivanovich Kalinin, President of the USSR! You poisoned him, when was it . . .'

'1946.'

'Right, 1946. Anyway, Misha was saying to me only the other day, Lev Davidovich, he was saying, it's getting quite like old times down here, you never meet anyone but old comrades. And he's right, you know. It's like Petersburg back in '17, you can't turn round without seeing a familiar face. Yagoda and Yhezhov send you their regards, by the way. No hard feelings. Oh yes, and I told Bukharin I was coming to see you. No message though. He doesn't seem to have forgiven you yet, Josif Vissarionovich.'

'Bukharin? Yhezhov and Yagoda? Kalinin? Where've you come from, Trotsky?' Josif Vissarionovich's damp brow furrows.

'You haven't guessed? Come on. Where d'you think?'

Josif Vissarionovich's mind is a blank. Then a thought passes through it. He turns his head to Trotsky and, hoping against hope that he's got the answer wrong, quietly says, 'Hell, Lev Davidovich?'

'Give the man a cigar! Considering you're so dumb it's a wonder you got so far, Josif Vissarionovich.'

'But what are you doing here? You haven't come just to pay a social call, have you? Lev, you haven't . . .'

'Oh yes I have, Josif. Come on, it's almost time to go.'

'Almost time?'

'Everyone's waiting.'

'Everyone?'

'Yes, everyone's waiting.'

'Waiting?'

'Give me strength! Yes, they're all waiting so they can start the trial.'

'The trial?'

'You graduating as a parrot or something? Yes, trial. Now hurry up, it's almost time.'

Josif Vissarionovich's eyebrows point down to the end of his nose. He sucks in his lower lip and scrapes it from between his loose teeth several times before glancing up at Trotsky.

'But . . . Lev . . . they can't . . . I won't . . . Lev, tell me what to do.'

'Me? Tell you what to do? Listen, you need my advice like I need a hole in the head!'

And as Trotsky leans over to squirt the small airbrush he's just taken out of his pocket into Josif Vissarionovich's face, Josif Vissarionovich reaches out to grab Trotsky's arm, but the spectre has already started to dematerialise and his hand falls through thin air. Josif Vissarionovich shudders. Hell? Trial? Everyone there. Everyone? Rykov? Kamenev, Muralov, Kretinsky? Nadezhda Alliluyeva? Gorky? And what about Vladimir Ilyich? In a final effort of will Josif Vissarionovich grinds his teeth and screws up his eyes. He won't go! They can't make him! He'll have them all arrested! Put on a show trial! Get Lavrenty back on to it, get him to stop it, stop it all, stop the whole fucking thing, stop it all.

Kuntsevo's cold. Even so, Molotov noticed a slight sweat break out on Stalin's forehead as he lifted another spoonful to his lips, but the dampness soon dried as the sudden spasm passed. Then the corpse began to cool.

Head Wound

Trotsky had earlier been elsewhere. More precisely, he'd materialised at the exact moment the hammer of Hitler's pistol had hit home, detonating the cartridge of the bullet destined to enter his gibbering brain at frankly incredible speeds. With a waggle of his fingers, Trotsky retarded the so far tiny explosion in the gun's chamber and the bullet proceeded down the barrel with excruciating slowness.

Hitler opened one eye, then the other, and bared his smelly teeth. Trotsky smiled infuriatingly down at him, and then seated himself between the Führer and the slumped body of Eva Hitler, whose recently acquired marital state did nothing to ameliorate her even more recently gotten and abidingly dead one.

'What are you doing here?' Hitler growled in his deep, gruff voice, squinting sideways at his visitor as he was unable, despite Trotsky's intervention, to move even an inch. The threads of History between the tip of the bullet and his grubby, moist and slightly sticky temple were by this stage too strong to break.

'Well, there's a question.' Trotsky leaned forward to help himself to a slice of pie from the dish on the low table in front of them. 'You might say that I've come to gloat. And why not? After all, that's my Red Army all round you out there. If it wasn't for me those brave lads would never have defeated the Whites and so, in turn, would never have ended up finishing off you and your crew. And 987¾ years earlier than you'd imagined, if my maths are right.'

Hitler wrinkled up his nose and twisted his mouth into a petulant snarl. Trotsky took a big bite of pie.

Just audible through the steel doors and the concrete and soil, soaked into a swamp by all the blood poured into it, they could hear the Soviet artillery, the shells they'd fired exploding and the buildings they'd aimed at collapsing, and as well as that strains of *Götterdämmerung* could just be heard playing interminably over a nearby wireless. Trotsky swallowed and licked his fingers.

'That,' he jerked his thumb in the direction of the music which feebly filled the foetid and dusty air, 'is just typical of you. "Twilight of the Gods"? Give me strength!'

Hitler grimaced and tried to shift his shoulders as best as he was able in the circumstances.

'Anyway,' Trotsky continued, 'although I admit the urge to gloat is very strong, I'm really here for another reason. On a freelance basis, if you understand what I mean.'

The Führer smiled weakly.

'You know, you speak very good German for a . . . um . . .'

'Jew? Russian? Or for a Red? Karl Marx was at least two of those, and he spoke it like a native, you *putz*. Why not for a pansy? That's one Stalin tried to stick on me because I could read and write and knew how to use a fork. Gypsy or cripple or mental defective I don't make a claim to, but I'd prefer the company of any of them to yours, in case you're wondering.'

'Then . . .'

'This is business. On a freelance basis, as I said.' Trotsky helped himself to another slice of pie. 'Incidentally, how many queer crippled retarded Communist Russian Jewish Gypsies do you suppose you've killed? I mean, the whole hog, with the lot going against them?'

Hitler closed his eyes as if immensely tired, or just simply bored at the childishness of the conversation.

'You think this is childish?' Hitler reopened one eye, and peered at Trotsky with growing suspicion. 'Then again, how many children have you killed? Had killed. Whatever. You know, gassed, or shot, or bombed, or tossed alive into furnaces. How many do you reckon? Hundred thousand? Million? Have a guess.'

Hitler sighed deeply. 'Is there a point to this?'

'A point? Look, I'll let you in on a secret. *There isn't any point to anything.* Although of course that shouldn't mean you stop trying, if you see what I mean. Anyway . . .'

Hitler interrupted him. He was beginning to feel the familiar rage growing inside, which was a shame as he'd composed himself with some care for his final action on Earth. His body pinioned by History, his emotions were only discernible, if at all, by a slight reddening of his ears and nostrils. Hissing between those vile teeth, he said, 'I get the point. You're the Russian Red Jew, and in a nice ironic twist you're here to take me to . . .'

Trotsky turned round on the sofa and held up a hand for silence. 'Now now, don't jump the gun. I've got a few other things to say first. Nice pie, by the way.' Trotsky munched away in silence for a moment or two, while Hitler rolled his eyes in despair. This really was intolerable!

Trotsky swallowed again, and dabbed at his goatee and brushed some crumbs from his lap before continuing. 'Now listen. You know as well as I do there's no point in going on about what you've done, and I'm getting bored with irony. The so-called saviour of Germany reducing Germany to ruins stuff doesn't really concern me. It might have been worthwhile making a point about morality once upon a time, but we all know the more morally certain you are, the greater the depths of immorality you'll sink to in order to remain moral, and it's a bit late for all that now. Although it's always worthwhile repeating that killing someone is always a more immoral act than anything that person, while alive, is capable of doing which you choose to perceive as immoral.'

'Huh!' Hitler pouted. 'You've changed your tune! What was that line you wrote about suppressing the Kronstadt Revolt – slaughtering the vanguard of your own revolution, no less? "There is a difference between the violence used by the slave owner to enshackle his slaves, and the violence used by the slave to break free from those chains, and anyone incapable of seeing the difference is a contemptible eunuch before the Court of Morality." Isn't that it? I always said you Reds were full of shit.'

'Fair point. I could mention how you started your brilliant career in murder by butchering your own butchers in the Night of the Long Knives . . .'

'Touché, I'm sure,' Hitler sneered.

'. . . and I could also say I've changed my mind, but who cares? All I wanted . . .'

'Although it's worth speculating,' the Führer interrupted again, 'on whether you'd have ended up killing more or fewer people than my old friend and ally Joe Stalin if your roles had been reversed. In fact, it's rather odd that you, of all people, should turn up at the moment of your own murderer's greatest triumph. Apart, that is, from murdering you, of course. Indeed, I'm surprised you didn't end up on my side against the, what did you call him, the "Cain of the Kremlin", I think it was. I nearly beat him, you know. I nearly freed the Russians from the monstrous and murderous tyranny you imposed upon them . . .'

'Right, freed them to be slaves to your master race, whom my subhuman countrymen are busy slaughtering and raping all around you, you schmuck. That's what I . . .'

Something flashed in Hitler's left eye. 'They deserve it! It's their own fault they're so weak! I could . . .'

Trotsky raised his eyes to the ceiling of the bunker, which intermittently coughed out little clouds of plaster dust with each closer explosion. 'Save it, pal.' Hitler calmed down and looked rather sheepishly at Trotsky. The bullet was now about halfway down the barrel.

'I know what you're going to say next,' Hitler said after a pause. 'Why the Jews? It's been asked before. If I hadn't insisted on a racially pure Fatherland we'd have kept hold of Einstein and the rest of those clever boys and we'd have had the atom bomb years ago.' He was speaking in a singsong voice now, having rehearsed the line many times in his head. 'Well . . .'

'No, honestly,' Trotsky interrupted yet again, 'it doesn't matter. It's done. They're dead, and ten times as many other people are dead too. Why doesn't matter any more. None of it can be undone is all that counts. If you want why, then everyone will always know why: that you and your gang of small-time deadbeat mobsters were just stupid and ugly losers who were driven crazy by anyone better looking or smarter or funnier than you. Why those clowns outside' – and as he spoke another seventy German ghosts evaporated into the roaring air – 'let you get on with it is anyone's guess, but that's people . . .'

'But they knew I was right. I had to make them believe in themselves again. That's why . . .'

'Believe in themselves? What, like they're Tinkerbell who dies if she doesn't hear a million of the *Herrenvolk* squeaking *sieg heil*?'

'Who's Tinkerbell?'

'Listen, I've got to know about people, and . . .'

'No, I mean it. Who's Tinkerbell?'

'There is nothing to know.'

'What?'

'That didn't come out right, but what I'm . . .'

'No, actually, you should have joined with us. Against Stalin. I might have let you rule in his place. Like I was going to put that queer playboy, whatsisname, the Duke of Windsor and that emaciated witch of a wife of his on the throne of England once we'd beaten them. Then the Jew Roosevelt and that fat drunk Jew Churchill . . .'

'Hang on, hang on. Churchill isn't a Jew.'

'I think you'll find I'm right.'

'But he doesn't even look Jewish!'

'Precisely.'

A particularly close explosion made Trotsky suddenly cringe, and then shake the dust out of his hair. Hitler remained immobile, except for the growing look of mad cunning in his eyes.

'And de Gaulle. Jewish, I mean. And Eisenhower. And Tito. And here's one you'd never guess. Franco. Yes, that treacherous little dago turns out to be one of the Chosen People too. Like Mussolini. And here's another.' Hitler peered at Trotsky with beguiling eyes, which then darted to and fro before he whispered, 'Stalin. Definitely. A. Jew. What do you make of that, eh?'

'What's that?' Trotsky said through another mouthful of pie, turning back just in time to catch the Führer's face collapse from glee to a growing despair. 'You talking about Jews again? Christ, you're a bore. Change the fucking record, can't you? Give us all a rest, you tedious little twat.'

In as much as he was able in the straitjacket Destiny had him held in, Hitler bridled. He even tried to puff out his chest and flounce, standing still the way he used to at the big shows, although of course that was, at the moment, impossible. His eyes shone red and yellow at their edges, and his nostrils flared. 'So, you've come here not to gloat, not to seek some kind of final explanation from me, not to hose Red Jew piss all over my final humiliation, not even to indulge me in my last seconds by joining in my little mind games. Dear God! Have you no curiosity? I am one of the greatest monsters in History! I have been directly responsible, through my deranged actions in pursuit of my insane belief in frankly ludicrous scientific theories jumbled up with a pathetic hotchpotch of half-thought-out mystical claptrap and embarrassingly kitsch folklore' – and he nearly bellowed the last word – 'for the deaths, yes, if you like the murders of sixty million people. Sixty million!' Hitler's eyes got wilder. His voice was growing louder and louder and he got angrier and angrier. 'I am the worst person who has ever lived, and my name will not, as I dreamed, be honoured for my great achievements, but will live in infamy for ever! My thousand-year Reich will be a thousand years of shame on the German people, the people I love and yet have brought to the position where their complicity in my crimes will dishonour this country throughout all time! I will be a byword for horror and murder and war and death and . . . and . . . and . . . you come here . . .' and he paused for a terrible instant, while the foam bubbled at the corners of his twisted mouth and the bullet neared the end of the barrel '. . . you come here just to insult me?'

'No,' Trotsky replied after he'd swallowed the last piece of the last slice of pie, 'I came here to tell you that that,' and he tapped Hitler's temple where the muzzle of the gun pressed in on the yellowing skin, while simultaneously scratching the back of his own head, 'is going to really really hurt.'

And without another word the apparition had gone, even before the blood hit the wall or the sound of the gunshot, an indiscernible note struck in the middle of a massive symphony of death, was heard by the henchmen cowering outside.

Goldeneye

In his early senescence the writer Evelyn Waugh was invited by his cousin Ann to stay at the Jamaican estate of her husband, Ian Fleming, also a writer. Despite a succession of pained excuses which Waugh insisted forbade travel, ranging from sciatica to crises of faith to incipient madness, he was eventually prevailed upon by his wife to accept the offer; so after various adventures at the departure and arrival desks of at least three airports, which left several menial employees of BOAC in tears, the Waughs arrived at Goldeneye.

Ann Fleming greeted her cousin with an appalling proposal. 'God, Evelyn, you look absolutely ghastly, positively *moribund*, but poor Laura looks worse. Darling, how *do* you put up with him? What *you* need is pampering, and I know just the place!' It transpired that Ann was cultivating an osteopath newly arrived in Kingston, who added to his manipulative powers a growing salon of the smarter women in ex-pat Jamaican society. 'A week under Mr Cruttwell's magical fingers, darling, and you'll be a new woman! And while we do that we can leave these two old buffers back here *writing*.' The two men flinched as she spat the word out, as both of them had been physically assaulted by Ann in the past, Waugh, publicly, twice and Fleming, privately and consensually, far more frequently. And now, helplessly overwhelmed by this pre-emptive strike, all they could do was eye each other suspiciously, each thinking, 'How the hell did she manage to pull that one and lumber me with this frightful Jewish pansy?'

117

Straight after breakfast the next morning Mrs Fleming and Mrs Waugh were driven down to Kingston and into the hands of Cruttwell, leaving their husbands sitting opposite each other on the veranda, shaded from the bright matutinal sunshine and the glare from the lush tropical borders beyond the small lawn, in silence.

Fleming, in a garish safari shirt, finally picked up a sheet of paper and rolled it into the typewriter on the table in front of him. Waugh noticed this and made a business of rearranging his own pile of blank sheets of paper, extracting his fountain pen from the inside pocket of his thick, large-checked tweed jacket and then filling it, emptying it and filling it again several times from the bottle of ink on the table. Fleming looked sideways at him from his studied pose, chin resting in the palm of his hand, elbow on the arm of his cane chair, legs crossed away from Waugh and pointing towards the garden, into which he was pretending to stare. For his part, as he repeated the operation with the pen a sixth time, Waugh sneaked the occasional glance at Fleming, who immediately looked away.

They continued in this manner for some time, until Fleming cleared his throat and, without looking at Waugh, addressed his typewriter and began clattering away. Waugh took his turn to stare into the garden, now and again clearing his throat noisily, alternating this with plumping his folded hands down into his lap or across his paunch with a sigh.

After a while an exotic bird of fabulous plumage landed in the garden and proceeded to stalk a lizard. Waugh surveyed the hunt with a bored intensity. The bird hopped this way and that, until finally flapping briefly into the air and falling on the lizard with its talons. Held fast, the reptile squirmed in defiance, even after the bird's beak began unravelling its guts from its fissured, pale belly. Waugh turned away, tired of the spectacle and unprepared to make anything of it, while Fleming continued typing, apparently lost in composition.

Waugh picked up the pen again, then thought better of it and instead took a number of small bottles from the various pockets of his jacket and waistcoat. These he now lined up, surveyed, rearranged, lined up in different order, constructed into a little pyramid, knocked over and then placed in a series of patterns, starting with a swastika and ending with a cross. Fleming typed on impervious, so Waugh now opened every little bottle and took out from each a small, coloured pill, which was now in its turn lined up with its companions in a series of patterns matching those constructed from the bottles. As the tablets were smaller he could be more delicate and intricate, and this time started with a swastika and finished with a rather lumpy hammer and sickle. Fleming looked up for a fraction of a second and then looked down again, back to his typing. Waugh saw this, so now took out a small hip flask and, putting the first pill (at the handle end of the sickle) on his tongue, washed it down with a quick slug of what-ever was in the flask, doing this with a great deal of gasping, wheezing, glugging and lip smacking. When he reached the seventh pill, Fleming stopped typing and Waugh froze, like an uncle about to smother his nieces and suddenly discovered by the constabulary. However, Fleming ignored Waugh and reached under the table for something, which turned out to be an ashtray. Waugh peered suspiciously at Fleming, who didn't return the look, and didn't do anything with the ashtray either. Instead, he resumed typing.

The bird was now finishing off the last scraps of the lizard, whose thin gore speckled the bird's beautiful beak. Waugh pushed the pill bottles aside and, after a great deal of puffing and gasping and fumbling, pulled a religious medal from his trouser pocket which he then breathed on so heavily that he started coughing and began to choke. Fleming continued typing, and it was only once Waugh recovered enough to conclude the operation by polishing the medal in a rather half-hearted fashion with his hankie and then collapsed, red-faced, back in his cane chair that Fleming paused again, this time looking straight at Waugh, who mopped his streaming face, kissed the medal and popped it in his waistcoat pocket.

'For Christ's sake, Evelyn.'

Waugh looked up at Fleming with a start, and shouted back, 'What did you say! I'm sorry, I'm very deaf!'

Fleming rolled his eyes to the dark underside of the veranda's thatched roof, doubtless nocturnally the home of bats, beetles and who knows how many species of venomous beasts. He shifted the ashtray slightly to the left of where it lay next to the typewriter. 'Honestly, Evelyn, I know you still blame me for not taking you aboard at the Admiralty during the War, but this is . . .'

Waugh cupped a hand behind his ear, widened his eyes, grinned in a pained kind of way and shouted, 'Sorry, Ian! Can't hear a thing!' Fleming ground his teeth and started typing again.

The exotic bird, meanwhile, had concluded its brunch and flew off from the lawn into the obscuring verdancy beyond. Fleming typed on. Waugh's face collapsed a fraction, folds of pink flesh shifting away from cantankerous mischief towards a kind of despairing pout, and he sniffed, stole a look at Fleming and then stared back into the garden, now birdless and, lest we forget, lizard-less too. Fleming hunkered down while, unseen by Waugh, keeping one eye on his companion.

It was only when he saw Waugh turn back to the table, unscrew the cap of his pen and begin writing that Fleming leaned forward over his typewriter and whispered, 'I saw Nancy the last time I was in Paris.' Waugh showed no sign of having heard a word, and gnawed his lower lip as he crossed out whatever few lines it was he'd written. Fleming leaned further forward and hissed, more quietly than before, 'She showed me her Order of Lenin.'

Waugh said nothing. Without looking up, he just sat there, seeming to swell slightly. Fleming sat back in his chair and watched the colour wash into Waugh's face in a kaleidoscope of deepening reds. Waugh bared his teeth, and tears began to well up in his now nearly circular eyes.

'What!'

Fleming smiled and pulled out his cigarette holder.

'WHAT!' Waugh bellowed, as the exotic bird, which had perched in a nearby tree, flew off in fright. 'SHE'S GOT THE ORDER OF FUCKING LENIN!' Waugh stared at Fleming, sobbing uncontrollably with rage and envy, before eventually mewing pitifully, 'Why haven't I got one?'

Fleming shrugged, extracted a cigarette case from another pocket and languidly screwed a Sobranie into the holder.

'WHY HAVEN'T I GOT ONE!' Waugh screamed, now purple and hyperventilating.

'Come on, Evelyn, don't take on so.'

Waugh struggled to compose himself, but just ended up opening and shutting his mouth like a beached carp, tears streaming down his chubby, puce cheeks. Fleming blew cerulean smoke out of his nose and raised his eyebrows in what some might have thought was a conciliatory way.

'Now now, Evelyn, it's only third class, you know.'

'THIRD CLASS!'

'Calm down, old boy. I'm sure you'll get yours eventually. Moscow Central tell me that they're still awfully pleased with *Brideshead*, you know, even if it didn't have quite the desired result.'

Waugh was still making considerable efforts to get a grip of himself. He dabbed his eyes with the hankie, blew his nose and slumped in his chair. When he next spoke it was with a terrible, resigned moroseness.

'Oh, Ian. What do they want? I did my best with that beastly *Brideshead* book, didn't I? How am I meant single-handedly to foment their precious lower classes into revolution with just one book? How was I meant to know that the pigs would like all that stuff in their horrid little book clubs and all that rot? I sometimes wonder if it's worth the money.'

Fleming suddenly felt sorry for the old buffer, worn out, burnt out, florid, ill and still doing his best to please their mutual paymasters in the Kremlin.

'There there, Evelyn. It's a long game, you know. No one expects immediate results, you know that as well as I do. Just look at these Bond books they've told me to write. Now I hear that they are, cumulatively, doing immense harm to Western Intelligence, but it's not going to happen overnight, for Christ's sake!'

Waugh pouted. Fleming rolled his eyes again. After a heavy pause, which gave birth to a comment from neither of them, they returned, in silence, to their writing.

Waugh had just crossed out the same sentence for the twelfth time when he looked up again at Fleming, sighed, and said, 'Sorry, Ian. I get frustrated. I've been faithful to the party ever since I was recruited in Abyssinia, and I just feel that I ought to do something more . . . more palpable. That's why I got so cross when you wouldn't fix it so I got that job at the Admiralty at the start of the War.'

'For God's sake, Evelyn! I wasn't even a member then! That's where *I* was recruited!'

'Good Lord! That's not what Graham told me.'

'Graham?'

'Graham knows all about such things, you know. Frightfully cloak and dagger. They say he still writes all his atheistical little books in invisible ink for purposes of security.' Waugh drawled the last words for laconic effect.

'But Greene's on the other side.'

'What?'

'He bats for the other team, Evelyn. You must have known that.'

Waugh's many-chinned jaw dropped. 'What? But he can't! He's such a beastly Red!'

'Exactly.'

'But . . .' This time the colour drained completely from Waugh's face. 'Oh my God. Oh. Fuck. Um, Ian, I think I may have done something rather silly.'

Fleming looked at him without speaking.

'I . . . um . . . I told him about Betjeman, and Tony Powell and . . . Oh Christ . . . even Ronnie Knox and Wodehouse.'

Fleming said nothing and fixed a fresh Sobranie in his cigarette holder.

'You did what?'

'It . . . it just came out in conversation. I was a bit tight, I suppose. It's difficult these days. I get so tired and . . . and . . .'

'Careless, Evelyn. That's the word for it. Jesus!' Fleming lit his fag and drew heavily on it, thinking carefully. 'Look, it's not really that important. Betjeman's a busted flush anyway, and Tony's probably a double agent. Knox is harder. Your friend the Pope . . . well, best not discuss that now. Wodehouse, though . . . Hmmm.' Fleming leaned his chin on the palm of his hand again and chewed at the cigarette holder, occasionally gasping out wreaths of purplish smoke which eddied away into the garden. The exotic bird had flown back onto the lawn, and was hopping around in search of fresh snacks.

Waugh's hands shook as he took out a cigar case, and from it a cigar which he lit with difficulty. 'Do you think . . . ?'

'Look, I'm sure it's going to be all right. I'll cable my control tonight on the scrambler. They know what they're dealing with, and as long as you didn't let anything else out of the bag . . . Hmmm.' They sat in silence for a long time, Waugh nervously puffing at his cigar, Fleming watching the antics of the exotic bird going about its business. Fleming finally swung round in his chair and, once more, faced his typewriter. However, his hands hung hesitantly over the keyboard, as if unsure of something.

'Evelyn.'

Waugh looked up with a frightened expression.

'What do you know about Koreans?'

'Koreans?'

'Koreans. Got a problem with the, whatsit, baddies.' He sneered the last word.

'Why Koreans?'

'Well, it used to be simple with baddies for those chaps before the War. Jews and Negroes were fair game back then, but my American publishers say they're now off limits, worse luck. The thing about the kind of stuff I write is that it helps with the villains if they're members of a race the reader will instantly recognise as quite beyond the pale.'

Waugh raised his eyebrows. 'How extraordinary. Have you considered the Chinese?'

'No, won't do. The Chinese are clever, everyone knows that. *Fiendishly* clever, so while they'll do for criminal masterminds, it's the devil's own business casting the thugs. I thought I might try out Koreans. What do Koreans make you think about?'

'Weren't the Nips awfully frightful to them in the War? And aren't half of them pinkoes or something?'

'Yes they were and yes they are, but does anyone know that, or really care? Do you see my problem? What do you think when you see the word "Korean"?'

Waugh looked back into the garden, where the exotic bird, a fast worker, was now pecking at the remains of another lizard. He turned slowly back to Fleming. 'I rather think Christopher Sykes might be Korean, you know. It might be thought rather bad form if you were to traduce his ancestors like that, don't you think?'

Fleming glowered at Waugh, looked back to his typewriter and started clattering away again. Waugh picked up his pen once more and held it over the paper as he stared into space.

Its latest meal concluded, the exotic bird took to the wing and flew into a nearby tree, where it gave voice to a hideous screech. Both men looked up with a start, then at each other. Waugh put down his pen and took out another cigar, making a pantomime of either offering it to Fleming or asking silent permission to smoke. Fleming pulled a face which seemed to decline the offer while sanctioning the act, and then took another Sobranie from the case in his pocket, screwing the snout into the end of the long cigarette holder which he then clenched, like Captain Hook, between his bounder's teeth. For a while the two men smoked in silence, Fleming gazing at the paper in his typewriter while

Waugh blew delicate blue smoke rings, occasionally brushing ash from his trousers and picking sour specks of tobacco from his tongue.

The sun rose to its zenith in the sky and the glare from the garden intensified.

After about fifteen minutes Fleming stopped again, stuck another Sobranie in his cigarette holder, and looked up.

'Um. Do you want to take that jacket off? You must be awfully hot.'

Waugh went on studying the doodles on the page in front of him. 'Before luncheon? Certainly not!' And so they continued, each ignoring the other and pretending to be entirely consumed by what lay before them on the table, until Fleming lifted his fingers from the keys and fixed Waugh with one gimlet eye.

'Evelyn.'

'Hmm?'

'Do you still find this kind of thing easy? The writing, I mean.'

'Absolute torture.'

'It's hell is what it is. You're lucky, you know. I get told all my plots, but this one's just frankly awful. I can't do a damn thing with it.'

'What is it?'

'They want to call it *Goldfinger*, about a sinister Lithuanian spy who wants to blow up Fort Knox. God knows where they get their ideas from, but it's beating me. What about you?'

'Oh, they want me to finish the War trilogy and I thought I'd butter them up with some rot about the Sword of Stalingrad and Guy Crouchback's dark night of the soul, although I can't for the life of me think how to pad it out and finish the wretched thing.'

Fleming sighed. 'Seems we're in the same boat, doesn't it?'

'Most ironic.'

'I just don't, what's the word, enjoy it as much as I used to. It all seems a bit, well, a bit formulaic.'

'Stuck. In. A. Rut.' Waugh puffed away at his cigar. 'I say, Ian, can't you call your native bearer and get us a drink?'

'That won't help.'

'Bugger off and get me a drink. In return I'll do yours if you do mine.'

Fleming's eyebrows shot up, he considered the proposition and so they stood up, ever so slightly unsteadily, and swapped places at the table on the veranda. Soon Fleming was scribbling furiously on Waugh's pile of paper, filling page after page with words, while Waugh typed two-fingered with surprising nimbleness and with equally surprising speed. By lunch time, after Fleming's long-suffering Jamaican servant had brought out several more Martinis, and with a fresh glass in front of each of them, they'd produced over 5000 words each. Waugh acknowledged his labours by finally taking off his tweed jacket and unbuttoning his waistcoat.

'You know, Ian, I'm surprised you've never made more of the fact that your man is so clearly a Catholic. One of the old recusant families, I'd say, with a private devotion in equal measure to St John of the Cross' – which Waugh pronounced, slightly slurred, to rhyme with 'horse' – 'and St Ignatius Loyola. Very sound on mortification of the flesh, don't you think. Or don't you?'

'I hope this isn't a theme you intend to expand on. Don't you think you might rather give the game away? Again?'

Waugh paused to relight his cigar and ignored the parry. 'I don't think they'll find out, do you, as long as you control your urge to turn Crouchback into a murderous satyr with half a dozen, what d'you call them, *gizmos* up his sleeve.'

'To be honest, Evelyn, I'm just about to contrive for the vile Corporal-Major Ludovic to start composing what is, to all intents and purposes, *Brideshead Revisited*.'

Waugh chortled, and both men returned to the job in hand beneath the shallow shadows of the veranda. Out on the lawn, the exotic bird blinked, taking another picture of the scene, the microphones hidden between its beautiful artificial feathers having picked up their every last word.

Film Studies

The meniscus on the ditches and bayous at the back of
the college crackled with ice, and behind him the busts
of long-dead alumni cracked into hideous rictuses in the
penetrating frost as Seumas Black pulled his beret
further down over his head and stuck his chin deeper
into the long, loose-knit mauve scarf wrapped several
times round his neck. His hands, in fingerless mittens,
were thrust into the high side pockets of his jacket, and
his narrow trousers tapered down to red shoes which
crunched across the clumps of white, frozen grass. The
back gate was, thank God, open, despite the earliness of
the hour and the fact that term had officially ended three
days before, at which point almost everyone had wisely
fled the crippling cold hanging, like the last breath from
a fresh corpse, around the Fens.

No, that wouldn't do. He tried to rework the trope as
he strode on, mindful of that thing he'd read in *Cahiers
du Cinéma* where Sam Spade had observed in *The Maltese
Falcon* that the cheaper the hood, the gaudier the patter.
Beneath the palest of pale blue skies, cross-hatched by
clouds of ice crystals high, high up, his denim satchel
swung as he walked, its contents of seminal texts and a
primitive videotape clattering together each time the
bag completed an upswing to return, with a thud, to his
hip.

The scarf smelled nice, and still, indeed, smelled of
Stephanie. He grimaced for a second as he turned the
corner towards the lecture site as he remembered, again,
their terrible row just before the end of term. He'd

thought it had been about Godard, but knew all along it was really about his refusal to go down as soon as term finished to her parents' place in Hampshire. Hampshire, for Christ's sake! It wasn't that he didn't like Steph's other friends (although obviously he didn't), but the thought of having to spend time in Hampshire with all those twats, so far from his natural habitat anywhere between Hammersmith and Camden, made him shudder. Anyway, she knew he had to attend Sykes-Wolsey's seminar, although she'd bordered on obduracy in failing to see how a seminar held under the aegis of a different faculty, far removed from his own subject, could be so important.

Things weren't helped by Sykes-Wolsey's idiosyncrasies, like insisting on continuing teaching after the end of term, although everyone knew that that was really just part of his pose, to reinforce his spiritual separation from the petty time constraints of the rest of the university in order to highlight his defining and fundamentally different seriousness. And, of course, his importance in a far wider arena than defined by the narrow-minded boundaries of this place. Seumas snuffled a laugh into the scarf as he again compared Sykes-Wolsey's celebrated rigour with the pitiful shortcomings of most of his own supervisors, particularly Pocock. He was no longer on speaking terms with his director of studies (which suited both of them just fine) as Pocock had clearly never heard of most of the people Seumas had cited in support of the analysis laid out with clinical precision in his last essay, and it was widely believed that the old fucker couldn't even speak French, let alone German. As he walked across the Sedgwick site Seumas was growingly conscious of the customary murderous rage that inevitably followed every time he thought of Pocock, and valiantly, and successfully, he exiled all such thoughts from his mind as he opened the glass and metal door to the department building and bounded up the stairs to the room where Sykes-Wolsey was lecturing.

Seumas was slightly abashed on entering to realise that he was the last to arrive. Two dozen similarly gaunt, slow-eyed faces turned on him as he stood in the doorway unfurling his scarf. At the top end of the room Sykes-Wolsey was sitting at a slight angle on the edge of the desk, next to a large TV set, which was currently hissing a black snowstorm of untuned static.

'Ah! More people. Come in, come in! Sit down . . . ah . . . there.'

Seumas smirked an apology as he sat down at the seat indicated by Sykes-Wolsey, pulling the small, integral tray over his lap as he pulled off his beret.

'Now, to recap for our . . . ah . . . latecomer. When seen in context the influence on the Bond films of the Carry On body of work is clear. Not just in terms of construction and narrativisation but, crucially, in terms of language. I'm indebted to the work of my colleague Dr Killane, who unfortunately has been detained in Hanoi, in this area, particularly for his close heuristics in analysing the ur-text or . . .' and Sykes-Wolsey waggled two fingers from each hand in the air '. . ."screen-play". . .' several students tittered '. . . in *Diamonds Are Forever*. We observed last time the use and interplay of double entendre in the obfuscation – literally, the disem-powerment of meaning – in both canons, the double-meaning/no-meaning nexus of ambiguity you should all be familiar with by now. But add to this the conscious borrowing of the language and practice of low farce deployed in the context of spy adventure. Moreover, the inevitably sexual dimension in these forays into the notoriously treacherous area of meaning denial/betrayal takes us towards the epistemological elephant trap, without us even beginning to explore all the other dynamics at play, from the objectification of the standard temptress role typified throughout the canon by Barbara Windsor, say, taken against the subjectification implied if not obvious in Bond's own internalised emotional dialectic, as the opposed but essentially symbiotic dynamics of sadism and masochism struggle for achievement of the final dominant synthesis within his, forgive me, libido . . .' and he waggled his fingers round that word too, while the same students sniggered knowingly '. . . placed ur-textually – and I'm very conscious of the inadequacies of these terms before you all start throwing things at me . . .' nearly all the students laughed here '. . . alongside Bond's perceived but only apparently externalised meta-dynamic with, in this instance, Ernst Blofeld.

'To return, then, to Killane's fresh insight in this area. The music hall vulgarity, for want of a better phrase, of Bond's language, particularly what my more old-fashioned colleagues might term "post-coitally", that is, if you prefer, post-partum in the context of the sex/birth/death mathene central to the so-called drama, can be seen highlighted in this section from *Diamonds Are Forever*.' Sykes-Wolsey slipped a videotape into a machine next to the TV set, which then stuttered into animation, but silently. 'As we observed last week, at this stage Bond and Tiffany Case are on Blofeld's oil rig, which, significantly, he has acquired by masquerading – and we've already covered masques, the carnivalesque and shape-changing within this canon of work, so I don't think I need to recap all that – as the billionaire Willard Whyte of, rather nicely, the Whyte House Casino in Las Vegas. Now you can see here Tiffany Case remove what she believes to be the real cassette tape which will implement the laser satellite's mechanism to destroy Washington, DC and replace it with what she believes to be the decoy, a tape of bagpipe music – with all that that particular choice of music connotes culturally but, more importantly, psychosexually. And here, the language consequence. The dialectic is worked out when Bond discovers what Tiffany has done, and says . . .'

Sykes-Wolsey turned up the sound and Seumas heard Sean Connery say to Jill St John, 'You twit!'

Sykes-Wolsey turned off the tape.

'I know many of you will have had the misfortune to attend Professor Jackson's rather futile efforts to breathe life back into the stale corpse of text studies, which still seem to hold a mystifying appeal to rather a lot of people in these parts . . .' more laughter '. . . but I should immediately add, before I get myself into even hotter water, that his so-called "deconstruction" in his recent lecture of the line "Jug jug jug jug jug jug" in a soi-disant poem by T.S. Eliot – and I won't for the moment comment on what I think of my friend and colleague Lavinia Sheet's description of Eliot as "numero-uno text-Nazi". . .' and there was even more laughter '. . . suffice to say, Professor Jackson's almost forensic autopsy on those six words was not without merit. I was there myself, and though it was, admittedly, a rather long three hours . . .' several students sniggered again '. . . it served to show how powerfully the errors of text-analysis maintain their stranglehold on certain sections of the Academy. Without necessarily agreeing with any of what these poor misguided people assert . . .' and Sykes-Wolsey paused to smile a beautiful smile '. . . it is still valid to imbue partially what Bond says with what Eliot and his muddle-headed followers still maintain that what they call text means or might now have or ever have had any possibility of meaning, as such.'

At the back Seumas glowed with an inner warmth.

This was just what he'd tried to explain to Steph, and why he had to attend Sykes-Wolsey's seminar, even though the subject Sykes-Wolsey specialised in wasn't even a part of any course the university offered, and he hung on to tenure, in the History of Art faculty of all places, by the skin of his teeth. But that was the point. He didn't belong here. He belonged in Paris, or Frankfurt, which made him even more special and exotic in Cambridge, as he used his fierce intelligence and limitless charm to smash down the ancient, arrogant ivory towers of error all around him to point a new way to new understanding. This was just perfect.

'Now we must move on to the bigger picture, as it were. When this film came out nine years ago, the events, the so-called "narrative" depicted, coexisted in spacio-temporal continuum with those, and again forgive me for using such outmoded terms, but they'll serve as shorthand until we've finalised a precise new heuristic lexicon, anyway, the events of *Diamonds Are Forever*, as we know, happened at the same time and in the same place, as the events "texted". . . ' and Sykes-Wolsey almost sneered his derision at the term he'd used '. . . in Hunter S. Thompson's *Fear and Loathing in Las Vegas*.' Seumas had missed all this, and now almost hugged himself with delight. 'Although the two ur-texts make no reference to each other, no more than *The Waste Land* false-text makes reference to the *Ulysses* ur-text, the inter-play of the two ur-texts is both obvious and inevitable. After all, Bond and Thompson were both in Las Vegas at the same time, and so it is quite beyond belief that they wouldn't have both met and inter-acted.'

At this point most of the students burst into spontaneous applause, which Seumas obviously joined in with, although he was slightly puzzled. Sykes-Wolsey waved his hands to hush his audience.

136

'No, no, please. This is not a conjuring trick, merely the inevitable truth that ur-textual tools lead us to. To hammer the point home, and for the benefit of some of us who have joined our little voyage of discovery rather late in the day . . .' Sykes-Wolsey beamed broadly at Seumas, who was beginning to feel rather uncomfortable '. . . the pioneering work by Schlefen and Crespolini in the sixties has now conclusively proved that we can no longer speak with any confidence in the ways that have held our subject back in the dark ages of understanding for so long. The arrogance, which still pertains, both here and in so many other places, that maintains the fictive lie, bolstered by the text lie, is frankly breathtaking. I will not now rehearse the battles we've had, but I can promise you this, that while we have more battles ahead, we will win this war!'

Sykes-Wolsey was now almost shouting, and his previously charmingly insouciant air had been replaced by something altogether more sinister. At the back Seumas glanced nervously at the faces of the other students, all of which had become masks of wide-eyed, joyous, unquestioning adulation.

'In short, we have proved, through rigorous analysis, that fiction does not exist and that, more precisely, the camera never lies. Close critical study over the last fifty years or so has finally taught us that, as an extrapolation from film studies, we can also prove that in every other medium everything depicted, in every poem, play, book or film, is, quite simply, the Truth. We know, through brain-scanning technology, that there is no such thing as 'mind' or 'imagination' or any of the other old lies that we've been fed with for centuries. Everything is merely a truthful documentary depiction of things as they then were. In certain cases, during the great modernist error, the shortcomings of the documentarist explain the apparent obtuseness of the document, certainly, but we can hardly blame Picasso for being such a bad painter, or having such ugly models, for his inability to produce clear document or ur-text. Similarly, we've seen how the false-text of *The Waste Land* is really the result of Eliot's badness as a writer, of his simple inability accurately and coherently to record an April morning in 1922 and his journey to work and his visit to a church, some pubs and the public library in his attempts to produce the ur-text. We're not playing the blame game here, merely tearing aside those veils of confusion and misunderstanding that have, quite simply, confused us.'

Seumas's eyes darted round the room and he hunkered down in his seat, hoping that he could make himself invisible. A horrible thought was infiltrating its way into his mind (along with alternating flashes of panic and puzzled disappointment), that, put bluntly, Sykes-Wolsey was fucking crazy.

'So, to return to *Diamonds Are Forever*. We know, because we've seen the documentary film, that the real person James Bond visited the Circus Circus Casino at the very time Hunter S. Thompson, significantly masquerading under the ur-text false-name of Raoul Duke, was drinking there with his Samoan attorney, both of them severely intoxicated by a cocktail of dangerous drugs. That they met is inevitable, as I've said, and Dexter Jakes at St Paul is producing very interesting work from a close analysis of contemporaneous police records and security-film footage. The question now before us is why, in their ur-text document, neither Bond nor Thompson make any mention of this. To what degree, therefore, can ur-text studies be obstructed by, on the one hand, artificially induced addle-headedness and consequent loss of memory, and on the other by the

necessary constraints of national security and the possibility of an unreliable documentarist resulting from
those two imported factors . . .'

Seumas had had enough, but as he slid stealthily from
his chair he knocked his bag over, and instantly every
face in the room turned on him, with looks of almost
murderous intensity.

'And where do you think that you're going?' snarled
Sykes-Wolsey, while far away in Hampshire Stephanie
laughed joyously at something a foppish boy called
Trubshawe had just said.

BEST FRIENDS

Best Friends

Trubshawe drank immoderately and often and, as a consequence, had no friends except for Stephens who, unlike all the others, was unswervingly loyal and never answered back. Trubshawe and Stephens lived together in reduced circumstances, shared each other's food, drank together and, as the years passed, grew to resemble each other more and more closely. And every night, when Trubshawe and Stephens entered the only local pub from which neither had been barred, Trubshawe carrying a bag of empty bottles and Stephens trailing behind on a slack length of string, the people would say, 'You and that bleeding dog get more alike each day, Trubshawe. You know what they say about people and their pets.' Except that Stephens was Trubshawe's friend, not his pet, and what people really meant was that they couldn't tell which one of them was smellier, dirtier or grumpier and which one wouldn't have been far happier if he were to be put down. Trubshawe grunted at the people's unkind observation, mumbled a few incomprehensibles as he paid for a bottle of Guinness and a Pernod and a packet of crisps which he shared with Stephens, who also grunted as he ate and drank his share. And, in their own odd way, they really were the very best of friends.

Until, that is, last Halloween. Trubshawe and Stephens had both got very drunk, even more than usual, and stumbling home after closing time they got into an argument. Afterwards, of course, neither could remember what it had all been about (which was probably, after the fashion of drunken disputes, nothing), and after Stephens had bitten Trubshawe and Trubshawe had bitten Stephens back, they both apologised profusely to each other, again in the lachrymose manner singular to drunks. Trubshawe hugged Stephens's huge, filthy, shaggy head to his own gaunt, unshaven jowls which Stephens licked forgivingly, and neither of them thought any more about it. Still, it had happened, and although neither bite was particularly deep or savage, neither healed. Trubshawe took Stephens to the People's Dispensary for Sick Animals where they fooled him into taking some foul medicine, and they both went along to the doctor's, where they pulled the same trick on Trubshawe. Indeed, so disagreeable was Trubshawe about his treatment that the doctor quite forgot to mention the weird things he'd noticed going on in Trubshawe's metabolism during the preliminary check-up.

The headaches, of course, had been going on for some time, although Trubshawe and Stephens hadn't paid them much heed as they weren't too qualitatively different from their usual matutinal hangovers, and if that familiar feeling was regularly a good deal worse than usual the morning after a full moon, the pair of them drew no conclusions from this, except that it was the obvious consequence of whatever they'd done the night before which, comfortingly, neither of them could remember. It must be said, perhaps, that Trubshawe felt a twinge of unease when, on such a morning, he caught a glimpse of the headlines on the day's papers on the tobacconist's counter, but this, he felt on reflection, was probably because he was about to be sick and he left without reading any more about the eleventh in a series of increasingly brutal and bizarre murders. Stephens couldn't read anyway, so after Trubshawe had retched a pool of pale, acidic soup over the pavement, they strolled off to the park together ignorant of either the police's continued bafflement or their ever gaudier speculations. All the victims had been killed on nights lit by full moons, all had been horribly mutilated and all, after death, had been chewed. Theories ran the whole gamut from psycho to satanists to some hideous and barely imaginable beast. Some people were even trying to prove a link with the dog killings, the eleventh just reported and, like the ten before it, the slain pooch had been butchered with stealthy, human dexterity by the light of the full moon. The police, however, considered the cases to be unrelated, while Trubshawe and Stephens didn't know and didn't care.

Another month went by, during which Trubshawe and Stephens spent a happy afternoon rummaging through Trubshawe's family effects. Stephens had laughed when Trubshawe put on his great-grandfather's Indian Army pith helmet, and Trubshawe had laughed when Stephens widdled on an ancient parchment relating the trial and execution of one of Trubshawe's eighteenth-century ancestors, where enlightened pleas of lunacy and superstitious accusations of witchcraft had both been rejected by the court, but they'd still buried the villain at a crossroads with a wooden stake through his wicked heart. Then they found Stephens's long pedigree, which seemed to have got mixed up with some birth certificates along the way, and then they set about matching up the labels on the silver bullets with names on Trubshawe's family tree, and both of them laughed like anything, though neither of them really knew why. Trubshawe then sold the silver bullets and the two of them went off on a mother of a bender, Stephens singing and Trubshawe howling as they stag-gered home in the late afternoon, man and dog, dog and man, silhouetted hand in paw against the rising red Halloween moon.

That evening their crapulous slumbers were disturbed by strange dreams. Trubshawe dreamed that he was Stephens, and Stephens dreamed he was Trubshawe, and at 9 p.m. Stephens rose from his basket, stretched, went off to find some clothes and got Trubshawe's lead. Trubshawe, curled up in the armchair, worried at the rags strewn over his body, leaped down and trotted after Stephens. Once outside, Stephens, or was it Trubshawe, unleashed Trubshawe, or was it Stephens, who loped off into the shadows, stopping to sniff the ground now and again, while his friend, checking the street, set off on his own mission.

Prowling the suburbs in a wild bloodlust, hungry for human flesh and his few thoughts filled with images of forests and the hunt, he was lucky it was Halloween, for he soon encountered a group of small children tricking and treating whom he devoured entirely before setting off in search of some more infuriating instances of humankind. His friend, meanwhile, pricked up his ears at the sound of distant barking, tracked down the source of the noise and proceeded to throttle the hapless cur, cursing it for its lowly station in the Chain of Being and its servile sycophancy to its human oppressors. His pelt glistening with gore, the dog pulled at the slithering lengths of gut and stuck his grinning snout into the still twitching corpse's eviscerated belly before pawing the ground and howling to the moon, while his master, standing ready to receive the leaping Doberman, grabbed its front legs, thrust them outwards and grinned with pleasure as the brute split up its thorax and spilled its bowels over the ground. Stupid animal, thought Stephens as he lit a cigarette. What a clever dog, thought Trubshawe vaguely as he picked up Stephens's scent and trotted into the pub.

'You and that bleedin' dog get more alike every day,'

144

said the barman. 'You know what people say about people and their pets.' Stephens sipped his lager and lime and smiled, sharing some pork scratchings with Trubshawe, and then they went home, silhouetted against the pale, setting moon, both their noses itching, Trubshawe getting flashes of indistinct memories from the back of his mind as he reared up to paw the front door, while Stephens's tongue hung out idiotically as he tried to remember something, before turning to enter the house, rummaging out a tin for Trubshawe's supper and going to the bookshelf.

But when he got there he could no longer remember what it was he was going to look up. He growled with frustration, and started reading out the titles of the books with increasing difficulty, before taking a couple of them over to the table. The mouldy smell of bound yellowed pages made him gag as he opened one of the volumes, then forgot why he'd opened it. He licked his fangs, yawned widely and padded over to where his best friend lay curled up in his basket, before absent-mindedly proceeding to lick the blood from his insensible face.

Joe's Last Dreams

Although dead, it took a while for the synapses finally to close, time enough to allow Stalin's cadaver to enjoy some prophetic posthumous dreams.

The first one was unpleasant, embarrassing, in grainy black and white but thankfully brief. Having vacated his own body, he watched it, lovingly preserved for ever by the skill of Soviet morticians, being placed in Lenin's Mausoleum next to Vladimir Ilyich. Lenin's corpse opened its eyes as soon as the morticians had left, looked at Stalin and then muttered audibly, 'Fucking hell, not you', before lapsing into a sullen silence for the next few years (which passed in fractions of seconds in dream-time) until Stalin was removed from the mausoleum in the small hours one morning and unceremoniously dumped in a grave next to the Kremlin wall.

But with the second dream Stalin dreamed of a time long after he had been removed from Lenin's Mausoleum and from a place in the hearts of his once loving if terrorised people.

He dreamed forward to the late eighties. In the Soviet Union, his heir Gorbachev would be continuing with his policies of dismantling both the old Stalinist Empire in Eastern Europe and the terror apparatus of the state. Meanwhile, Reagan's rearmament programme had plunged the American Federal Government deep into deficit. Then, at just the wrong moment, the neo-liberal New Order would get its first shock with the stock market crash of October 1987. Stalin dreamed that the panic would be so great, worst of all in the banks, that,

147

fearing a general banking collapse, they would call in the US Government's debts. The Federal Government would naturally default, and would be declared bankrupt. At this point, in California, the new technology companies – many with Japanese backing and a Pacific, rather than Atlanticist, Cold War frame of reference – would start thinking politically as well as merely commercially as all those Pentagon contracts disappeared because the Federal Government would have no money to pay for them. With a massive hike in Federal taxes, more and more Americans would join the growing tax strike, as History had taught them was the founding American Way. More to the point, the Californians, seeing a brighter future on the other side of the Pacific, would secede from the Union, and, in one of those mysterious, unfathomable but defining moments in History, the United States would rapidly collapse, with each state seceding in turn, and with absolutely no public support for an already discredited Federal Government using armed force to halt the disintegration. Reagan would thus become the last President of the United States and sink into senile obscurity. And Washington, DC would fulfil the manifest destiny foretold by Gore Vidal's grandfather, Senator Gore of Tennessee, who said of the Federal capital's new buildings, 'They'll make magnificent ruins.'

The rich, money-making parts of the former United States (as the world would now learn to call it) would quickly regroup, with California and New York State being the leading partners in the new Western and Eastern Confederacies of Independent States. Texas would try to go it alone and would be reannexed by Mexico, while the remaining forty or so states would break down into lawlessness and almost permanent minor border warfare. The ten-foot-high fence stretching the length of the new Mexican border would succeed pretty well in repelling economic migrants from the north, although an occasional former professor of economics from Chicago would now and again slip through to scrape a barely living wage as a domestic houseboy in Acapulco. The Branch Davidians would prosper in Waco because the new Mexican masters of Texas wouldn't care, and anyway they'd be indistinguishable from all the other tin-pot micro-governments made up of former militiamen and gangsters oscillating between fanaticism and corruption that would pepper what was once called Middle America. Washington State would vote, in Proposition 591, to become part of Canada, meaning that Bill Gates and Microsoft would come under the suzerainty of the Queen and the Commonwealth. The missiles meanwhile would rust in their silos in Utah, heavily guarded by troops of the United Nations (which would have decamped to Moscow). That move would be necessitated by the obvious fact that the Soviet Union would now be the Sole Remaining Superpower, to repeat an annoying phrase much beloved of the media. And yet the removal of the greatest threat to World Peace would have an effect on the Soviet Government few of the more hawkish members of the now defunct US Administration might have anticipated. The group of young reformers surrounding Gorbachev would seize the opportunity to slash military spending, to reinvest in and fundamentally reform the Soviet economy. In Stalin's dream, the gamble would work, and the first free elections in the Soviet Union would see Gorbachev returned at the head of a hugely popular, reformed Communist Party government promising domestic prosperity, a free press and a Truth and Reconciliation Commission to investigate the former crimes of the state, while the former head of the

KGB would languish in prison awaiting trial. In rapid succession the Soviet Union and the newly independent states of Eastern Europe would join the EU while their neighbours in the West, with the addition of Canada, Mexico and the Eastern Confederacy, would join the reformed Warsaw Pact. Somewhere an idiot would write about the End of History. A series of unforeseen historical accidents would lead to a growing belief that State Socialism, albeit now with a more human face, would have triumphed over Free Market Capitalism because it is intrinsically morally better. Sleek, smooth young men from Gosplan would start journeying to the former USA to give advice to the emerging nations of the Midwest on Planned Economy Reforms. The new State Socialism World Order would rigorously regulate the multinationals until many would voluntarily liquidate themselves (in an unfortunate turn of phrase) and become state-owned enterprises, committed to public ownership and common benefit instead of private greed . . .

At which point the last synapse in Stalin's brain disconnects, his ultimate thoughts a distinctly disagreeable vision of a future world completely lacking in the poetry of revolution, the beauty of terror. Not that it mattered much, as he was now, finally, well and truly dead.

Cyberspace

Cynthia's Green Line bus was late both arriving in and leaving Dunstable. According to the conductor a road gang the other side of Whipsnade had a steamroller which had blown a gasket, and she kept glancing anxiously at her watch as they rattled through the country lanes that lay between the hedgerows in the early spring sunshine. A flock of sheep, being driven between non-adjacent meadows, delayed them further, and so she was quite out of breath by the time she'd run from her stop to the gatehouse.

A military policeman leered at her with the kind of other-ranks familiarity she could have done without. She fumbled in her bag for her security pass. Her ration book and lipstick fell to the painted tarmac as she delved deeper and finally found the little cardboard booklet, bearing her photograph and thumb prints, both over-laid with a dozen or so official stamps.

'First day, love?' grinned the MP, winking. Cynthia grunted something non-committal as she bent, at the knees, to pick up her stuff. Thus rebuffed, the MP switched his mood to officious. 'Name?' He waved a clipboard, laden with carbon copies of lists and lists of names, which he'd previously been hugging to his chest.

'Cynthia Mal . . .'

'First name only,' he barked, then winked again and tapped the side of his nose before ticking her name off on one of his lists. After a cursory look at her pass he pointed towards a low blockhouse abutting the enormous hangar which dominated the surrounding landscape. Everywhere, Cynthia noticed with an inward smirk, hung signs declaring the hangar to be an official secret under the Meaning of the Act.

'You better look sharpish, ducks!' the MP yelled after her. 'You're under Mrs Pettifer, and she's a fuckin' dragon, that one!'

Cynthia quickened her pace as best she could while holding her bag against her side with her elbow and trying to bring some order to her hair. She opened a dully painted green door into the blockhouse, to find another military policeman sitting behind an empty desk and reading a three-day-old copy of the *Daily Mirror*. He didn't bother to look up, but just gestured sideways with his head towards a tiny and terrifying-looking middle-aged woman standing on the other side of the room.

'Cynthia? I'm Mrs Pettifer, and you're late.'

Cynthia blushed, and tried to stammer out, 'Sorry, Mrs Pettifer,' but was cut short.

'We don't expect sorry, we expect punctuality. Don't let it happen again or you're out, understand?'

'Yes, Mrs Petti . . .'

'You've signed the Official Secrets Act, I assume? Very good. Follow me.' And with that Mrs Pettifer turned on her heel and marched through another set of dull green doors with Cynthia, feeling very small, following.

They walked on in silence down a seemingly endless corridor lined with thick grey metal pipes, mostly inexpertly lagged. Wires drooped from and cross-hatched the ceiling at regular intervals, coming together in ancient metal junction boxes held to the ceiling by enormous bolts occluded into shapelessness by generations of layers of dun paint.

Eventually they passed through another set of doors

whose rubber skirts at top and bottom stuttered mutely against the concrete floor and ceiling. Inside, the hangar was even more enormous than it appeared from the outside and was filled with a grid of thousands of nests of desks, each nest partitioned from the next by chest-high walls of wood and canvas. Phones rang constantly in a chaotic campanology, although through this noise Cynthia could also detect the deeper noise of the constant low hubbub of human voices answering calls and then transferring them elsewhere within the hangar.

Mrs Pettifer stood for a moment looking with pride at the pandemonium of human industry before them. Her sharp little chin held high as she surveyed the scene, she was as good as saying to Cynthia, This is what *I* can do! And what can *you* do, skit? Out loud, Mrs Pettifer said, 'Where were you before, dear?'

'IT in Luton, Mrs Pettifer.'

'Well, that means that you will have some of the basic grounding, although you'll find that I do things slightly differently here. Things have got rather slack in Luton since Marjorie Pettigrew retired. Not pregnant, are you?'

'No, Mrs Pettifer!'

'Well, who knows what goes on in Luton these days.' Mrs Pettifer raised her thin eyebrows in an expression combining disgust, judgement and intimate yet unabashed knowledge of the vilest vilenesses the World could throw at her. 'Just make sure it stays that way. Come on.'

The noise inside the hangar almost drowned out the clacking of Mrs Pettifer's high stiletto heels as they walked down the central aisle before stopping about midway down and entering one of the oases of desks, these ones centred round some kind of telephone-exchange apparatus. About ten girls, all roughly Cynthia's age, were answering the ringing phones and then connecting and transferring the calls by plugging and unplugging the jack plugs with such speed that it made Cynthia dizzy just looking at them. Mrs Pettifer clapped her hands loudly. The girls all looked round, but didn't stop their plugging and unplugging, their connecting and disconnecting.

'Girls!' Mrs Pettifer barked. 'This is Cynthia, just joined us from Luton. It's her first day so I don't want anyone covering up for any mistakes she makes. She'll never learn that way.'

'Hello, Cynthia!' several of the girls cried out, waving, then winking and mouthing reassurances once Mrs Pettifer's back was turned. Cynthia smiled weakly back at them and hurried after her supervisor.

'Now, dear, that was the log-on pool for the sector you'll be starting in. They receive the incoming calls. *This* is where you'll be working.' Mrs Pettifer ushered her into another wood and canvas encircled kraal of desks. Here sat another dozen or so girls wearing headsets, all of whom had a shelf containing about six box files in front of them. Each girl now and again shouted 'Wilco!' or 'Okey-dokey!' into the curved Bakelite mouthpiece set into the wall in front of her while, with extraordinary speed, finding and extracting the required document from one of the box files before her and, without looking, placing it in a wooden tray attached to the back of her chair. Beyond the pool of girls stood an oldish man with a small, yellowing moustache and wearing a cream and orange sleeveless pullover and dirty woollen tie. He leaned over a large wooden-topped table which, apart from a bank of black Bakelite telephones, bore a large metal rostrum, attached to the top of which was a Super 8 cine-camera.

'Morning, Ted!' shouted Mrs Pettifer. The man looked up and gave them a thumbs-up sign, flashing for an

156

instant the yellow to brown teeth clamped round his smoking pipe.

'Ted is the camera operator for this section, and to begin with your job is to collect the images from the download pool' – Mrs Pettifer indicated the girls with the box files – 'and get them over to Ted sharpish. Once he's snapped them – and this is very, *very* important – you must record the time, the serial number of the image and the reference numbers given by Log-on and Download on one of these envelopes' – she picked up a foolscap brown envelope, trailing red string from its flap, from a pile next to her – 'then place the image in it, but only after you've recorded the details, and then, according to the reference number, you place it in one of these pigeonholes where young Sam takes over.' A spotty youth with brilliantined hair grinned evilly at Cynthia as he carried on taking envelopes from the pigeonholes and, on opening them, clipping the images to a constantly moving wire passing above their heads and chucking the envelopes in a large hessian sack at his feet.

'Clear?' Mrs Pettifer glowered at Cynthia.

'Um . . .'

'Oh, don't worry, dear, it's not difficult!' Mrs Pettifer sounded tetchy. 'Let's run through the whole thing from A to Z.' And with that she grabbed a headset from one of the girls in Download and held one earpiece to Cynthia's head and the other to her own. They listened to one of the girls from Log-on.

'Fifteen-year-old male from Carthage, Texas, callname "Dweeber", requests A/HS/AN/BJB/156328/f32/ ACGP/8, copy.'

'Okey-doke,' Mrs Pettifer yelled into the mouthpiece, and turned to Cynthia. 'Filthy little beast! I'd chop their hands off if I had anything to do with it!' Then she pulled out box file A/HS/AN/BJB/156328/f32/ACGP from the six in front of her, opened it and quickly extracted image eight, which was a high-resolution colour photograph of a naked white woman inserting a huge, green dildo into her vagina while fellating a large naked black man who was, simultaneously, being sodomised by a long-haired white man who was probably older than he first appeared.

'Over to Ted with it now!'

Cynthia picked up the image and scampered over to Ted, who slowly and carefully took the photograph, secured it to the table top beneath a sheet of clear glass, and then pressed a switch on the side of the Super 8 camera which, Cynthia noticed, was connected by a series of black and yellow fabric-covered plaited flexes to the bank of Bakelite telephones.

Ted puffed on his pipe as the camera whirred for an instant, then pressed down a small black switch by the phones marked 'scrambler'.

'All done!' Ted stretched and smiled at Cynthia. 'Thanks, miss. New, aren't you? You'll like it here.' Then someone handed him a photograph of several naked men, women and animals, while Cynthia took image eight over to the pigeonholes and started filling in its details on the back of one of the envelopes. When she'd finished she walked back to Mrs Pettifer, who was deep in conversation with another middle-aged woman.

'So I said to her, come in painted like that again, young lady, and it won't be Neo-Nazi Conspiracy Theories or Kiddiporn you get sent back to, it'll be Local Government Records and Personal Homepages for you, mark my words! Well, that settled her hash,' said Mrs Pettifer, a note of triumph in her voice.

'Quite right too, Beryl,' the other woman said. 'That's the trouble with these youngsters, think they can come in here, green as you like, and start straight away in Genealogy and Search Engines!'

'The very idea! Oh, have you finished, dear?' Mrs Pettifer turned back to Cynthia and sounded almost friendly.

'Yes, thank you, Mrs Pettifer.'

'This is Mrs Challoner, she'll look after you from now on. Good luck.' And, smiling really rather beautifully, Mrs Pettifer bade them farewell to check up on another part of her empire.

'Don't worry about her, dear,' Mrs Challoner said to Cynthia. 'She's a love really. Bark worse than her bite, y'know. Ooh look,' she squeaked, turning round to one of the many enormous clocks hanging from vast pillars round the hangar, 'it's only five minutes before tea break. You run along to the canteen and you can start properly after. All right, dear?'

'Thank you, Mrs Challoner,' Cynthia said politely, and left the sector for the canteen, looking in her bag for her luncheon vouchers. The youth Sam ran after her until he caught up.

'Hello, luv! Fancy sharing a Wagon Wheel?'

'Well, actually . . .' Cynthia was about to mention Roger, her on/off fiancé of the last six months, when a series of klaxons almost made her jump out of her skin.

'Don't worry about that, darlin'! Just a minor crash over in Chatrooms. Now have you ever heard about what happened when they got gremlins in Webcams?'

As they passed a nest of desks covered in log tables and slide rules, Sam's hand, very slowly, started moving towards Cynthia's more distant shoulder, while all around the phones kept ringing incessantly.

Ape

The knotted timeline untangled at the very moment that Seumas tripped on the top step before the half landing, sending him tumbling forward and through the bathroom door, although the only thing he noticed was the famous, previously young but still short novelist, on tiptoes, wanking into his hostess's bathroom sink. The timeline in question, one of the thicker strands in the plaited crochetwork that flows eternally onwards, shouldn't be confused with the smaller, thinner, more subjective timelines, although they get knotted all the time, which was happening to Seumas's personal timeline about every thirty seconds as, without him willing it, yet another piece of the scattered jigsaw of the previous night's events came back to him. As he stumbled, backwards, out of the bathroom, he now remembered the dog that man Trubshawe owned, who'd joined them after they'd gone on, and on, from the restaurant, and had spoken at length about the Vorticist poet Julian Sykes-Wolsey while the full moon rose above the city and was mirrored, in shards, in the filthy river.

It was just coincidence that it was a reissue of Sykes-Wolsey's second, slim volume of poetry that was being celebrated tonight, downstairs in Seumas's editorial director's house near the Heath, and nothing to do with the knot in the timeline, although it had become knotted as the dog started to speak. Seumas shuddered, fell back against the half-landing wall and slithered into a sitting position, leaning against the Anaglypta, where he lit a fag. Downstairs Sykes-Wolsey's book continued to be launched, like the *Titanic*, more and more bottles of cheap red wine being smashed against its flimsy prow. For his part Seumas had had both wines too many and wines too various, and when he inhaled the first drag of the cigarette, his eyesight started strobing in the gloom halfway upstairs. He knew he should get downstairs again. The book was his baby, so to speak, the first one he'd brought to completion since he'd joined Grabber's six months ago. And Sykes-Wolsey was a seller, part of the backlist that cross-subsidised the publisher's usual output. This explained the turnout tonight, which wasn't bad for an author who'd been dead for forty years, but which had included Sykes-Wolsey's great-nephew Damien, who Seumas was still eager to avoid ten years after their first and last meeting. Trubshawe had also turned up, without his dog, although Seumas wasn't overkeen on seeing either of them again after last night.

Trubshawe had claimed – had, in fact, used it as his entreé into Seumas's company – to be an old friend of Seumas's wife, Stephanie, although this news hadn't broken the silence which greeted him this morning as he crept from the spare room into the bathroom where Steph, newly pregnant, was being sick. If anything, Trubshawe's name made things worse as she stiffened and, still silently, withdrew any small twinge of sympathy she may or may not have been pushing Seumas's way. Despite the huge range of pantomime faces he'd pulled in apology, she remained steadfastly and mutely enraged and disgusted, so he'd showered, shat, kissed her unresponsive cheek and stumbled off to work, where the two packages had been sitting, waiting, on his desk. Since then he'd spent all day lassoed by his subjective timeline, hog-tied, hobbled, and dragged behind the wild mustang of his guilt through ever more lucid memories of roaring through town in a quest for another drink, another venue, another planet, clubs, acquaintances, crises, cocaine, Camelot and finally a cab home. It wasn't surprising, then, that his mind had not been entirely on his work, and he opened the two packages with shaking hands and diminished critical faculties, although not so diminished that he'd failed to notice that he had before him two exact, word for word copies of *Paradise Lost*, one typed, the other in longhand. He'd been in no fit state to deal with inexplicable conundrums like that, and anyway the phone on his desk then rang. He'd groaned inaudibly, and braced himself for the surges of remorse, nausea and self-disgust that were about to break over him as soon as Steph's sobs started hammering against his oversensitive eardrums, and without thinking – almost instinctively, perhaps – he'd initialled the typescript and tossed it into the out tray, while binning the handwritten manuscript.

This was when the timeline had been knotted for about eight hours. As I say, this type of thing happens all the time, the resulting triple simultaneity of this particular knot being just one of those things. It made no difference to the individuals concerned anyway, as neither Seumas, nor Elizabeth Milton, nor Tristan Tzara knew it was happening, and normally there would have been no long-lasting consequence arising from the fact that Mrs Milton and Tzara both posted their identical manuscripts of *Paradise Lost* to their publishers at precisely the same time, although, they believed for they had no reason to do otherwise, 250 years apart.

Things are made more complicated by the fact that, because of the knot, there was a slight fraying in the spacio-temporal strand interwoven into the timeline, which meant that the packages sent to Clerkenwell from Chalfont St Giles in 1667 and from Zurich to Paris in

1916 both ended up on Seumas's desk, in Bloomsbury, around the end of the twentieth century, as well as at their intended destination, at the time desired.

The second drag on the snout was better, or less alarming in its effect, than the first, although Seumas's head still swam. Downstairs he could hear Grabber's MD introduce his wife on the harp, accompanying another member of the Sykes-Wolsey clan singing some of old Julian's verse, set to music years before by Constant Lambert. Seumas decided that they wouldn't, for the time being, be missing him, so he stopped where he was, and belched something nasty into his furry mouth, having no cause to wonder why, in the first place, the Dadaist impresario Tristan Tzara should have wished to submit a typed manuscript of *Paradise Lost* to him or anyone else. For his part, Tzara never reflected on such things for long, and certainly drew no conclusions. It wasn't up to him to make judgements about why or how he'd bought 750 orang-utans dirt cheap off a bankrupt Croatian circus, whose business had been fatally crippled by the European War, which itself was as impervious to analysis or explanation as the reason why Tzara had chained the apes to 750 typewriters in the basement of the Cabaret Voltaire, or why the fat orange bastards had then typed out *Paradise Lost*. All Tzara had done was to glance at the typescript, recognise it as just the kind of meaningless bullshit he needed for the next Dadaist manifesto and, without a second's thought, sent it off to the publishers. During the simultaneity, slightly earlier than Tzara had walked to the postbox, Milton's long-suffering second wife, who'd taken down her husband's dictation of his satirical masterpiece in longhand, spent no time at all bitterly recriminating with him for refusing to buy her a typewriter, in order to avoid the outcome we've already observed, although her heart sank as she trudged back home through the lanes of Buckinghamshire.

And anyway, the simultaneity finished when the knot in the timeline unravelled, and that would have been that, had not a parallel, double simultaneity – abutting Irwin Piscator and Kit Marlowe into a far closer proximity than the mists of time would normally have allowed – meant that as it unravelled, the knot causing the triple simultaneity snagged on a randomly generated memory burr, spored from Seumas's vibrating personal timeline. This, of course, meant that the apes' version of the poem instantly became the standard text, and always had been.

Seumas woke up with a jolt as the burning end of the cigarette scorched his index and middle fingers. He groaned, and shifted stiffly where he sat outside his boss's Hampstead bog. At least downstairs the music had stopped, although he could clearly hear the psychotic Damien Sykes-Wolsey starting a fight over his latest deconstruction of Books Three and Four of *Paradise Lost*, which overturned decades of neo-geneticist literary theory in rereading Lucifer as aspirant supra-ape ur-hero. Seumas was just lighting another fag when the short novelist stepped out from the bathroom, insouciantly pretending to read F. Scott Fitzgerald's translation of *Omar Khayyám*.

The Twelve Point Path to Personal Enlightenment

Stephens eventually died of cirrhosis of the liver, as he'd sort of always known he would, although the subjective prescience stroked the objective certainty with the fingertips of self-knowledge so softly and gently that the whole thing was rendered almost imperceptible. In fairness, it should be pointed out that this failure to achieve catharsis was far more related to the debilitating effects of drink rather than those concomitant with Stephens being a dog, albeit one who either enjoyed or endured human status once a month. Had he thought about it, Stephens might have recognised that he had much more in common with a tampon than he might first have imagined, given the unremitting regularity of the cycle which converted them both from being furry and fluffy to being a mess. As it was, he hadn't thought about it, so let's leave it at that.

Their crimes had remained unsolved by the authorities at the time of Stephens's death just as much as they remained unremembered by Stephens and Trubshawe, and they now ceased anyway. Whatever dark imperative it was that defined Trubshawe's lycanthropy clearly regretted the absence of the neat cross-species dimension from the monthly horror. The new asymmetry, by and large, ruined the point.

So, when Trubshawe howled to the moon in his grief, pissed out of his head on Guinness and Pernod, he howled for his dead best friend entirely and exclusively in human form.

The howling and the drinking helped, of course, although not to diminish his grief. After a while this failure in amelioration no longer mattered. The howling, the drinking and the night were so enjoyable, both separately and together, that the justification for their combination receded in importance with the increasing frequency with which he gave himself up to this divine ritual of self-indulgence, and Trubshawe had already forgotten why it was that he should so regularly feel compelled to make such a dick of himself.

It must now be said that we made practically no effort previously to explore either Stephens's or Trubshawe's back story, beyond the common bond of their lycanthropy. We should remedy that before we go any further, for as things stand you have no idea that Trubshawe (although hardly anything has been said to the contrary) is in fact decently the right side of forty, wealthy through one accident of birth and both enduringly and endearingly good-looking through another. They were, just to ram the point home, the bruised, floppy, broad-grinning and ever so slightly out of focus good looks you're probably familiar with, and want either to smother with kisses and cuddles and look after or else slash with a cut-throat razor depending on what, precisely, is your cup of tea. Trubshawe, effortlessly, had proved to be the cup of tea of an apparently endless cavalcade of nice, rich, usually blonde and Alice-banded and invariably optimistic young girls of a certain class, three of whom had been dumb enough, over the years, to marry him. This was despite the permanent fucked-off-his-facedness that had been his defining schtick since his mid-teens.

He treated them all appallingly, of course, but there was never any intentional malice aforethought, no actual causal meanness, just the teeth-rattling, numb-ache-at-the-back-of-your-head unbelievable selfishness which, because it came in equal measures from his class and his temperament, was his birthright. It manifested itself, without a thought for anyone else, but also with no thought that anyone else would mind, care or notice, in the barrage of shouted-out-loud soliloquies that disturbed the denizens of too many streets round Pimlico, too late at night and too often, and went far beyond what anyone watching (which, by Trubshawe's lights, they obviously weren't) would immediately recognise as a textbook case of drink-related psychotic solipsism.

Most of the nice young girls, particularly the ones who'd married him, gave up at this point and decamped to surer certainties with equally nice young men called Piers or Gavin in the Home Counties, there to burn a hopeless but, through the delicious lambency of its hopelessness, inextinguishable torch for Trubshawe. One of the ex-wives, incidentally, had bequeathed him Stephens, and one of her nastier successors got to the point one night when she found Trubshawe sobbing beneath the stuccoed portal which gave ingress to his house, entirely unpaid for except by his ridiculously, perennially generous family.

She looked down at him, wiping a cocktail of nicotinal snot and tears from his face.

'For Christ's sake, Trubshawe, it was only a fucking dog,' she observed correctly, then rolled her eyes and left for ever. Trubshawe knew that the love of nasty, clever, unforgiving women was infinitely better than the adoration of nice girls, was what he needed and what he didn't, under any circumstances, deserve. The only bad thing, in fact, that one can say about the clever, nasty women, the last example of whom has just left our narrative having hardly entered it, is how any of them could ever have been so blindly kind (it's the besetting sin of their sort) to have entertained his brand of winsome bollocks in the first place.

None of which made any difference to Trubshawe, who mistook the reality of final abandonment for the illusory triumph of personal freedom, so he went on a prolonged bender, savouring every joyously self-destructive moment of ever more disgusting degradation, not as a monument to the depths of his grief for Stephens but as another little victory for his inalienable right to implode into the ravenous black hole of his own self-regard. The alternative, to shine with incandescent effulgence in the nebula of self-awareness, could, on the whole, wait for something else to turn up.

It was when he woke up one morning, around 6 a.m., on a piece of abandoned land abutting the westerly reaches of the Westway, the rising sun over White City neatly highlighting the arabesques of dried puke on his overcoat, that he realised that enough, probably, was enough. He'd always eschewed the higher drugs, and had stuck to seeking catharsis, or a catalyst, or communion, or whatever the fuck it was, through booze alone. This was because he liked the taste. It had other attractions. It meant he was invariably vile to the ones he loved and who loved him until they'd had enough. It meant that he was beguilingly full of promise, interesting to know (at least until about halfway through lunch), deliciously irresponsible with his gaunt cheekbones and blurry eyes and, although shit in the sack and permanently engulfed in a miasma of foul proportions, probably a bit of a character.

But he was also pushing forty, getting paunchy and irredeemably fucked. He was aware, with the lucidity that, oxymoronically, often walks hand in hand with being totally off your face, that his tone of voice was getting perilously close to the cadences of a small boy always about to burst into tears, which is the exclusive prerogative of the chronic lush and, occasionally, the gaudier kind of shameless statesman. And he was also aware that something had to be done, although what it was, and what its consequences might be, temporarily eluded him. As, for the record, did his home address.

Later, surveying his beetroot eyeballs and thinning hair in an unforgiving mirror in the nicely outfitted bathroom of a sort of friend he'd met after finally finding egress from his bower of shit and nepenthe in Paddington, it came to him. Self-improvement. He had to get a grip. Take control. Beat down his demons (the demons, barely alive and with splitting hangovers, shrugged their agreement) and show who was boss. He splashed more water on his face to wash away the tears of self-pity, glowered at himself again in the mirror with a few more shouted imprecations and, in a blinding (and it certainly was) moment of inspiration, suddenly conceived in almost its entirety the Twelve Point Path to Personal Enlightenment.

That he spent the next twenty minutes retching into the bidet is, for our purposes, very much beside the point.

Any prior exploration of Trubshawe's philosophy would probably have marked him down as an orthodox, almost zealous Cartesian, immovably wedded to the proposition that the body is merely a locomotive system for the brain, which in turn functions purely as the seat of the soul. The body, therefore, exists to allow the brain to get to the next drink, so the soul can get pissed, and if it suffers any collateral damage along the way, it's not that important and you can always get a new one. The Twelve Points, however, marked a complete rejection of this previous belief, being far closer to Buddhism than anything else previously recognised. They were:

171

1) We're all fucked up because our brains are too big and don't have enough to do, so we fill the endless empty moments between birth and death thinking up ways to make ourselves and everyone else miserable, like politics and art and religion and love.
2) All human cultures and societies have devised some kind of psychotropic catalyst to beat down their too big brains and make them feel better. These include booze, fags, drugs, meditation, chanting, religion, Benylin cough expectorant with vodka chasers, art, politics and so on.
3) There is nothing wrong with wanting to feel better, even if it makes you feel worse.
4) All hangovers are actually rather enjoyable.
5) The greatest insights a person is capable of often coincide with being unable to get your key into a lock at 3 a.m., in the rain.
6) The dialogue with the self, even if shouted and involving violence, is the most rewarding.
7) The awareness of profundity in oneself last thing at night is never invalidated by the recognition of its crashing banality the following morning. Self-loathing is merely self-criticism, and should be ignored.
8) There is a restaurant in central London where you can get a particular brand of clear plum brandy which has been blessed by the Chief Rabbi of Budapest and which, once drunk, makes you forget everything that happens to you in the next six hours. Who knows what heroic cosmic journeys you might travel on or what transcendental adventures you might undertake during that time? Embrace the infinite, even when you don't know you're doing it.

172

9) A throat oyster hawked up from the tar and phlegm of your lungs can prove a welcome refreshment on the path of life.

10) Getting off your face is the surest way to get into your head, wherein lies wisdom.

11) Surrender yourself to your desires and feel appallingly guilty about it afterwards. This guilt is the engine driving you on to further abandonment of the self.

12) There is no twelfth point. You have attained Personal Enlightenment.

Looking at the list (which was hard, given his problems with both seeing and handwriting), Trubshawe felt rather pleased with himself. The twelfth point, he conceded, was a bit of a cop-out, but as he'd forgotten what it was by the time he'd found the biro, he'd had to wing this one, and it had the right feel about it. He rewrote the list with a steadier hand and, as an afterthought, added the phrase 'Recognise this, then forget it' after each point. He then felt a terrible burden in his bowels and reluctantly judged it time to venture the first shit of the day. Twenty minutes later he fled his sort of friend's flat and the horrors he'd bequeathed it, walked out into the lunch-time sunshine and went for a pint, feeling rather pleased with himself.

The Twelve Point Path to Personal Enlightenment came out to no fanfare at all, in tiny format, at the expense of yet another nice girl. Trubshawe dedicated it to Stephens, who wagged his tail in Doggy Hell, and he wept when he thought of his dead friend. This struck the nice girl as really rather sweet, but Trubshawe, freshly empowered with the spirit of self-improvement (among other things), took his destiny in his own hands for once and dumped *her*. For its part the book underwent a rapid odyssey from the Mind and Spirit shelves of small independent bookshops, to their bargain bins, to charity shops, to obscurity. Trubshawe, sticking to his Twelve Point Path, was feeling better and better and stronger and stronger every day, so didn't bother to torment himself by speculating on any alternative odyssey the book might have undertaken.

Obviously he rapidly drank himself to death. Almost at the end, as he half fell off his bar stool to go for a pee, knocking over his pint in the process, he had a vague intimation of his approaching death, for he was very conscious of the sense that he would soon be reunited with Stephens. In the Gents he fumbled for what would, one day, become a rare and precious first edition of *The Twelve Point Path to Personal Enlightenment* and opened it at the dedication page, equally oblivious to the hair that had started sprouting on his back and palms and that he was pissing down his left trouser leg. The dedication was to his friend Stephens, who once more wagged his tail in Doggy Hell, and Trubshawe started weeping uncontrollably, the tears of pure alcohol streaming down his elongating muzzle. He pushed his way out of the Gents, his cock still hanging out of his soiled trousers, and through the pub into the night air. The full moon was rising over Vauxhall as he tried to gulp in some oxygen and belch at the same time, to feed his collapsing lungs and dissipate the poisons pumping into his guts from his exploding liver. The belch turned into a howl as he fell on all fours, slavering and puking simultaneously. Then, in his last semi-conscious thought (down, it must be said, to drink rather than his imminent death), he remembered the twelfth point with a startling and awesome clarity. For an instant he sobered up and stared with clear-eyed terror into the oncoming infinite void, before falling dead to the pavement.

And the twelfth point, the random unconnectedness of which underscored its unquestionable truth, was this: you don't piss Guinness, you shit it. Recognise this, then forget it.

The Intercession of Saint Lucy

'In the beginning was the Word, and the Word was with God, and the Word was God.'

The above words – spoken, incidentally, in an archaic kind of Greek – echoed through the coffers of the vaulted ceiling, above the clouds of incense, the tinny clang of bells and the voices of differing pitch.

The church, an Eastern aberration in an occidental suburb, wore its golden onion dome rather dully, and the émigrés, exiles, economic migrants and converts who passed the booted old Tolstoy on the steps thought little about he to whom the place was dedicated.

Not that Saint Lucian Stylites demanded much contemplation, as practically nothing at all was known about him, and some years ago Pope Paul VI had pronounced him apocryphal. So the communicants knew nothing about the trembling girl who heard the word of God: acting on it, she'd obeyed the Divine Order and jumped, tumbling to the ground, death, hagiography (of the undiscriminating kind they practised in the fourth century) and obscurity.

'. . . and Levites from Jerusalem to ask him, Who art thou? And he confessed, and denied not; but confessed, I am not the Christ . . .'

And beyond the church, now empty of the bobbing grandmothers, on all sides the secular woke and had their breakfast.

Corrugated steel shutters stayed pulled down over shop windows in the city centre, while in the suburbs wire grilles were clanked up by adherents to different faiths.

177

An occasional dog or cat scampered through the high narrow streets of the old city, and a Protestant stepped briskly out of the Calvinist cathedral.

Otherwise nothing disturbed the already silent and muffled Realm of Rex Mundi.

The priest, Father Gregory (which was not, of course, his name), removed his cope and tugged at his beard as he joined the grandmothers on the steps outside, spitting in the dusty shrubbery as he went.

His deacon, meanwhile, spoke to a rough man holding the hand of his blind, deaf-mute daughter.

Miracles don't happen too often nowadays, observed the deacon, especially for someone like him.

The rough man said he still believed in miracles, and the deacon replied nastily that it was a miracle he wasn't in The Hague right now.

The two men glowered at each other, but let it pass, knowing that neither was without sin, and you don't keep a low profile if you start throwing stones.

They spoke of other things instead, above and around the little girl, who scraped a scummy residue from a table with her thumbnail.

Throughout the lethargic city nothing much was happening.

As the deacon, the rough man and the child walked to the trolleybus stop to travel to the man's suburban apartment, an old woman walking her small and over-dressed dog swore at them in trans-Jurassic French.

They ignored her, as they had to.

Back at the apartment block, still gaudily bright with the primary colours an optimistic architect had thought would keep it decent two decades previously, children fought in the dust and youths loitered, hunched up, trying to pout meanness into their unlined faces, and scared stiff.

Fifteen floors up the rough man glanced over the city and towards the distant lake, great, grey and turbulent like the sky, then looked back at the deacon who was placing a cross, a chalice and other knick-knacks on the kitchen table, peeping in a mirror at the girl's family.

The mother crunched nuts between her teeth and tried to look at ease, while an older brother gawped out of the window at a seagull resting on the layers of wind. Beneath it, great industrial processes concluded and others began, at each stage evacuating more filth somewhere or other.

And, overtured by the distant thrumming of commencing traffic, in order to restore her sight and hearing through divine intervention, the girl's parents and some of her other surviving relations prayed to Saint Lucy who, rather surprisingly, immediately manifested herself to the little girl, who squinted up at the saint hovering outside the low, large, open window, conscious, first, that she could see and, second, that the apparition had interrupted the stream of instructions coming straight from God to which she had been listening carefully since before her birth, and with the first words she ever heard on Earth, among the screech of horns and screaming children and approaching sirens beyond the window.

'Go on, love. Jump!'

The Towers of Babel

Among the dust and debris of desktops, disks, door-
mats, dermatitis, dingbats, dinner plates, dentures, Dicta-
phones, dental plates, Danish pastries, duodenums,
deodorant, dishcloths, dividing panels, documents,
driving licences, drink dispensers, dollar bills, drinks
cabinets, coffee machines, contact lenses, carotid arteries,
cakes, Coke cans, cocaine, cartilage, cover notes, canti-
levered box files, corrupt programmes, Cartier watches,
crucifixes, carpeting, carpet cutters, cardboard, cup-
boards, coupons, crossword puzzles, canary yellow
overalls, compacts, compact discs, computers, cata-
logues, cartons, concrete, condoms, calling cards, credit
cards, cap badges, Canadian bacon, cue balls, Calvin
Klein boxer shorts, carrier bags, baseball caps, broken
biscuits, brainpans, boxes, bureaus, bodies, brassieres,
brass doorknobs, biros, Brookes Brothers suits, boiler
rooms, brushes, brooms, bubblegum, best friends,
brothers, buckets, bathrooms, boots, Ben and Jerry's
ice-cream tubs, buttresses, books (and bookkeepers),
bubbles, beef, Buddhist pamphlets, bullhorns, bad
accounts, accountants, air-conditioning systems, aero-
sols, appendages, Armani jackets, arms, accoutrements,
ancillary staff, airline meals, antipasti, antihistamines,
apples, anterior lobes, axis vertebrae, armature, armaments, aeroplanes, aortas, aniseed balls, artichokes,
aunts, answering machines, anarchist texts, alabaster,
actuaries, apologia, asthma inhalers, amphetamines,
alphabets and air-fresheners, along with copies of the
Koran and three well-thumbed editions of Trubshawe's

little book, *The Twelve Point Path to Personal Enlightenment*, were seven people who'd never previously met.

Intermingled with Episcopalians, evangelists, Methodists, Muslims, Moonies, Mormons, Baptists, Buddhists, Baha'ists, Lutherans, Roman Catholics, Confucianists, Armenians, Arminians, Greek and Russian Orthodox, Jews, Jehovah's Witnesses, Wesleyans, Wiccans, Calvinists, animists, Zoroastrians, Taoists, Shintoists, spiritualists, Scientologists, Seventh-Day Adventists, pantheists, atheists, Anabaptists, Quakers and assorted devotees of various New Age groupings and communicants of no faith at all, were Eliot, who was Jewish, but not so you'd notice, and had held down a good job with good prospects. Jesus was a nominal Catholic, and had had a lousy job with appalling prospects. Mike had had a good but potentially hazardous job and was also a nominal Catholic. Maria was Catholic too, and had had a truly dreadful job no one officially knew about. Consuela, confusingly, was a Pentacostalist, and had had a reasonably okay job which had been due to end shortly in her well-earned retirement. John, who used different names as he went out and about, had a rewarding job and had been born a Baptist, later becoming a Muslim before entering, finally, into a trenchant and bitter atheism. Suzi had been born and bred as a Buddhist, married an Episcopalian but had recently been dabbling with a curious, westernised variant of Hinduism. Together, mingling with thousands of others, they billowed out of the sky, atomised.

'Jesus fucking Christ!' Eliot yelled. 'Did you *see* that? Holy fuck!' Then he did a double take. 'Hey! What the fuck's this? Can anyone else hear me?'

Several hundred voices answered, most of them telling him to shut the fuck up. Those closest, with whom his disintegrated self was now engaging in an appalling kind of Brownian motion, along with some of the material paraphernalia of his earthly working life, spoke loudest.

'Hey, Jew boy! Can it!' Mike was pissed off, and sounded like it. A few of the other voices close by protested at his outburst. 'Gee, sorry. I'm not prejudiced, it's just that . . .'

'That's okay, honey,' said Consuela. 'We're all aggravated. I was coming up to retirement!'

'That's a bitch,' John butted in, then apologised. 'Sorry 'bout the language. Sheeee-yut.'

Everyone was quiet for an instant, then Maria spoke, surprised that, limited in life to Isthmaic Spanish, she was widely understood for once. 'So what was all that about? Someone said it was a plane crash or something. I don't work near any windows so all I saw was lots of people rushing about before the flames reached me.'

'God. It must've been terrorists or something,' Eliot said. 'Two planes. Two planes there were. I saw the second one just before I got fried. What kind of fucker does that kind of thing?'

'I reckon it's them fuckin' ragheads,' John ventured. 'I know those muthafuckers, so just believe me.'

'So why us? Hell, what I ever do to them, handin' round sandwiches?'

'Why any of us, sweetheart? I'm Jesus, by the way.' Several people round and about laughed at that, and Jesus laughed too, as he could see the joke.

'You know,' said Suzi, 'I wouldn't be surprised if it was the CIA or someone.'

'Yeah, right!' Mike laughed. 'So's Bush can whack Iraq.' Several people close by muttered how they'd never voted for that son of a bitch, while others yelled at them to pipe down.

'Come on!' Mike yelled back. 'What odds does it make

now?' Despite himself, he was beginning to laugh. 'Hey . . . uh . . . Eliot, right? Who d'you think really done this? The towelheads, like the brother over here says?'

'I know them, Mike,' John interjected.

'Yeah, sure, but so what? Well?'

Eliot pondered for a moment. 'There's something about this that stinks, you know,' he said, beginning to giggle. The tiny corporeal remnants of thousands of people jeered or laughed at that, but Eliot cut across them. 'No, listen. This is one big fucking thing that's happened here, and who the fuck knows what's going to happen as a result, yeah? This could, like, be the end of the world, you know?' A few evangelicals fluttered in the wind in something like rapture. 'But there's something fishy, right?'

'Go on,' Mike guffawed.

'Yeah, hang on.' Eliot raised his voice. 'Hey, Chuck!' In the cloud someone shouted back.

'That you, Eliot? What the fuck you make of that, huh?'

'Too damn right, buddy. But d'you remember that stuff that was coming up yesterday? No, this is serious! That trading you thought was kinda weird?'

'Hell, that's right! Looked like someone somewhere knew something big was gonna come up. That fucker made a fucking killing outa what went down here today.'

A loud burst of laughter volleyed through the widening cloud.

'That's what I'm saying, Mike, right? You can say it's terrorists or some kinda government set-up case or whatever. I'm looking criminal mastermind here!'

'Get outa here!' Mike was now having trouble speaking through the gulps of hilarity.

'Just think about it, you miserable Mick Polack asshole!' They both laughed as their ashes wafted

together and then apart again. 'Perfect cover if you get
some dumb buncha terrorists from Palestine or Iran or
wherever to think they're stomping on old Uncle Sam,
you put up the money and go along with the whole
crazy fucking line but all the time you're using them to
pull off the biggest heist in fucking History! You do the
insider dealing through the brokers in the WTC and then
destroy the fucking evidence! The Government goes
after your patsies in the jellabas and you're home free!'
'Yeah!' shouted Chuck. 'Then you whack the fucking
whole lot into armaments and airlines, now the price is
low!'
'You just stole that from *Die Hard*!' someone laughed.
'Yeah, so why couldn't someone else? I can see him
now, on his secret island somewhere . . .'
'Stroking his fucking white cat!' John interrupted, and
they all started laughing so hard they nearly choked.
And down they tumbled, all those atomised people
suddenly so cruelly reduced to motes and specks falling
from the cobalt sky, people from Manhattan and Queens
and Brooklyn and from Jersey and Manchester and
London, with their origins in California or Hampshire or
Lahore or Tokyo or Karachi or Dahomey or Benin or
Shanghai or Timbuktu or Tashkent or Bombay or Pretoria
or Manila, Germans, Italians, Scotsmen, Irish, Poles,
Russians, Mexicans, Guatemalans, Haitians, Indonesians,
Australians, New Zealanders, Cajuns, Dutchmen, people
from Iberia and Scythia and the Indus Valley and the
Arabian Peninsula and Mesopotamia and Phoenicia and
Babylon and Caesarea and sub-Saharan Africa and the
Kalahari and the Gobi and remnants of the Golden
Horde and the peoples who'd crossed into Europe and
over Alaska into the New World and sailed the Pacific
from island to island and the Atlantic in slave ships and
steamers from Liverpool and all of them could have

traced their ancestors all the way back to the Rift Valley, all those people mixed up together in that morbid thunderhead obnubilating the narrow canyons below.

They were all still laughing fit to bust when Consuela shushed them.

'Hey, everyone! What's that noise?' Some feet below they could now hear not laughter or the cacophonous rumbling as their own molecules collided and displaced vast volumes of surrounding air, but instead a piteous moaning and wailing.

'Jesus!' said Jesus. 'Isn't that Mohammed?'

'Fuck me! You're right!'

'Yo, Mohammed! Chill, brother!'

Beneath them the wailing ceased for an instant, then started again.

'No! No! This isn't right! This isn't what's meant to happen! What am I doing here?'

'Hey, folks!' John shouted breezily. 'Poor ole Mohammed here thinks he should be in Paradise right now, lickin' pussy with 20,000 vestal virgins!' The laughter was now even more uproarious than before, but Mohammed didn't join in.

'Keep away from me! Keep those women away from my body! This is not right! Those women must not defile my body!' The sky now filled with expanding laughter, increasingly happy and joyous and filled with an exponentially growing, unconditional, universal and carefree love.

'Come on, girls,' Maria cried out to Consuela and Suzi, 'let's show poor little Mohammed how things stand round here now!' Consuela and Suzi whooped with almost hysterical joy, and swooped down after Maria to engulf Mohammed, whose screams of dismay were lost in the babel of cackling and chortling, tittering, sniggering, smirking, guffawing and helpless, helpless laughter as

186

they all high-fived the dead Algonquins and Apaches and Armenians and Albanians and Argentines and Bulgarians and Biafrans and Cubans and Chileans and Chechens and Cambodians and deviants and the disabled and Ethiopians and East Timorese and Filipinos and Guatemalans and Gypsies and Haitians and Iraqis and Iranians and Jews and Jews and Jews and Kurds and Kosovars and Lithuanians and Letts and Laotians and Mexicans and Mayans and Nicaraguans and Olympian gods and occultists and Poles and Palestinians and quislings and Russians and Serbians and Tutsis and troublemakers and Uranians and Vietnamese and witches and Xhosas and young babies and Zulus whose subatomic particles ubiquitously and completely filled the skies along with their laughter, making it blue over the edge of a republic constantly spawning Coriolanuses to battle for autistic hegemonies. It took a while for Mike and Jesus and Eliot and John to be able to speak again. Eventually, breathlessly, John said: 'You know, there is one thing I don't quite get . . .'

And then they all understood everything, and there was no further need to speak as they settled, like snow on Christmas Day, over the mistakes of Manhattan.

Candide In Las Vegas

Candide in Las Vegas

Candide and Cacambo shook hands and slapped each other on the back as they raked up their winnings from the table and went to cash in their chips.

The House, naturally, took a sixty-five per cent commission on this transaction. Such insane levels of generosity on the part of the mobsters who ran the casino revealed them for the cautious and conscientious businessmen they surely were. When Candide had arrived in Las Vegas, only a week after Cunegonde had left, he'd been burdened with so much dirty drug money that he didn't know what to do, so Cacambo had arranged a meeting with the mobsters, who were only too happy to help, although Candide's simplicity of soul and trusting manner had terrified them so much that they handled such an obviously unscrupulous and ruthless big shot with extreme care. This was prudent. Even after a further thirty per cent State Gaming Tax had been levied, Candide still had more money than most of the mobsters had ever seen, so his hosts treated him with respect bordering on panic.

'Thanks to the head of the Eldorado Cartel,' said Candide, smiling at the quaking cashier, 'I can now marry Cunegonde. Once we've bought her back off the head of the Five Families, that is. As my teacher Pangloss so correctly observed, all is for the best in this best of all possible worlds!'

'Sure thing, boss,' replied Cacambo. 'Shame the old doc got blown into tiny pieces by that Yardie rocket as we were leaving Eldorado.'

'But if Pangloss had not been in the second helicopter, then he would have been with us, and as it was surely preordained that that was the precise time at which that dear philosopher had to be blasted into so very many atoms, then we would have been blown to bits as well. As it is we escaped with nearly all the cocaine, and now we're in Las Vegas with enough money for me finally to marry my beloved Cunegonde! And don't forget, had the Jesuit guerrillas not . . .'

'Yes yes yes,' interrupted Cacambo. 'Come on, let's eat.'

After Candide had tipped the cashier somewhere in the region of thirty times the terrified man's annual salary, he and Cacambo were ushered, with due deference, into a private bar high above the casino floor and reserved for the exclusive use of its most exalted patrons. The two friends were given tall glasses filled with a very cold liquid the colour of swimming pools. Slowly Candide's eyes grew accustomed to the gloom in the room, and he saw that they were not alone. Hunched round the bar in the near total darkness sat eight shadowy figures, idly and silently nursing their drinks.

A man in an elaborate uniform entered the room and crossed over to an elderly mustachioed gentleman drinking Chivas Regal.

'Senator,' said the soldier, 'the management sends its compliments along with your winnings, which I have safely strapped to my body. When you are quite ready the car awaits to take you to the show at Caesar's Palace before your appointment at the clinic.'

The elderly gentleman grunted and the soldier withdrew, to be replaced almost immediately by another lackey, wearing completely opaque dark glasses in spite of the darkness of the room, and with one hand held to his ear and the other stuffed inside his jacket. He went to another elderly gentleman who was smiling round at no one in particular.

'Mr President,' shouted the man in the dark glasses and suit, 'your wife is collecting her winnings and is ready when you are! I'll take you down to the car momentarily!' The elderly gentleman kept on smiling and nodding his head as the man in the dark glasses withdrew. He was replaced by an employee of the casino, who approached a third man, who was wearing glasses and drinking an enormous Bloody Mary.

'Doctor!' cried the casino employee in delighted tones. 'It's always a real pleasure and privilege to welcome you here! Here's your winnings and your car will be ready when you are!' The doctor thanked him with a guttural snarl and the casino employee withdrew, to be replaced by a tall and dignified Englishman, who approached an elderly lady drinking a large Scotch.

'Baroness, here are your winnings and the car taking you to your lecture is ready when you are.' The Baroness thanked the man, who in turn withdrew, only to be replaced by an anxious-looking foreigner in an ill-fitting suit who hurried over to a bald man at the bar drinking vodka in large gulps.

'We're fucked,' the foreigner whispered in the bald man's ear. 'They won't give us any more credit and I've just blown the last of the foundation money. I'll keep the car running for ten minutes while you try and make it out of here without anyone stopping you!' As the foreigner hurried out he bumped into another foreigner, this time a Frenchman, who went over to an elderly black man at the bar.

'Okay, Your Imperial Highness,' the Frenchman sneered, 'playtime's over. I've got your winnings and we leave in ten minutes.' The elderly black man said nothing, and as the Frenchman withdrew he almost knocked into a smartly dressed man, who went over to an elderly, oriental man sitting at the bar with a beer. They had a brief exchange in a language Candide could not understand, but as they both looked at their watches he assumed the conversation was roughly similar to the others that had taken place in this extraordinary bar.

Finally, a frightened young man sidled in furtively and went over to the last person sitting round the bar, who was drinking orange juice.

'My brother!' whispered the young man anxiously. 'We will be found here for certain. In the name of Allah we must flee!'

'There is no hurry, my brother,' the man at the bar replied. 'Collect my winnings and all will be well.' And he smiled serenely at his friend, who hurried away.

Candide turned to Cacambo. 'Did you hear all that? Where on earth can we be, that we're drinking with presidents and emperors?' And saying this Candide carelessly pulled out a vast bankroll to get the barman's attention.

'Big deal,' muttered Cacambo. 'And for God's sake keep your voice down! They'll all start telling us their life stories if we're not careful!'

But it was too late. Each of the drinkers round the bar had seen Candide's enormous roll of money, and each now, in turn, introduced themselves with the greatest courtesy.

'Good day to you, sir,' said the elderly man with the moustache. 'I am Senator Pinochet, formerly President of Chile. I saved my country from anarchy and Communism, and governed it with a firm hand until it was time for me to stand aside. Although I no longer have any power, I am beloved of my people, despite the best efforts of traitors and Communists. As the desert air is good for me I am in Las Vegas for my health, but also to play the tables.'

'Hiya,' said the next elderly man, 'I'm Ronnie.' The man next to him interrupted.

'Forgive him, he is very old. This is Ronald Reagan, former President of the United States of America and therefore once the most powerful man in the world. And now look at him! If you were of an ironic bent, my dear young man, you could make something of that! As it is, he is here to visit his old showbiz pals and for his wife to play the tables. For my part, I am Dr Henry Kissinger, former United States Secretary of State, winner of the Nobel Peace Prize and the world's greatest living expert on diplomacy and realpolitik. I was just passing through on my way to another international seminar when I decided to stop and play the tables. Although I'm delighted to meet both you, my dear sir, and my old friend the Senator!'

'As are we,' said the elderly lady. 'Of course I'm Baroness Thatcher. I was Britain's first woman Prime Minister and a strong and robust leader who made Britain great again! I was elected by my people three times in succession, they loved me so, and would have been elected again had it not been for a conspiracy of weak-minded moaning minnies! Although I, like my friends Augusto and Ronnie, am no longer in a position of power, all around the world I am courted for my opinions, and my example will influence generations of leaders both at home and abroad. And, of course, I am still loved by my people, who yearn for me to return when they look upon the pygmies who have succeeded me. I am here in Las Vegas with my husband to deliver a lecture on the Triumph of Freedom and Free Markets, and to play the tables.'

'Jesus Christ!' moaned the bald man. 'If I'd known

193

you lot were in here I'd have found some joint down the strip! My name is Mikhail Sergeyevich Gorbachev. I used to be General Secretary of the Communist Party of the Soviet Union and President of the Soviet Union, until they closed the fucking place down. I was once the second most powerful man in the world, able, had I chosen, to destroy all life on Earth. Instead I tried to bring my people a measure of freedom and prosperity, for what good it did me. Instead of what I offered, they wanted total freedom and free markets, and so for the past decade have been ruled by gangsters and thieves and have seen their standard of living and indeed life expectancy tumble. I was here to play the tables as it's the only way I can make a living these days, but it seems the very last of my luck has run out. I'd give myself up to despair but I can't, honestly, be bothered at this stage.'

'You're lucky!' drawled the elderly black man next to him. 'I am Emperor Bokassa, currently in exile from my Empire in Central Africa. I am the natural son of General de Gaulle, you know. Once I ruled over a nation racked by poverty, where I stole nearly all the money for my own use and killed anyone I cared to. For this I was denounced as a mad cannibal tyrant by the Europeans, despite the fact that they placed me in power in the first place, and I only did what they had been doing to my country and all the rest of Africa for centuries, although I admit I did it with more flair. Then the Europeans got fed up with me, deposed me and I now have my court in exile, a virtual prisoner of the French. Now and again they let me out to meet some old buddies, and I am in Las Vegas with Idi Amin and Baby Doc Duvalier to play the tables.'

The oriental man next to Emperor Bokassa now turned to Candide and said, in perfect and unaccented English,

'How do you do, my dear young sir. My name is Pol Pot, former leader of the Khmer Rouge and undisputed necrocrat of Kampuchea, also known as Cambodia. You'll be happy to hear that reports of my death have been exaggerated, although naturally I prefer everyone to think otherwise. In my time, courtesy of the good offices of Dr Kissinger, I was in a position to murder millions of my compatriots and make the lives of those I didn't murder a living hell. All this I did because, like all my friends here, I genuinely believed that it was essential to kill people in order to persuade them that we were trying to make their lives better. Senator Pinochet killed his countrymen to save them from wanting to be Communists or socialists or liberals or trade unionists. President Reagan killed people because he wanted to save them from wanting to be Sandinistas or to vote for who they wanted to in Grenada or, in one memorable case, because a rather small child wanted to continue to be Colonel Gaddafi's infant son. Dr Kissinger's fame, of course, precedes him wherever he goes, like the stink of the charnel house. Whatever the people of East Timor or Chile or Cyprus or my own poor country wanted or didn't want didn't really matter: they had to die because they wanted something different from what he thought the United States wanted. Baroness Thatcher has far fewer corpses to her credit, although she made the lives of millions miserable beyond belief because she wanted them to want to be free to spend money she made sure they didn't have. Of Comrade Gorbachev I despair. It's half-arsed liberals like him who give Communist despots a bad name. Had I been in his position I would have wiped out half, or maybe all, of humanity without a second's thought, in order to make it better. Instead of that, unlike my other friends here, he is a pauper, a forgotten and embarrassing relic from a bygone age. You could say the same of Emperor Bokassa here, but he doesn't really count. I don't believe for a moment that he slaughtered his countrymen for any other reason than to steal money, stay in power and because he felt like it. Such charming and old-fashioned motives can only serve to enhance our over-ideological times. But I'm going on far too long. I am no longer involved in politics, although I'm still responsible, directly or indirectly, for the deaths of hundreds of thousands of people all round the world, although nowadays I afford them the dignity of a little enjoyment instead of indoctrination before they die. Just like you, my dear Monsieur Candide, with all the money you stole from the Eldorado Cartel, I am here to launder drugs money from the poppy plantations of my homeland in order to maintain my now lavish lifestyle.'

When Pol Pot saw Candide blush he looked abashed. 'Oh, my dear young sir! Forgive me! But there are no secrets in Las Vegas! As I'm sure our friend Osama Bin Laden will tell you!'

Candide turned to the last figure seated at the bar, who bowed low. 'Blessings be upon you,' he said. 'I am, as the atheist infidel hypocrite says, Osama Bin Laden. I am nothing, nobody, but the servant of the Prophet, peace and blessings be upon him, and of Allah, and as such, with my brothers, sweep aside the cities of the unbelievers with one wave of my hand and make the leaders of the infidels quake with fear at the mention of my name, I who am nobody and nothing but the tool of God's wrath against the blasphemers and secularists and the uncircumcised and who was Lord of the Islamic Caliphate of Afghanistan in all but name. The Communist speaks of death as if it is something to fear, for in his blindness to the mercy of God he is ignorant and in darkness of the promise of Paradise. For you godless fools, death is a terror. For us, martyrdom is the most beautiful thing imaginable. You love life. We love death, and the life after. Death, then, to those who defy God and break his holy laws. Death to you all!' And Bin Laden smiled serenely and sipped his orange juice.

'Excuse me, sir,' said Candide after a while, 'but could you tell us why you are in Las Vegas? Are we all about to die, for I would be most disappointed if this were to be the end, without me ever finding my Cunegonde.'

'Fear not, you infidel pig,' smiled Bin Laden. 'I'm merely here to launder my drugs money, like you and the Communist hypocrite. I am not so foolish as to destroy my bankers or declare war against the Mafia. Until we restore the caliphate we must needs occasionally compromise our principles, like I did when I took money and guns and cheer from the Thatcher Whore and the Satan Reagan when I fought against the godless Russians ruled by Gorbachev. You might care to dwell on the ironies involved here, as I know you westerners do.'

'Don't fucking talk to me about irony,' Gorbachev mumbled.

'Forgive me,' said Candide, 'but I'm confused. If death is not to be feared, like you say, why do you kill so many people you don't like?'

'You are naturally ignorant, for you are a godless infidel who has chosen comfort and the ways of Satan instead of the blissful comfort of the teachings of the Prophet, peace and blessings be upon his name, and therefore . . .' But before the gentleman could finish explaining things to Candide, Cacambo crept up behind him and waved a long stiletto under his nose.

'Like I always say,' Cacambo explained to the famous terrorist, 'never talk religion or politics.'

'Schwarze putz!' Bin Laden muttered under his

breath, before getting off his stool and quickly leaving the bar. Cacambo grinned at the other people in the bar, who finished their drinks and left with cursory nods to Candide, who insisted on giving Gorbachev and Bokassa 30,000 dollars each.

Cacambo sighed. 'You know, people take advantage of you. You're just too kind-hearted.'

'I know. But their stories were so sad. There is something very affecting about the idea of worldly power and then losing it, don't you think, Cacambo? I wonder what poor dear Pangloss would have made of it all.'

At that point, to Candide and Cacambo's amazement, Pangloss himself entered the room, looking even worse than ever.

'I would observe, my dear young sir, that we should leave the poignancy of their present condition for more sentimental writers, and reflect instead on the consequences of their periods in power, for had not Dr Kissinger helped Senator Pinochet to prove the effectiveness of monetary theory in Chile, it would not have been adopted by President Reagan and Baroness Thatcher in their far more powerful economies, which in turn would not have become so prosperous and proved so beguiling to President Gorbachev's former subjects, causing the collapse of the Soviet Union and its replacement, in the natural dualist geopolitical order, with the severe Islamism of Reagan and Thatcher's former client Mr Bin Laden, and had he not declared war on the Western Way of Life, with such savage and tragic consequences, we would not have enjoyed the level of security now pertaining in the United States, and I, as a friend of a highly valued customer of this casino, would have been unable to secure a safe and carefully guarded parking space beneath this building for my car, which at this very minute contains your beloved, the lady Cunegonde!'

'But why didn't you say so?' cried Candide, who rushed from the room to the arms of Cunegonde. Cacambo gestured at the barman and ordered another drink and something for Pangloss.

'Okay,' he said, gingerly picking the little paper umbrella out of his glass, 'I can see how Kissinger engineering the Chilean coup led directly to Cunegonde sitting downstairs in your car . . .'

'Thus proving,' interrupted Pangloss, 'that all is for the best in this best of all possible worlds!'

'Absolutely,' Cacambo continued. 'But how do Bokassa or Pol Pot now being a drugs lord fit into it all?'

'I'm still working on that. When I've figured it out I'll write an article for the *Atlantic Monthly* about it.'

'And what about all the people they all killed?'

'Really, Cacambo!'

'Okay, okay. So how's Cunegonde?'

'She's got a raging crack habit and suspected Aids, and I only managed to get her away from the head of the Five Families by challenging him to a game of Angolan roulette . . .'

'What?'

'Same as Russian roulette, only with hand grenades. Anyway, in the process I regret to say that both the old lady and the Baron perished in the most horrible way imaginable, and I hear that the head of the Eldorado Cartel is not, as we had hoped, dead after all.'

'And you still say all is for the best in this best of all possible worlds?'

'My dear Cacambo, if I've learned nothing else since our adventures began, I've learned this: that there is, ultimately, a time and a place for philosophy, and this is not it.'

'At last. Come on, let's go.' With which words Cacambo and Pangloss left the bar, failing to notice the deceptively youthful James Bond and Raoul Duke comparing prescription tabs in the corner.

The Mexican Ambassador

The Mexican ambassador smiled, only half to herself, as she stirred tiny dry specks into her hot chocolate, stretched, yawned and carefully sloughed off the ceremonial cloak made from the tiny iridescent feathers of thousands and thousands of humming birds, thanks to the Primitive People's Exclusion Protocol (Wildlife) she herself had negotiated in the last GATT round, despite strenuous objections from the Europeans but with the last-minute support, surprisingly, of the Americans added to the Mexican, Brazilian and Inuits bloc. She chucked it now, rather carelessly, onto the double bed and smoothed her hands down the flanks of her Armani suit, the lining of the jacket still stuck with sweat to her back. It had been, she reflected with a grin, a long and difficult day, finishing only an hour ago and long after midnight. But she'd got there. The last-minute, skin-of-your-teeth, back-from-the-brink breakthrough (which was, she conceded, her forte), then the agreed statement and the smiles for the world's media (though the Yankee Secretary of State's forced rictus looked, as the ambassador glanced sideways, far from joyous). Hence the humming-bird cloak which, ever optimistic, she'd instructed her aides to have ready for the (as she always knew) inevitable compromise.

The ambassador ran her hand through her still thick, still black hair and put a videolink call through to her President. He was still up, apparently drunk, although he obviously wasn't, and was both gracious and generous considering their previously acrimonious political differences. Still, whatever you might say about the President (and the ambassador had said almost all there was to say during last year's election campaign, but only almost all), he was always able to recognise a job well done, especially if, in the process, the Americans got shafted. And that, the ambassador acknowledged with a short bark of laughter, they had well and truly been.

Because, she convinced herself with a certain level of self-justificatory humbug, she was very tired, she allowed herself a small indulgence by deciding to summon the embassy valet to put away the feather cloak, although to do so went against her higher principles. Usually a loyal daughter of the Revolution, she was meticulously democratic and egalitarian in all her dealings with the embassy staff, and in normal circumstances would have hung up her clothes herself as a matter of course, common decency and political correctness. But tonight, tired and triumphant, she could, she reasoned, reward herself with a little pampering. The refrigerated wardrobe in which the cloak was stored kept humming at her, as if in reassuring assent.

It was only when the line to the embassy's chief of staff connected that she remembered.

'The valet, Comrade Excellency?'

'Yes yes, I'm sorry. I only remembered this minute. It's been a long day.'

'Of course, Comrade Excellency.'

'How did it go?'

'He comported himself with pride and dignity, Comrade Excellency. You would have been proud.'

'We're all proud.'

'Especially of your triumph, if I may say so, Comrade Excellency.' The ambassador grimaced for an instant at this piece of unrevolutionary fawning, but let it pass.

'The . . . um . . .' It was one of the minor irritations of foreign postings, particularly in the United States, that certain consequences of the maintenance of the purity of Mexican culture and traditions involved so many tricky diplomatic niceties being observed in order to keep the host nation, with its own, frequently incompatible, culture and traditions, sweet.

'The orphanage, Comrade Excellency.'

'Of course. The Cardinal is a generous and understanding friend.' Both of them, at either end of the internal, but probably tapped, phone line, reflected for a second on the benefits of the ecumenical spirit of the times.

'Well, goodnight, Quetzy.'

'Goodnight, Comrade Excellency.'

So the ambassador hung the cloak up herself, glad, in the end, that circumstances had forced her to stick to her principles. She twirled the combination lock on the door of the frosty glass case, finished undressing and ran herself a bath. Lying in the warm and fragrant water for a few minutes, she then buffed up the circle of pinprick tattoos round her left breast with a piece of good Mexican pumice. Then, as she dried herself back in the bedroom, she glanced at the clock on her bedside table and saw that it was a lot later than she'd thought, being now about an hour before dawn. Well, strictly speaking her presence wasn't required anyway, even on such a glorious morning as this, and in another tiny and forgivable act of self-indulgence she climbed into bed and fell asleep immediately, so she didn't hear the soft tread of feet ascending to the roof, or the low ululations and chanting that followed from the pious throats of the diplomat-priests and the more devout embassy staff as the sun rose, red and angry, over Capitol Heights.

The ambassador wasn't given to dreaming. Or, more correctly, she never remembered her dreams after she'd

205

had them. Unbeknownst to her, they were almost invariably in black and white, although this signified nothing. Nonetheless, her failure to be aware of her dreams could explain, for those who sought an explanation, why she was not particularly religious and so seldom rose in time for the dawn service, apart from dutiful attendance every tenth day. This was not held against her. Along with many of her university-educated, technocratic generation, her secularist outlook was recognised, tolerated and forgiven by her more devout compatriots while she, in turn, tending to view their religion as quaint and faintly ludicrous, also recognised, again with that tolerance that famously defined the Mexican character, the central role religion played in Mexican society.

In her youth, to be sure, like the President she'd flirted with outright atheism, but that surely was just the kind of conformist non-conformism both desirable and forgivable in the young. Again, such things were tolerated, even though the President's continued vehement and outspoken atheism struck the ambassador as rather embarrassing in a man in late middle age. But again, the President's eccentricities were tolerated and had proved no obstacle to his repeated re-election by an electorate which, in any other country (and particularly, the ambassador often thought, in Mexico's exuberant, exasperating and frequently deranged northern neighbours), would have got him lynched. At the end of the day (and the ambassador snuffled with amusement at this point in her unremembered dreaming) she and the President were, above all else, Mexican patriots, and as such they would fight to the death to defend their country's culture and traditions. So the ambassador could sleep on in peace, certain in the knowledge that this zeal – in a country otherwise remarkable for its endemic lack of zealotry – was shared by almost all Mexicans apart from

a few peasants, their minds poisoned by Yankee mission-
aries constantly trying to foment low-level rebellion in
the northern provinces.

The ambassador slept on as the sun rose higher over
Washington, unaware (except in the unconscious sense
that it was a routine daily occurrence, and was therefore one of the expected small defining parameters of
every day) of the ancillary staff on the roof cleaning up,
and dreamed her unknowable dreams. They were not
in the slightest bit interesting, neither terrifying nor rev-
elatory of either a higher cosmic truth or a deep, hidden
internal malaise. Instead, that morning, she dreamed
prosaically of her country's history as, although of
course she never knew it, she did every night. She was,
it should be remembered, a servant of her country:
Mexico had made her and, boringly enough, informed
her nightly reveries.

Had she been conscious of them, the ambassador
might have been slightly abashed by how dull those
dreams were. Like most modern Mexicans who'd
received at least a part of their education north of the
border in the shining land of individuality, therapy and
a carefully nurtured culture always aspiring towards the
condition of solipsistic madness, she fancied herself, like
her erstwhile hosts, to be far more psychologically
complex and therefore interesting than she really was.
Abashed but, unlike the Yankees, not ashamed. That
distinct Mexican trait of shamelessness was hardwired
into her. Perhaps 'shamelessness' is too strong a word:
it was far more like a happy and contented fatalism that
had no room for anything as self-indulgent as shame
and its implications of a personal route to salvation or
damnation. That was deeply alien to the Mexican
national character, which was viewed with equal measures of envy and disgust by other, unhappier nations.

Needless to say, her contended demeanour and happy smile had served the ambassador well, and during fraught negotiations had driven more than one US President into such rages of impotent frustration that, crucially for Mexican interests, the President had always blinked first.

But let's return to the ambassador's dream. It was, first of all, simple and linear with none of the disjointedness and absurd intrusions which typified the dreams of Anglo-Saxons and other European races. It told, with clear narrative cohesion, the history of Mexico since the foundation of the modern state in a way familiar to the youngest Mexican schoolchild. And it told of how, following the volcano, the remnants of the Aztecs had returned to Mexico to excavate their ruined city and repopulate it, at the same time reaffirming their faith in the gods of the Aztecs and the liturgical practices performed to propitiate them. How, thereafter, the previously subject surrounding nations had joined Mexico in the new, democratic and tolerant Aztec confederation, united in mutual respect and multiculturalism, and how they had easily rebuffed the second Spanish invasion. How the lessons of the first invasion had been learned, and how methods of warfare had been refined and the rigidity of the old eschatology had been redefined to make it much more pragmatic and practical. How the primacy of personal conscience within the context of mass society had been institutionalised in the reformed calendar and how Mexico, as it expanded to the Rio Grande and the foothills of the Andes, was welcomed by its new citizens and won converts to its religion and its ethos through example rather than conquest. Then she dreamed of the decades of border wars with the Spanish Empire at the south of the isthmus until an uneasy peace had finally been negotiated, and how, later,

Mexico had aided, armed and funded the South American liberation movements that had finally driven the imperialist European tyrants and despoilers from the Southern Continent. Then she dreamed of the disastrous consequences of similar attempts to aid the indigenous nations to the north in their wars with the Anglo-Saxon invaders, and how European perfidy and rapacity had succeeded in the Northern Continent where it had been expunged from the lands south of Mexico. She dreamed of the humiliating US–Mexican War of 1832 which had led to the overthrow of the now corrupt and dissipated old Aztec monarchy and the establishment of the First Mexican Republic, and how the revitalised Mexican people had finally, after years of brutal warfare, driven out the Yankee invaders, restored Mexican territorial integrity and saved their nation from the depredations of European and Christian hegemony.

She dreamed on, of how, after peace was finally established with the defeated Americans, Mexico entered a new golden age which it still enjoyed, when Mexican tolerance made it a beacon for intellectual enquiry and technological advance. Of how this had been underwritten by Mexico's enormous wealth of natural resources including, of course, gold. But also of how the centuries of mathematical expertise acquired within the ranks of the priesthood had allowed Mexico to lead the world in the development of the computer sciences, so that by what the Europeans called the twentieth century of their biscuit god's era Mexico was the most advanced and prosperous nation on Earth, fierce in her neutrality but noble and generous in her dealings with all other nations. She dreamed of how the Yankees had never been able to understand how the Mexicans, unlike themselves, were not maddened by imperialist ambitions of conquest and the forcible imposition of alien cultures on indigenous peoples, and how, after the Second World War, in a second front in the Cold War, the United States had taken Mexico's tolerant and friendly relations with the Soviet Union as a pretext to destabilise President Xlabpak's moderate Pan-Mayan Government, leading to the temporary dictatorship of Generalissimo Teotihuacin as the United States' satrap, until the Revolution, in which she had played her part in her youth, brought about the establishment of the Fourth Republic and the tumbling of the world towards the brink of nuclear war. And now the ambassador dreamed about the last-minute intervention of the Soviets, and the subsequent decades of relative if uneasy peace until the collapse of the Soviet Union.

And now she dreamed of the new instability, the new and terrible types of intolerance that had filled the void left by the Soviets, which seemed to be bringing the world to new, and perhaps final, catastrophes as the Americans policed a non-consensual world with growing insensitivity and brutality, and of how the Yankees, triumphant, were also bankrupt, and how, again at the last minute, Mexico had come forward as the honest broker, the friend to and equal of all nations, and bailed out the Americans, along with certain conditions which, thanks to the ambassador's skill and cunning, would be ratified in the morning.

And as she slept on, in the last remaining minutes before she awoke, she dreamed a dream of which, on waking, she retained, this as every time, the glimmer of recollection. It was about how the whole of Mexico's glorious and inglorious, triumphant and abject history had been informed by one defining factor: the centrality of human sacrifice to the success and prosperity of the Mexican state and people, the willing and voluntary and loving submission of the individual to the needs of the

210

many, the still-beating, torn-out heart of selfless commun-
itarianism. And then, as she always did at this stage of
the dream, she woke up, smiling.

The phone was ringing on the ambassador's bedside
table to tell her it was 9.15 a.m., and although she wasn't
due at the White House for lunch until 12.30 p.m., she
had to hold several press conferences after briefing her
old friend and foe the Mexican President on the full
details of the treaty by videolink. The ambassador, as on
every morning, had been filled with an unconditional
love for all mankind by her dream, although, as we've
said, she hardly knew why. She sang loudly and joyously
in the shower, and as she dried herself she turned on
the TV. CNN was carrying live coverage of the US Vice-
President's flight to Mexico City for his engagement
with Mexico's President to celebrate the mutually
triumphant conclusion of the negotiations. Watching the
plane as it crossed the Rio Grande and the miles of fence
to repel migrant workers from the north which Mexican
troops, in their brightly coloured ponchos and smiles on
their wide, Mayan faces, were already tearing down, the
ambassador thought how, despite his avowed atheism,
the President was always fastidious in carrying out
his largely ceremonial duties as constitutional God
King, and respected him all the more for it. She said so
during their videolink, and the President mumbled self-
deprecatingly but rather curtly that each of them knew
their jobs, before lightening the mood by joking about
the US Vice-President's famously dodgy heart condition.
Given the diplomatic sensitivities involved the ambassador didn't repeat the joke during her press conferences,
repeating, instead, the importance of maintaining mutual
respect in the relations between nations, including, most
importantly, tolerance of different cultures and traditions. In fact, she thought she sold what was already

being called the 'Aztec Doctrine' of tolerance and multiculturalism rather well, even if the American President looked strangely pale as he welcomed the ambassador to the White House and they walked together into the Oval Office. In one corner a television, also tuned to CNN, was showing live pictures from Mexico City of the Vice-President's goodwill visit, and the President grew even paler as his deputy, clearly heavily drugged, was guided up the stone steps of the pyramid towards the Mexican President, glorious in his magnificent robes of feathers and the pelts of jaguars, who, once the Vice-President had been secured, raised his onyx knife high above his head as the chanting and ululations reached a crescendo. And the ambassador, ever the diplomat, pretended to ignore her host vomiting noisily into a wastepaper basket as lunch was announced.

The Practical Applications of the 12 Point Path to Personal Enlightenment

The Practical Applications of the Twelve Point Path to Personal Enlightenment

The Princess Michael of Kent Function Room at the Moat House Hotel on the outskirts of Guildford was an unforgiving venue, and Colin knew he was dying the death. It wasn't that he'd lost the audience hours ago – that was only to be expected; it was that he'd lost himself. The slogans, homilies and nostra came out in the right order and everything, but they no longer held any meaning for him.

Is this what it feels like to a priest who loses his faith, Colin wondered, as the mesmeric bullshit poured from his mouth undiminished. A sweat broke out down the middle of his back, sticking his business shirt to his pale skin. Colin shuddered inside as he came to the close. Magic marker in one hand, the other all juju-waggling fingers, he jutted out his jaw, smiled through his crippling hangover, and spoke the laid-down form of words, not believing in a single one of them.

'Remember, you're all members of a team, and there's no "I" in the word team. So get out there, touch people, make deals, be there, do it.' Which was meant to be the end, except that, from nowhere, or from some long unvisited dungeon in Colin's subconscious, he dredged up and added: 'Recognise this. Then forget it.'

There was some desultory applause from the middle managers who'd been attending the course. They were even more hung-over than Colin, and packed up their presentation packs with an aguish deliberation. All of them understood the nature of the bargain they'd just been party to: in return for allowing them to get away from home and the office, to stay up drinking in the bar till three in the morning and essay a shag with always otherwise unattainable colleagues, these crapulent employees, like their brothers and sisters throughout the western world, were quite prepared to listen to some shit in shirtsleeves talk bollocks at them about management theory, as long as they weren't expected to listen too hard. Colin knew all this. He'd once built a whole weekend course around the idea that working together in order to waste your employer's time and steal his money was the sincerest form of team building there was. After all, a team member who gets away with stealing a stapler is a happy, there-fore efficient, and therefore profit-making team member. It was his bad luck that he'd pitched the idea at a particu-larly unreceptive group from an old family firm of stationery suppliers. They'd gone into liquidation shortly afterwards, but even Colin couldn't pretend that it was because they hadn't responded more positively to his spiel. It was more to do with old-fashioned, cold-blooded management stupidity and incompetence, compounded this time by congenital idiocy through three generations.

Colin blinked several times, quite savagely, to exile the irrelevant memories of the stationers from his fuddled mind. From somewhere inside the Mondeo came the noise – the outward and visible sign – of the indicator indicating that he was pulling to the left, into the middle lane. It clicked with the deliberation and regularity of a death-watch beetle. It clicked again as he took the turn-off to Ripley. The car stopped on the gravel of the Half Moon's car park with a familiar, marine susurration. Elsewhere, far away, waves crashed on beaches, just as waves of nausea and waves of guilt and self-loathing broke on the beaches of Colin's stomach and soul.

216

His colleague Trevor passed him his pint. 'Feeling a bit under the weather, eh, Col?'

'Fuck off, you cunt. Christ, I should have gone to bed after we all went for that bloody curry.'

'Yeah. And preferably in your own bed in your own room, you dirty dog. Any good, then?'

Colin shuddered. 'God, Trev, I can't remember.' He could. Clearly. The careful way she'd coaxed him, prone as he was, to heights of sexual bliss, and then quite deliberately rifled through his wallet until she found the pictures of Kaye and the kids, and made him talk all night all about them as they drank their way through the minibar. She'd left with a smile just before dawn to go to present her own management course, leaving him utterly broken.

'Who was she, anyway? Not on the course, I trust. Very unprofessional.'

'No no no, just some woman.' Another tsunami of guilt and disgust crashed on Colin and he gave a tiny, involuntary grimace. Trevor looked at him and lit a fag.

'You all right, Col? Not still pissed, are you?'

Colin groaned. 'You noticed, didn't you, Trev?'

'Yep.'

'It just, I dunno, it just came from somewhere, something I read once. There I was, saying all this stuff, all this bollocks they've all heard a thousand times before, none of them listening anyway cos they all got pissed up last night as well, and it just came to me, y'know, almost as if it wasn't me speaking.'

'Yeah, Colin. Dead mystical. And the scales fell from your eyes on the road to Dorking. Actually, your eyes . . .' Trevor went through a little, ironic pantomime of disgust. 'Although, it must be said, it was fucking brilliant.'

'What?'

'Their MD was having a chat afterwards while you were throwing up back in the room, said it was the best course he's been on, and the clincher was that stuff about recognising and forgetting. Said it put everything in perspective for him. How you built up experience through self-discovery and self-awareness, but always had to maintain the capacity to forget all you've learned in order to discover new ways of doing things, to, what was it, create the enabling environment for perpetual renewal. That's what he said.'

'Jesus! What a wanker!'

'You said it. Another pint?'

Campus

Sykes-Wolsey's memory was not what it was, although he remembered clearly both last night's activities with the divine Dyan from the much diminished Department of International Relations and also, over twenty years previously, that he'd lost tenure at Cambridge over the Seumas Black Affair. Seumas had been far too cool to press charges in respect of the allegations of false imprisonment and aggravated assault that had arisen from the fifteen hours he'd endured the rather primitive attempts at brainwashing, more mindful by that stage of his forthcoming career in the media, but the authorities didn't care. Things hadn't been helped when Sykes-Wolsey nearly blinded a venerable old Marxist with a broken sherry glass in a College Senior Parlour a few evenings after he'd been released on bail, even though the antique Red had, as it turned out, given as good as he'd got with a smashed decanter full of port. And of course Sykes-Wolsey had been goading his college, the faculty and the university into martyring him for so long that to deny him the consummation he sought so eagerly would have been inhuman, which his enemies, despite his best agitprop efforts to brand them as such, weren't quite.

This glimmer of humanity was their mistake, as it had allowed Sykes-Wolsey to dress his dismissal up as the gravest attack on academic freedom since, I don't know, Galileo or someone. However, it was his mistake that a nice little broadsheet media frenzy fizzled out almost immediately after he appeared on a smartish late-night TV show on the infant Channel 4, and blew

221

it by sidestepping all questions asked him by concentrating instead on an elliptical deconstruction of the *Guardian*'s typeface along with the bizarre insistence that Basil Brush, in rigorously applied ur-terms, was a real fox. This just bored everyone, including the alliance of Marxists, structuralists, traditionalists and even a few old Leavisites who'd really got rid of him because they were maddened with envy by the way he'd got away for so long with having torrid, dirty sex with most of his undergraduate and all of his post-graduate students, while, simultaneously, being a raging alcoholic and jabbering coke-fiend.

He also remembered that he was still thin if fifty and all dressed in black, and he grinned winningly as he crossed the campus of an obscure Midwest American college away from the lecture theatre, although he'd already half forgotten what he'd said to at most about fifteen students, who unknowingly marked the depth of Sykes-Wolsey's fall from academic and critical grace. Whereas once his students had fought for closest proximity to him, and were invariably cosmopolitan, modish, stylish, well connected, rich, clever and eminently (and often imminently) fuckable, this lot were a complete turn-off to anyone except one of their own number, slouching at the very back of the hall, all dressed identically in their cheap, casual uniforms borrowed distantly from the sartorial choices of fifties' truck drivers, gormlessly chewing or twiddling pencils or fiddling with packets of fags, the contents of which they were strictly enjoined from smoking. They'd hunkered down furiously making notes, occasionally peering up like lumpy, bored gazelles round a drying waterhole in the savannah, and almost certainly not listening to a word he was saying. As he now couldn't remember what that had been, this didn't really matter.

His subject, incidentally, had been America; more precisely, he'd been continuing his series of lectures on American popular culture, post 9/11, concentrating today on the comic book as narrativising and denarrativising heuristic tool, taking as the ur- and supra-texts a single frame from both a Spiderman comic and a recent Spiderman movie. He'd concluded his exegesis in a muck-sweat of excitement, having indestructibly proved his point once again to his audience who packed their bags and exited morosely.

It may be observed at this point that all this was not without certain levels of irony, most of which Sykes-Wolsey had forgotten, while others had eluded him from the outset, as you'd expect. One of these was his subject. He ended up in American Studies just as the subject was consumptively wheezing its last speckled breath. Almost everyone now accepted that the study of America, Americans, American ways, American movies, musicals, literature, poetry, jazz, art, politics, cartoons, workplace ethos, comic books, racism, shopping, capitalism, protest, folk songs, atom bombs, architecture, ghettoes, space exploration, diners, torch songs, frontiers, immigration, teenagers, wars, roads, genocides, landscape, recreations, travels, self-awakenings, dancing, religion, management theories, energy, cars, quilt making, exploitation, jukeboxes, furniture construction, rap, graphic design, accounting, radicalism, militarism, imperialism, rock 'n' roll, science and TV were not only obvious and therefore deeply uninteresting, but were also faintly embarrassing. More to the point, following the Mexican loan the new generation of Neo-Geneticist critics proved beyond question that *they always had been*. Sykes-Wolsey had read Thawpit and Dabitoff's latest seminal work, *Not Melting Pot but Dog's Dinner: Further Examinations of the American Mistake*, with increasing dismay, but was comforted, dimly if definingly, by the fact that first he knew he'd never get tenure anywhere else and second he was increasingly unable to remember anything he'd recently read almost as soon as he'd read it.

Another irony that was equally lost on him was his indestructible Englishness, of the kind which once appealed to Americans but, in their new irrelevance, was now seen by them in their turn as more than just faintly embarrassing. Despite his efforts to adopt an international, or at least European, pose, he stank of a deliciously destructive kind of English faggotry, which manifested itself in a mawkish love of a countryside his class had expropriated, despoiled and destroyed, arts which reached their height in a capacity to pretend to be someone else, but speaking in modulations which never normally issued from human lips, and a political culture whose elite regularly betrayed the people they presumed to rule with breathtaking levels of institutionalised craven cowardice, and finally in Sykes-Wolsey's capacity to remember, unlike so much else but like Clement Attlee, the names of every boy in his class at his minor public school till the day he died. Which, for the record, was going to be today.

This was another irony, dramatic in at least two senses of the word, which we won't detain ourselves with here, but returning to the last one, his bloody awful sniffy sentimental Englishness could be seen in the way he'd gently but cruelly forced his star pupil and one-time drinking buddy Trubshawe into doing a PhD which centred round counting the phonemes in some of the works of P.G. Wodehouse, and how he'd done this as they'd got pissed as parakeets watching a cricket match out at Fenners in Cambridge. Sykes-Wolsey smiled to himself at the false memory of sunshine haloed in emptying glasses, attainable youths in clean, bright clothes, the smell of new-mown grass wafting on the warm, cocooning, cripplingly corrupt air, punts distantly plopping along the Cam, the sluggish water chorusing the barely perceptible squawks of well-heeled laughter while ducks quacked a selection of the more plangent parts of the oeuvre of Vaughan Williams, and it didn't matter that Trubshawe went rapidly off the rails and thereafter downhill, or that Sykes-Wolsey, after many adventures, had ended up in this wind-blown concrete and steel dump in the middle of the prairie. He'd heard a while ago about Trubshawe's premature death after half a lifetime of silence, and had even seen a copy of *The Twelve Point Path to Personal Enlightenment*, which struck him as disappointing before he forgot about it, but still half in love with hard death, Sykes-Wolsey almost skipped into the refectory, passing a posse of Trubshawist management consultants nursing hideous hangovers on their way to sort out the Admissions Department.

As soon as he got into the body of the hall, he forgot why he was there, then looked at the cafeteria's distant bulwark dispensing food, remembered to pick up a tray, but then forgot what he liked to eat. He remembered just in time to pick up his cutlery, but then, at the checkout, realised that he'd forgotten his wallet, containing both his money and his security pass. The old woman at the checkout waved him through, familiar with his ways and not in the slightest bit impressed with what she imagined was a carefully cultured Limey affectation towards dippy eccentricity. For a moment Sykes-Wolsey stood staring about him, having completely forgotten where he was and what he was doing there, until a woman he thought he knew waved at him from across the hall, so he eased his way through the tables and sat down opposite Dyan. She leaned forward on her folded arms and whispered, 'Christ, Damien. You look fucked. You still having the memory problems?'

'Um . . .'

'Look, babe, I know you like it weird, dirty and often, but you gotta quit doing that stuff. People will talk.'

People were talking all around them, in a whining babel of bollocks, some of which Sykes-Wolsey over-heard and then immediately forgot. 'Yes. Yes, Dyan. You're right. Decrease the dosage. I think I'm going to, um . . .'

He trailed off and stared at some tofu and a beaker of turnip juice on his tray. Dyan leaned over and kissed him, then held out his security pass. 'You dozy prick. I found this in my bathroom this morning. I washed it for you.'

Sykes-Wolsey took the plastic rectangle from her with a winsome smile, and frowned, as though puzzled at something.

'Jesus. You don't remember, do you? This is the day.' Sykes-Wolsey raised his eyebrows pleadingly. Dyan rolled her eyes in despair, and leaned closer. 'The day. God, the day when we do it.' She mouthed the last two words noiselessly, and Sykes-Wolsey smiled.

'Of course. And everything's . . .'

'Of course. I linked up the ur-probe to the university mainframe last night, and we're reckoning synthesis as soon as you give the stuff, you know, the *things* to Mustapha and Corin over in the Strategic Department basement this afternoon. This is it, babe! We're finally gonna link up the ur- and supra-mathene! Christ, I'm so excited I could almost come!'

Sykes-Wolsey leered, and remembered last night, although not how he'd lost his pass. The students they'd chosen for the initiation were keen, if maladroit, and rather toothsome, as he'd put it, licking his lips as they'd tied them up. Yes, it was all coming back now. This was the big day, the Day of Synthesis, when everything would come together and Everything Would Finally Be Clear and Understood. He flashed a foxy smile at Dyan and leaned forward to take her hands in his.

'And you know what to do when the mainframe crashes?'

'Of course I do, babe. After the explosions I reboot and download the ur-theory module into the auxiliary system, while Kemal, Ruben, Sophie and Dan take the Admin. Block, neutralise the databases and the false-text lackeys and then execute the Principal, the Vice-Principal and the heads of all the Humanities departments while Leroy, Buster and Laverne dynamite the library.'

'Yes. Yes.' Sykes-Wolsey's eyes shone, even though he'd already forgotten what she'd just said. Dyan stroked his cheek.

'Gee, this must've been what it was like in the sixties! A Revolution in Ideas becoming the Revolution in Reality!' She was panting with excitement.

'I was fifteen when the sixties ended,' Sykes-Wolsey observed, and Dyan smiled sweetly. It was just this kind of gnomic utterance that made Sykes-Wolsey so cute, and his ideas so intoxicatingly wonderful. The way he'd realised that the point to terrorism was that it had no point, and therefore it made perfect sense, or ur-sense, for bitter ideological foes to act together in the advancement of the supra-atrocity. She almost hugged herself at the thought of the mayhem to come, the fruition of months of planning, countless hours of frantically filthy ur-tantric sex, weeks lost to addlement from a pharmacopoeia of chemicals mostly unknown to medical science and decades of frustration at the continuing false-text doctrinaire hegemony that had stifled so many independent

227

minds like her own in this soulless academic gulag. Once they'd had the Purge, and destroyed for ever the Fictive Lie, Everything Would Be Real. Thinking about how she'd rebuild International Relations as a respectable discipline, after she'd tortured to death all her enemies across the country, she leaned over and kissed Sykes-Wolsey passionately on the mouth.

Elsewhere across campus teenagers clipped magazines into their automatic weapons, while down in the basement of the Department of Strategic Studies Mustapha and Corin hunkered down nervously next to the dirty bomb they'd built from a blueprint downloaded from a patriotic website Corin subscribed to. They'd just prayed together, in their different ways, and nervously punched their fists together in a tremulous high-five. Although studying different subjects, they'd both been mesmerised by Sykes-Wolsey's vision of a World Free from Lies, where everyone would finally understand that everything was true. A few hundred metres away Laverne tied a mauve bandanna round her forehead, took out a small Bible and kissed it, while Dan and Sophie wrapped the corsets of explosives around each other's lean young bodies. Sykes-Wolsey swallowed the last mouthful of tofu without expression, immediately forgetting what it tasted like. Dyan stood up, and taking him by the hand led him out of the hall and into a janitor's closet, where she gave him a quick blow job before carefully repeating the instructions he'd laid out that she was to repeat to him if he forgot them. He smiled shyly as she tucked his cock back into his tight black corduroy trousers and leaned up to kiss him on the cheek.

'You okay, babe?'

'Um . . .'

'I got Margaret and the kids away okay. They'll be in Canada by tonight.'

'Who?'

'Your wife, you dummy!' she smiled, kissed him again, and stealthily exited the closet.

In the darkness Sykes-Wolsey took a small pill from a round, silver box in his pocket and popped it in his mouth. A sudden metabolic rush made him dizzy and the back of his head vibrate as his eyes went in and out of focus. Yes. That was it. A blow. Um. But then he remembered he had to get to Strategic Studies, so, staggering slightly, sneaked out of the closet in his turn, left the Refectory and walked towards a large building, guarded by military policemen, and sponsored by any number of different Merchants of Death. The guards were jittery, as the News from Everywhere was just awful, but Sykes-Wolsey had forgotten this, although he suddenly remembered something that had been puzzling him for decades, and which now re-entered his mind unbidden and unwelcome, fatally disturbing his determination to keep the tattered shreds of his short-term memory focused on where he was going, who he was meeting and what he had to give them and why. Damn! Um. Yes. It was the ur-text, that was the thing. Today was the day. Smash the lies. Expose the Fictive Lie and reveal the coming reign of the ur-text, the truth behind everything, that everything is True. Yes. Um. Damn.

In his completely fucked-up mind the uninvited thought was deftly slitting the scrawny throats of all his demented ideas and plans, and he stumbled for a moment as he neared the Strategic Studies building, banging a fist against his temple. No. It was gone. The thing he had to remember, so important that Dyan wouldn't repeat it over lunch, even if he could remember lunch. Gone, gone. The guards watched him lurch towards them and fingered their weaponry, but nodded him through as he flashed the precious security pass. No! He screamed inside himself as the thought now expanded to fill his entire consciousness, and all else was occluded, obliterated, lost.

He got through the revolving doors with difficulty, unable to focus on anything except the mystery of how David Lean had been able to use colour filmstock to make his documentary about Lawrence of Arabia, when colour film wasn't invented until years later. Fuck! Sykes-Wolsey knew the answer to this. It was either a trick of false-chronology, or an obvious ur-riddle. He ground his teeth and spun round on his heel as he almost fell towards the sophisticated scanning equipment in the lobby of the department.

'Yes!' he shouted. Several people looked round, including some more red-eyed Trubshawist management theorists, who acknowledged in quiet triumph the disgraceful drunkenness of one of the university's more senior academics, but Sykes-Wolsey forgot about them as soon as he saw them. No. Yes! That was it. It was the supra-time conundrum, where ur-text and supra-chronology meet to create a beguiling mirage of false-timespace. This was elementary stuff, and he cursed himself for being momentarily bamboozled by such childish nonsense, and, grinning, pulled himself upright just as he passed the first of the network of invisible, highly sensitive and proactive lasers criss-crossing the lobby, unfortunately having forgotten that last night he'd concealed the detonators for Corin's bomb up his arse for safety's sake and which, triggered by the lasers, now exploded within him in a splashy deconstruction.

The Time Portal

'Oh God! Oh fucking Jesus God!' Stephanie sobbed, looking at the mess in their kitchen. 'What have they done?' Seumas looked round the door frame and flinched. 'Jesus Christ, Steph. What's happened here?'

'What the fuck do you think's happened?' There was more than a hint of hysteria edging into her voice now as she surveyed the wreckage along the work surfaces. 'It's them again. They've fucking eaten everything.' A few limp strands of rocket clung to the tiles above the sink, but all else was gone. 'Everyone's going to be here any minute now. What are we going to do?' The last word was almost howled, and then Steph started sobbing again.

'Look, I'll have a another word with them, okay?' Seumas said rather feebly, and flinching again, this time unseen, he walked tentatively down the hall towards the children's rooms. The television was horribly loud, and he recognised with dismay that they were playing the tape of Andrew Davies's adaptation of *Pride and Prejudice* again. The soundtrack was accompanied by raucous laughter and, he heard with relief, the occasional happy gurgle from the twins. He knocked on the door before opening it, just in time to see Dirty Susan ease her naked buttocks onto the window sill and shit noisily into the Islington street. She cackled madly as she saw Seumas come in, while Tom and George turned round, raising cans of lager in a loose kind of salute, and tapped grubby forefingers against their grubbier temples as they rolled their eyes at Dirty Susan.

'Told you she was just Bedlam totty, master,' George drawled, continuing to bounce a twin on either knee. 'Thanks for the wittals, though, master. Fancy enough grub you have these days, would explain Susie's shits, eh?' Tom guffawed into his lager.

'Um, yes,' Seumas ventured, rather lamely. 'It's about the food and . . .' But Stephanie's latest screams distracted him. She'd just discovered the true nature of the contents of the sink. The three asylum seekers all burst out laughing again, so much that George's tricorn hat fell off and Susan shat out of the window again.

'Um . . .' Seumas ventured, when the doorbell rang.

When the practical applications of the principles of time travel were first developed in the middle of the opening decade of the twenty-first century, it was widely recognised as a triumph for British science, despite the limitations to the process that soon became apparent. Chief among these was the fact that you could only travel through time that had already elapsed, so while it was possible to travel forward to past futures and thus, thankfully, return to the present, the future itself, as viewed from the present, remained an undiscoverable mystery. Likewise, inherent instabilities in the infinitely complex interweavings of the millions of threads of the spacio-temporal continua meant that it was only possible to travel with any hope of safe return to a period of roughly fifty years spanning the end of the eighteenth and beginning of the nineteenth centuries. But even with these limitations, when the Starbucks Goldman Sachs Time Portal, named after the project's two principal corporate sponsors, was opened at the British Chrononautics Institute in Kent, for a while at least it served to make the nation feel good about itself once more, at a time when it seemed there was so little else for it to feel good about. Indeed, the technical glitch at the portal's inauguration that sent the Earl and Countess of Wessex irretrievably back to the late Cretaceous period seemed only to inflame the general sense of national euphoria.

There were, however, other drawbacks. Only a week or two after the royal visit, the first portal suddenly imploded, taking a mobile phone, a pager and a sizeable part of the Kentish Weald with it into the unknowable past. Thereafter all further attempts to transport non-organic matter back through time were abandoned. (In the eighteen months it took to build the Mark II Time Portal, this time near Folkestone to facilitate rail connections with the Channel Tunnel, scientists at the BCI claimed to have discovered a previously unrecognised time 'gene' lurking within the interstices of the DNA of all living beings: in other words, time was to all intents and purposes a subjective construct and, outside the organic matrix, non-existent. Therefore it followed that moving any non-organic material through time was, literally, impossible. Naturally, this gave rise to considerable anxiety in all the other physical sciences, and Professor Stephen Hawking's reputation never truly recovered from his assertion that that thing which had previously been called 'time' in all the equations was obviously still 'time', but with a different name. His income from advertising work dwindled away to almost nothing as a result, sending shock waves throughout the whole scientific community.) Unfortunately for the project itself its two chief corporate backers withdrew their financial support once the implications of the untransportability of non-organic material sunk in: first off, Starbucks would be unable to exploit the potential for expansion in the non-contemporary sector if it was unable to kit out its new outlets in Regency London with the trappings of its specific corporate branding (despite increasingly frantic efforts to create an entirely organic *cafe latte* machine); then Goldman Sachs, unable to send bullion back in time, was unable to invest it in high-yield, long-term unit trusts, and thus any further support for the project was not in the interests of its investors. Soon afterwards, seeing no commercial advantage in their continued support, all the other sponsors, including the cartel of bookmakers and several Cork Street galleries, withdrew too.

This might have proved the end for the project had not the Government, at just that time, been particularly self-conscious about its place in History and in History more generally. Despite the excitement that had greeted the unveiling of the first time portal, the nation remained stubbornly ill at ease: despite the increasing prosperity of its citizens, there was a collective sense of mild despair abroad, a dissatisfaction with the modern world and all its myriad wonders. The Government, recently re-elected and still phenomenally popular, was grumbled about everywhere and, oxymoronically, was the most unpopular popular government since records, as they say, had begun. Cultural commentators and columnists, sniffing the national mood, ascribed it to a simple cause: lack of national confidence due to being cut off by the trappings of modernity from the ancient soul of England. It was time, in short, for the nation to reconnect with itself. And what better way was there than for the nation to revisit its former self, on the threshold of its nineteenth-century glory? And, thus inspired, work together to forge an even greater national destiny? Through English ingenuity and invention, this was now literally possible. The Government was massively in surplus due to prudent management of the economy (as well as the windfall resulting from the recent demise of the agri-cultural sector, a previously considerable drain on the public purse). With hardly any hesitation, therefore, it nationalised the time portal in a return, as many commented at the time, to the Good Old Days. And thus, beyond the huge, shapeless, colourless void that now constituted what had once been the Medway Valley, beyond the now empty fields of mid-Kent, returning to an uncultivated, ungrazed state of natural innocence and beauty, the Mark II Time Portal was opened, with little fanfare, by the newly created Minister for Time, who inaugurated it with a brief trip to a Thursday afternoon in late June, 1787, from which he soon safely returned, to polite applause.

Its proximity to the population centres of Northern Europe meant that the time portal's potential income from tourism was incalculable. The edifice itself was unassuming, being merely a rather short tunnel attached to some simple if mystifying machinery, but it was soon housed in a vast and magnificent building designed by England's greatest living architect, combining the ultra-modern, more contemporary design, and pastiches of the neoclassical and the neo-Gothic, alluding to the period of England's history to which the day visitors would be transported. Having been conducted through a series of interpretation centres, the visitors, before being sent back in time, had to change from their modern clothing into garments fashioned from imported silk, flax and wool, and to remove all non-organic matter from their persons, including spectacles, contact lenses, wristwatches, wedding rings and false teeth. People equipped with pacemakers and non-wooden artificial limbs were, regretfully, turned away. Each visitor then had to spend half an hour being briefed about ways to conduct themselves in the past, and then had to sign a legally enforceable document freeing the time portal holding company from any liability whatsoever for anything that might befall them on their Journey into History. Only then, accompanied by specially trained guides, could the visitors, in small groups of up to five, pass through the portal. No one quibbled at the charge of one hundred pounds a head, especially as the Government was paying for every schoolchild in the country to visit its past; the time portal was a genuinely universal attraction, bringing in all classes, all ages and all ethnicities and sexualities, and had the effect of uniting the nation in a ferment of excitement, expectation and hope unseen for generations.

After all, this was the stuff of science fiction, which may (the time portal's PR company accepted) be a cliché, but which proved (they added with quiet satisfaction) that clichés are clichés because they're true. By visiting Yesterday, it allowed the people of Today to get a perspective on Tomorrow, not just for individuals, but for the nation as a whole. It was, indeed, Incredible. Unbelievable. Awesome. And an appalling flop.

For a start there was the queuing, which was horrendous, as there was only one portal. And of course before that you had to have a series of painful inoculations and vaccinations. Then there was changing your clothes, being disinfected, having cosmetics or deodorants with even the tiniest non-organic compound scrubbed off you by vicious old women in overalls, and then the final indignity of signing away your rights. Worse, the actual experience of time travel was far from pleasant, a bit like being in a plummeting lift while having your fingernails dragged down a blackboard, making many of the visitors physically sick (although those who were unable to produce certificated evidence that they had only eaten organically reared meat and vegetables in the past forty-eight hours had already had their stomachs pumped). For reasons no one could adequately explain, travelling from one instant in time to another took about twenty minutes. And for equally unexplained reasons, despite leaving the twenty-first century in Folkestone, the spacio-temporal threads led, in the past, to the northern mudbanks of the Thames just below the Tower, and although the coordinates were always set for low tide, mistakes happened.

Even if you didn't drown, it was a long and unpleasant walk to the relatively more salubrious parts of London, but even there it stank. Because it was impossible to send money into the past, there were no catering facilities, nor the possibility of buying anything at all by way of a souvenir, as you couldn't return with it; nor could you bring back photographic or video mementoes of your trip. But worst of all were the people.

Most visitors were so shocked and disturbed at the condition of their ancestors they demanded to be returned to the present almost immediately. The depredations of disease and poverty were visible everywhere, and even visitors with stronger stomachs didn't last long. Amateur genealogists gagged at the sight of their great-great-great-great-great-great-grandmother's nose eaten away by syphilis and face ravaged by smallpox. A party of bibliophiles, having previously conjured up a romantic vision of a world of learning and respect for beauty evoked every time they stroked a musty old vellum-bound volume, toured a printing works in growing horror as they watched old women arrive with baskets full of dog shit, harvested from the stinking streets and then rubbed (and euphemistically redubbed 'pure') into the leather to soften it prior to binding. At least the bibliophiles got as far as Clerkenwell. Most never made it past the Fleet Ditch, with its constant flow of blood and guts from Smithfield (on top of all the shit and rubbish and dead cats already bobbing along on their way to the Thames). A few especially brave souls tried to meet up with celebrated historical figures, but in the subsequent interviews, apart from the mutual incomprehension arising from accent and idiom, the foulness of the breath of the famous, the rankness of their clothing and the general choking mist seeping in through the windows or arising from the floor, soon drew the encounters to a close. A very, very few could stand it long enough to make a break for the country-side surrounding London, a short distance away but a long walk, through the encircling heaps of dumped trash and human excrement, but a dead baby abandoned beyond Borough or a mounted figure eyeing you hungrily from the side of a windmill near Archway usually made them turn and hurry back to the present. One or two made it to fresh air in Lewisham or Highgate, but stayed out too late and got murdered for their hair.

After a few months, the only visitors to the time portal were historians and perverts. The interpretation centres, cafés and shops around the portal were closed down, and the whole thing was passed over to the British Museum.

Strangely, the modern world's encounter with its past did have a salutary effect, despite the universally negative response of the day visitors to their experience. Perhaps, in finally recognising how utterly revolting the past was, the people of England started to appreciate the benefits of the present and look, once more, with hope to the future. But such speculation is academic, because around this time the first asylum seekers started arriving.

The aspect of the time portal which most vexed its developers – not because of the problems it presented to the smooth operation of the process, but because it was inexplicable – was the way it would not allow travel into the future from the present, but would allow travel into the future from the past. That is, it was possible for someone living in the eighteenth century to travel over 200 years into their, subjective, future, up to the point of present time, but no further. This phenomenon was in danger of stumbling into the realm of metaphysics when a greater problem arose. It had always been assumed that visitors to the past moved through History in stealthy incognito, their true identity disguised from the denizens of that former epoch, not least of all because a revelation of who they truly were – People From the Future – would be incomprehensible and, probably literally, mindblowing. The twenty-first century's forebears, however, weren't as dumb as their descendants might have imagined, and across the whole period accessible through the time portal the stinking inhabitants of stinking London had grown accustomed to the time tourists during their brief invasion of their past. As the visitors to the time portal had chosen destinations across the whole period from roughly 1770 to roughly 1820, they were, in fact, an almost permanent feature of late Georgian and Regency London life, spewing in the streets, holding coarse linen handkerchiefs over their mouths and noses and, invariably, never spending a penny. Their total poverty and transience (yet ubiquity) resulted in most of the population paying them no attention once it had been established that they came from 200 or so years in the future, and had nothing to contribute but their disgust.

Meanwhile, the location of the portal was discovered at various times across the fifty-year period, and it became briefly popular among certain classes (having been nabbed, claimed and exploited by different generations of the same family almost as soon as it was discovered) to

travel, for a small fee, from, say, just after the Battle of
Waterloo back to the eve of the French Revolution to
have dinner with one's grandfather and discuss, in a
disinterested and civilised manner, the vicissitudes of
History. Likewise, young bloods across three generations
would go for a jaunt to sneer and laugh at the
sartorial experiments of their predecessors, legatees or,
indeed, older selves and sometimes beat themselves up
after a heavy night's drinking. The portal was a harmless
distraction, a bit of a lark after Vauxhall Gardens or
before Drury Lane, and so no one took it particularly
seriously.

Even when people started travelling to the twenty-first
century, it had little effect on the leisured and
respectable class of persons whose exclusive use of the
portal was guaranteed by the monopolistic practices of
its family of owners. The two-way traffic was hardly
noticed by its users in the future: their time was so
conditioned in the practices of heritage that the organic
clothes they made the day visitors wear were, of course,
of an eighteenth-century cut and style, so when genuine
inhabitants of that century passed through the portal in
Folkestone, arriving from the past, no one paid them
any attention and they, in their turn, had a look around,
wrinkled up their noses at the artificial smells of the
future, and then went home.

However, news of the portal, and the world of the
future, started to trickle down the strata of society. One
or two visitors from the past, of a scholarly bent, had
spent longer than a few minutes in Folkestone. Indeed,
one antiquary (or 'anti-antiquary', as he wittily restyled
himself), did what Goldman Sachs couldn't, and
invested wisely enough to be able to live extremely
comfortably, if discreetly, in twenty-first-century London
for several years, before returning to his own time and

writing a short monograph about his adventures. Rumours of the wonders and unimaginable comforts of the future world began circulating in ever more exaggerated form among the lowest rungs of society, in the rookeries and the collapsing tenements, among the dog-shit collectors and road sweepers and prostitutes and pickpockets, those for whom their lives were mere existence, and that existence hardly bearable. And soon, across the whole fifty years, the lowest of the low, the truly desperate, started slipping, when no one was looking, through the portal to the easy life of the future.

'They're even worse than that Kosovan girl Peter and Alice got,' Stephanie whispered across the candlelit table, her shaking fingers abstractedly reducing a poppadom to a fine dust.

'I thought she was a Serb, wasn't she?' The remains of the takeaway steeped in the waving shadows, dahl and korma tenebrous and increasingly tepid.

Simon didn't wait for an answer to his wife Kate's question. 'But can't you get rid of them?'

'How?' Stephanie nearly shrieked. Seumas winced again and looked furtively down the hall, from whence the sound of the TV battled for audibility above the noise made by their three servants. Stephanie calmed herself. 'It's not as if they came from an agency or anything. They just came off the streets like all the others. And what if they came back for the twins? That Susan bitch . . .' But Steph's sobs prevented her from speculating further on what Dirty Susan was capable of doing. Seumas hugged Stephanie tight but helplessly, and looked pleadingly at Simon and Kate.

'But this is ridiculous,' Kate hissed. 'You should get the police involved or something! What about social services?' Another crash from down the hall once more distracted them for an instant.

And of course it was all easier said than done.

At first the refugees went almost unnoticed, and even when their numbers increased it might still have been possible to accommodate them somehow or other. Having a poxy drab as an au pair or some noseless cutpurse as a handyman held a certain cachet in some social circles for a while, until reports of the experiences of people like Seumas and Stephanie started gaining circulation. The problem soon became obvious: any threats made or implemented against the refugees had no effect. Nothing the twenty-first century could throw at them could possibly be worse than the routine horrors of the eighteenth-century life they'd left behind. Sack them, and they'd camp on your front door. Arrest them or detain them and they'd escape, go back through the time portal and then turn up again before you'd sacked, arrested or detained them.

The same problem beset all attempts to police the point of entry. Despite twenty-four-hour surveillance of the portal by snatch squads of private security guards, news had got round the rookeries and thieves' kitchens of 200 years previously, so the refugees simply started arriving before the security measures had been implemented. Because of the anomalies of time travel the authorities were unable to respond in kind: from the constantly progressing present, despite the frantic efforts of the British Chrononautical Institute's scientists, it still remained impossible to travel back to any time except the Georgian era, not to last week, nor yesterday, nor even to a second ago.

Things were becoming desperate. The streets of London and the towns left in Kent teemed with filthy, lousy, stinking beggars demanding money, medicine and the miracles of modern life with menaces. Highwaymen had taken to lurking around motorway intersections on the M2, M20 and M25. Worse still, they brought with them not only their attitudes to personal property and hygiene but also their diseases. When bubonic plague and cholera broke out in Reigate, sterner measures were clearly needed.

A daring scheme was suggested by some of the BCI's more adventurous scientists. As they were unable to return to five years before to prevent themselves from making the instigating breakthrough which had allowed them to develop the technology of time travel in the first place, instead they volunteered to return to Georgian London in order to ensure that the circumstances which would eventually allow the time portal to be built could never come to pass, even if this required them to murder their own ancestors and thus immediately snuff out their own existence.

The risks were immense. Nobody could even guess what effects tinkering with the past might have, so it was with extreme trepidation, mingled with a little hope, that the team of scientists entered the portal and travelled back in time.

The effects were immediate. For a split second the scientists who'd remained in the twenty-first century, or most of them, found themselves dressed in smocks: instead of the time portal, they beheld an immense Gothic cathedral and gaggles of laughing, flaxen-haired children weaving tapestries. A second later everything disappeared, leaving a flat, vulcanite wasteland across which lumbered huge, pangolin-like creatures. A second after that things got back, more or less, to normal, although it was now apparent that almost as soon as the squad of scientists had left, the time portal had now been in operation for five years longer than it had been previously, the number of refugees was thus instantly quadrupled and, coincidentally, skirt lengths in 1958 were from now on remembered as being marginally shorter.

'Christ, Steph,' Kate whispered, after a terrible silence. 'I think she's dead.' She turned back from the window and the view it held of Dirty Susan, floppy and partially impaled on the railings in the street below. Stephanie started screaming hysterically, despite Seumas's attempts to hug her into silence, and his repeated mantra: 'It was an accident. Wasn't it? It was obviously an accident. Just an accident.' George hid the twins' faces behind his filthy cuff, while Tom gawped idiotically at his employers.

Stephanie was acquitted of murder, but convicted of manslaughter and given a three-year custodial sentence. The judge in the case, in his arcane robes, with his patrician manner, antediluvian attitudes and the untypical courtesy with which he'd listened to the evidence from Tom and George, was turned overnight into a national hate figure by a furious popular press, for a change reflecting public opinion rather than seeking to manipulate it. Moreover, Stephanie was middle class and a media professional, as well as being a friend of several of the Government's junior ministers. Dry academic observations that the public mood was identical to that which had informed the Wilkesite and Gordon riots in eighteenth-century London (which Tom, if not George, had joined in) cut no ice, and a few lone voices defending the judge in particular and the refugees from the past in general were drowned out, even in the liberal papers that usually observed similar eruptions of ill-informed public hysteria with a disapproving if faintly amused disdain. A growing hatred of the past and everything associated with it became widespread, and when the British Museum was firebombed one night the Government finally acted with speed. All citizens were now obliged to carry their birth certificates with them at all times, and were to be subjected to spot checks by the newly established Time Police. Possession of a forgery, or failure to produce a valid certificate, resulted in immediate internment prior to deportation back in time. An inspector in the Time Police then worked out how to make the measures effective across the period in the twenty-first-century the time portal was in operation. He and a female colleague volunteered to go back in time with the specific purpose of producing a dynasty sworn to the secret possession of the facts of the dangers of the time portal until such a time, centuries later, when the thing was built, at which point the latest scion of the family was to inform the proper authorities. Amazingly, this worked, and from its inception the time portal was now surrounded by vast open prison camps, their inmates each awaiting transportation to the vile era of their origins.

This was done with despatch, or even haste, with nobody bothering to observe the usual niceties. No effort was made to discover from which particular time within the fifty-year period of the past the deportees had come from, nor did anyone really care what happened to them when they arrived. Had they done so, they might have been shocked to observe how certain of the anomalies inherent in time travel automatically corrected themselves in various cases, albeit with apparent randomness. So, if someone was returned to their own time even within weeks of when their own death should have occurred had they not travelled through time, they fell to dust as soon as they exited the time portal, in the Thames mud. Likewise, returning to a period approximating to the time of one's birth resulted in the unfortunate returnee instantly imploding in on him- or herself, with a nauseating sucking sound and a shower of blood, afterbirth and amniotic fluid. And then, of course, there were the thousands who arrived in the present to be forced at gunpoint back to their own time, arriving at high tide. Many of the bodies that floated in the Thames in the last decades of the eighteenth century bore bullet holes from ordnance quite unknown to the gunsmiths of that period. Soon rumours spread of certain powerless undesirables born in the later times being bundled into involuntary temporal exile along with their ancestral equivalents, though these stories gained little currency when the rumour-mongers mysteriously disappeared too.

As Stephanie was released early from prison with a full pardon amidst jubilant scenes outside the gaol, earlier Wordsworth looked in dismay at the clumps of bloated corpses brought in by the latest tide and caught around the piers of Westminster Bridge. He crossed out the line he'd just written in his notebook and stomped off to find Coleridge in a nearby pub, the melancholia growing in his heart. The dog and horse and human shit started drying in the streets as the sun rose towards its zenith, and when Wordsworth finally tracked him down, Coleridge was maudlin and pretty smelly himself. They drank in silence for a while, and earlier John Wilkes, now Lord Mayor of London, swigged from the bottle as he reread the latest report on the influx of returning refugees. Later, Lord Byron wept on the steps to the House of Lords as a young woman, prematurely aged by her experiences in the future, proffered him her dead baby from beneath the folds of her shawl. Earlier, William Blake thought he saw an angel tumble from the time portal, surrounded by several veterans of Nelson's fleet, lacking limbs, falling backwards, dead from a volley fired over 200 years hence. In his laboratory Joseph Priestley stared into a belljar and in Finsbury, earlier, people who, in truth, were as yet long unborn, a forlorn gang of derelicts, lunatics, paedophiles, small-beer radicals and drug dealers and abusers, milled around behind stockades as philanthropic clergymen wondered what on earth to do with them. Gillray rubbed his eyes as he etched a satanic figure, in twenty-first-century dress, impale an infant on what looked like a TV aerial. Earlier, Tom Paine cut his thumb as he sharpened his quill to berate the Government for the wretchedness suffered by the returnees at the hands of their descendants, as, later, did Hazlitt, Cobbett, Hone and, earlier, Dr Johnson, while Charles James Fox lambasted Pitt the Younger in the House of Commons, spurred on by Sheridan, about the state of the poor, exiled from the future, and the Prince Regent sent ten shillings to help relieve their suffering. George III was, throughout the whole period in question, driven mad as he tried to take it all in.

Finally, they met, ministers, writers, poets, natural philosophers, inventors, aristocrats and radicals, each travelling through the time portal to 15 May 1800, and then walking the short distance to the Tower and their secret conclave. After introductions had been made, Burke spoke first, and beautifully, balancing felicitous phrases describing the paradise of comfort and ease and unimaginable material benefit which, it seemed, was humankind's destiny in the not too distant future, with thunderous denunciations of the depths of moral depravity and inhumanity to which such comfort would lead the race. Lord Liverpool pulled a nasty face, while Turner scribbled something on his thumbnail. The Duke of Wellington damned the eyes of the future, and suggested invading it, until several of the scientists there pointed out the physical impossibility of such a course of action. And thus the debate proceeded, getting nowhere, until a young man whose name History has forgotten rose to speak.

'My Lords,' he said. Several bobbed their heads in acknowledgement. 'I believe us to be skirting this problem. Are we concerned here with provision for our fellow men and women driven onto our charity by the cruelties exacted upon them by the inhabitants of the future? If so, this is a problem of administration, and easily settled. Or are we filled with despair and disgust at the sight of what, it seems, we will become? Or are we, like the poor, filled with wonder and awe at the sight of the future one minute, and then consumed with rage and jealousy the next when it becomes clear that our progeny will selfishly refuse to share their magnificence with us, their ancestors? If the second, we reflect on it and hope, in as much as we can understand these things, that they will turn out differently. If the last, then perhaps we should *arrange* things differently, to ensure a different outcome.'

'What? What?' the Prince Regent blustered, and was about to propose, again, that a delegation of great men (himself included) go into the future to implore their descendants to see sense, when, as deferentially as he knew how, Wilkes intervened with a question.

'I'm confused,' he leered. 'How can we change the course of the future? We are all gathered here only because that course cannot be changed. I am me here from my time twenty-five years ago as surely as His Highness,' he bobbed at the Prince Regent, 'will be as he is here fifteen years from now. This is clearly set, and we've seen enough movement through these times to see that nothing will alter events as they are clearly predestined to be, now, a couple of decades hence and 200 years from now. God knows, the Duke here tried to assassinate Bonaparte back in 1791, and the bullets

250

melted in the air. All of us have sought ways to stop ourselves dying, or from making that terrible mistake which, in retrospect, has altered our lives for the worse, or even tried to change our destinies by saying yes when we'd previously said no and vice versa. We can't even use our knowledge of their new-found knowledge to change our circumstances in any way at all. Their medical and technological discoveries simply cannot be applied in our time. None of it works. Things are as they are and always will be, which was why the time portal was merely a harmless distraction, an unimportant amusement until our underclass realised that they could use it to escape from us and our terrible times.'

'Ah, but,' Erasmus Darwin interrupted, 'we only know that this time, our time, and their time, for somewhat in the region of five to ten years in that particular future, are set, so to speak. We cannot go to any time in between, and neither can they. Could it be that our times and theirs are exceptional, and that what we might do now could effect the intervening period and thus their seemingly certain future that we know of?'

'Your Highness, my Lords, we seem set on a course we have not agreed upon, hmph?' Fox sat down with a thump, then stood up again. 'Are we to wreak our vengeance on our future because of their treatment of our citizens? All their behaviour suggests to me is the enduring beastliness of Man. If we condemn them, we must just as surely condemn ourselves and be done with it all. Hmph? Is this . . . revenge altogether wise?'

'In answer to that, wisdom doesn't enter into it. Anything we do to them obviously can have no effect on us at all, except while the time portal remains open and they send back our beggars and theirs to contaminate our times.'

'This is too deep for me,' said the Duke of York (who'd

chosen to appear in slim youth). 'These people in the future, we've all seen them, are disgusted by us, and we by them. Let's blow up the damn portal and be done with it.'

'Impossible, Your Highness. Can't be done.'

Then the young man forgotten by History spoke again. 'My friends, we are going in circles! This is clear-cut. I have seen the future, as many of you here have. As Burke has said, it is a paradise. The diseases that ravage you . . . us . . . have been all but defeated. The depths of poverty that degrade us have been all but destroyed in almost every case. The simple human quests for food and warmth and light are taken for granted by the vast majority of people in the future. Is it any wonder that our poor sought refuge in that fabulous time? And is it not the greatest crime imaginable that those people of the future – as I say, our legatees, the beneficiaries of our sacrifices and the sweat from our brows – refuse to share their wealth and comfort with the generations that preceded them, and laid the foundations of their luxury?'

Several heads nodded in agreement.

'Now, we know we can do little about this, and to our envy is added the appalling problems arising from the influx of these returning beggars as well as our horror as the people of the future thoughtlessly demonise, mistreat and frequently slaughter hundreds of our fellows. But remember, these future generations are our legatees. We are creating a revolution in industry that will ultimately give them their world, a world of technologically-based luxury alongside computers and forms of transport and so many other marvels we'd find unbelievable had we not seen them. We will give them, thanks to friend Jenner here, their ultimate victory over pestilence. You could even say that the agitations of our radicals' – and here the young man's chest puffed up ever so slightly – 'are creating the conditions that will give them their New Jerusalem of Freedom, Equality and Democracy.' Half the great men there sneered and coughed, although it was the surgeon John Hunter who then said, 'Are you suggesting that we stop all that . . . all our . . . work, our enquiry, staunch our curiosity about the world just to teach them a lesson, so their lives will be as bad as ours?'

'Oh no. In our time, the work of our friends thirty years ago is slowly, sometimes perhaps imperceptibly, improving our lot, and that of our children twenty years from now. And we know, from that future time's history, that our immediate future hereafter is one of endless progress. For our immediate descendants, things do only get better, ending in that time we now confront. No, I suggest instead we do something that will do nothing to harm us, nor the many generations that succeed us, but will destroy *them*.'

'Destroy?' Fox jumped up. 'Why should we destroy them? We're speaking of the future of our species, our own great-great-great-great-great-grandchildren.'

'I say destroy because we need only look at those kin of ours. Look at their careless hubris. Look at their cavalier prodigality. Look, most of all, at their terrible, thoughtless impatience. We've seen how they blithely assume, thanks to our originating endeavours, everything is not only possible but essential: the barren are rendered fruitful; genders are changed at a whim; their medical advances have made them assume that every natural death is unjustly and tragically premature; the very atoms of life itself are meddled with in order to sate their insatiable thirst for ever greater levels of luxury. They even think they've mastered the secrets of time itself. And still, and still, my friends, they are not happy! Theirs is an age of universal discontent, because they've come to believe that nothing is ever good enough for them. They stand not in awe of their achievements, but resentful that they haven't achieved yet more. And to what end? So that they might lead lives of infinite ease given up to the pursuit of the trivial and banal and ugly and cruel. I say destroy because if theirs is the certain future, for all that it might seem at first sight like paradise to us, then it is a paradise they have inherited where the air is filled with ceaseless complaints about the deafening sound of angels' wings beating, and because their paradise is never, ever good enough for them. If that is the paradise that we bequeath them, then it is not worth inheriting.'

There was a terrible and compelling finality to his words that none of them could gainsay. Almost all of the company had journeyed at some point into their nation's future, and been, as Burke had said, both amazed and appalled by it. After several minutes' silence, Pitt said, 'How?'

'Ah, my friend' – several of them were now suspecting the young man of being a Quaker or something worse – 'I have this all worked out. My lord,' and here he bowed to a bewigged grandee across the room, 'several years ago – forgive me, in your period – you elected to power your forges and ironworks and manufactories with water, did you not?'

'I did, sir, with amazing results. It outperformed the burning of coal a hundredfold. Moreover, we are even now, sorry, then, whatever, conducting trials for a water locomotive which is massively more powerful and speedy than anything else we've seen.'

'Precisely. Our water and also our wind and our geo-thermal engines are fuelling our industrial revolution and our social revolution and entirely changing the ways we will live. Correction; not us, but our descendants. Our ungrateful, unthinking, callous descendants will reap the fruits of our labours, and we will all be dead. We had a chance to share in those spoils, which our children's children's children – our kin – have rudely and brutally denied us. So let's deny them something too.'

'Yes, yes, yes, but how?'

'I propose we shift the entire basis of our industrial revolution to another method of fuel, which will have no consequence for us, but which will, for them.'

'But we can't! We've tried to alter the course of events and . . .'

'Please. Friend Harrison has identified a Saturday afternoon at the very end of March in 1784 where there are, let us say, certain anomalies in the passage of time. I believe that if we begin the process then, it will work. Now, you are all of you, I'm sure, unfamiliar with the notion of the emission of carbon particles into the atmosphere. Friend Priestley will explain.' Somewhere close by, the lions in the Tower menagerie began to roar, either in triumph or in lament.

History was inexorably changed, although no one in the twenty-first century had any memory whatsoever of the way things had been a second before their vengeful ancestors implemented their plan, changing the future but also, though they'd never know it, the past as well. No one in the present remembered the water-driven cars they'd once owned, nor the geothermal springs that had lit entire cities, nor the natural elements harnessed and harvested to power space rockets and airliners and marvellous industrial processes and all the other everyday taken-for-granted miracles of their times. Nor could they remember the other things that had suddenly been blotted out of History by the actions of their forebears. They had no memory, for instance, of the friends and relations who could no longer exist because their parents or grandparents or great-grandparents had been killed in the two great wars that had previously never happened, in that dark age inaccessible via the time portal, or of the unicorns at the zoo or the industrious and wily Neanderthals who inhabited Switzerland. All History hitherto was not so much rewritten as cloaked under a universally obscuring palimpsest, so they took their new History entirely and unthinkingly for granted, along with, among so much else, petrol cars and gas and coal-fuelled power stations and the highly polluting system which now powered the time portal instead of the complex arrangement of vinegar, brown paper and spa water previously but unknowably in place. And the carbon particles had now been building up for over two centuries as the trapped carbon of the billions of dead trees and tiny creatures, laid down over millions of years, were released into the atmosphere in an infinitesimal fraction of the time it had taken to trap them deep in the earth. And the temperature rose. The spot where the time portal gave ingress to eighteenth-century London on the shore of the Thames was, by the early twenty-first century, well below the low tide mark, and Stephanie and Seumas and the twins dodged the mercenary gangs of vigilantes who'd taken over from the police in many parts of Southern England as the climate had worsened and the fuel ration became ever more severe, to make it, in desperation, through the lashing rain and gales to Folkestone. Here a semblance of order remained, as harassed but caring people sent each fresh wave of refugees through the time portal to seek some kind of asylum in the past, before everything went so horribly, inevitably, predictably wrong. Stephanie held one twin while Seumas held the other, and they each held the other's hands during the nauseating twenty-minute journey back in time, and each briefly gagged on the miasmatic stench of the past before the ranks of grinning redcoats moved forward, and there was the briefest moment of recognition before Tom and George, proud in their smart new red uniforms, drove their bayonets mercilessly through the clutched infants and then deep into the hearts of their parents.

It's a Wonderful Life

At the precise moment of his detonation, Damien Sykes-Wolsey exited his exploding body in ecstasy and was greeted by his guardian angel who, to his delight as a professional film buff, proved to be Clarence Oddbody who, as Sykes-Wolsey knew from his careful and close reading of the documentary footage, had helped an American called George Bailey through a dark night of the soul on 24 December 1945.

'I knew you were real,' Sykes-Wolsey gasped, now ecstatic in more than one meaning of the word. Clarence had won his wings after he'd stopped Bailey despairing of life, and stood before Sykes-Wolsey in the blood-spattered lobby of the Strategic Studies building trans-formed; no longer a rather quaint, folksy little man but now a vast, Blakean figure, muscular and magnificent, his great eagle's wings flapping with enormous power, and a blinding green light emanating from his celestial core. Clarence stooped slightly to take Sykes-Wolsey's hands, but then paused for a second, furrowed his brow and looked skywards.

'What's that, Gabriel? Oh no! Not again? But he's . . . Oh, all right then!' Clarence pouted, and looked down at Sykes-Wolsey. 'Well, Damien, it seems I've got to show you your life and how things would have turned out differently if you'd never even been born. They keep on pulling this trick, though I don't see how it's going to make any difference now,' he whined, and stepping over the broken husk of Sykes-Wolsey's corporeal incarna-tion, led the way out of the building and onto the wind-blown campus. Sykes-Wolsey's eyes shone with excitement as Clarence looked up to Heaven again and flapped his wings twice.

Sykes-Wolsey blinked. 'What? Was that it?'

'What do you mean?' Clarence whinged.

'Well, all I got then was about half a second of jumbled images, shot in what looked like bad sixties Technicolor stock.'

'Yes?'

'Well, it all happened so fast I couldn't even tell what was going on. How would things have been different if I'd never been born?'

Clarence frowned and gnawed his lower lip. 'Oh, really, Damien. You should have been paying attention! Now I'll have to do it all again!'

So he flapped his wings again. Sykes-Wolsey blinked again.

Clarence glowered at him impatiently, and mewled, 'Did you get it that time?'

'Um . . .'

'What's that supposed to mean? Did you see what things would have been like if you'd never been born?'

Sykes-Wolsey grimaced slightly and cleared his ectoplasmic throat before answering nervously. 'Um. I saw an old radiator.'

'And was it hot?'

'Um . . . Yes. Yes, it was hot.'

'So there you go. That's what difference you being born made. If you'd never been born that radiator would have been hot. Don't you see? *Because you were born Mr Kenworthy never fixed it,* and one of those kittens didn't make it through the night, just because you abused the precious gift of life. You never realised how lucky you were, Damien, never even thought about the difference one person can make to the lives of all the people and creatures around him. Come on, I've got to take you downstairs now.'

'Mr Kenworthy? Who the fuck is Mr Kenworthy?'

Clarence sighed. 'It's too late to worry about that now. You should have thought about that at the time. Let's go.'

'But . . . but . . .'

Clarence flapped his wings a third time, silencing Sykes-Wolsey by cocooning him in a tight webbing of fire. 'I don't know, Damien. I think they're getting slack upstairs, always giving people like you a last chance to see the error of their ways. It's just a waste of time with some folks. What?' Clarence looked up into the grey sky. 'What's that, Gabriel? No! No, sir. I wasn't complaining. It's just . . . Oh, all *right* then!' And so Clarence tetchily flapped his wings one last time and, amidst the pandemonium of alarms and sirens, and the smoke and screaming, and damaged people issuing from the building behind them, took Sykes-Wolsey in his arms and sank, unseen, into the earth.

Heart of Darkness

The soft ground bristled under the shower of shrapnel. Lucy threw herself behind the abandoned and blackened shell of the burnt-out UN jeep as another of the hospital's outbuildings buckled under a direct hit from the advancing rebels' rocket attack. The outbuilding – really nothing more than a roofless breeze-block sty – must have contained all the remaining oxygen and fuel supplies, as it now went up with a God almighty bang, bringing down half of the main hospital building in the blast, rushing, blazing, outwards in all directions. Lucy cringed, huddled in her hiding place, her eyes squeezed tightly shut as she heard all sorts of stuff, large and small, soft and hard, organic and otherwise – the usual airborne flotsam and jetsam of modern war – spatter and thud against the other side of the jeep and onto and into the receiving earth outside its shadow. Eventually the roar of the explosion gently subsided like a blanket pulled slowly and carefully away, exposing a soiled soundscape of groans, feeble death rattles, the crackling of burning wood and masonry and, in the distance, the rather vague stutter of automatic gunfire somewhere off in the jungle.

Lucy finally opened her eyes and saw, lit obliquely by the burning hospital, an artificial leg, lying exactly parallel to a real child's leg of precisely the same length. They lay about twenty centimetres apart. At the end of each leg the feet were turned outwards, finishing off the perfect symmetry, and all they lacked was a half-metal, half-flesh torso, head and upper limbs to fit on top, although doubtless several of those components were also lying, strewn, close at hand.

Lucy looked away, feeling no more numb than before, and squinted around to see where she might flee to next. At last, past the bombed ruin of the Epicurean Brothers' feeding station, beyond the rubble of the Aids clinic and the overgrown, exposed beams of the old Mission School, towards the fringe of the jungle she saw her haven, an old rectangular pit with sheer, vertical sides, long since drained of whatever it was that had defined its original or later function. She waited for the inevitable rocket that would get the other half of the hospital, and when it came she ran like hell across the 300 to 400 metres between her and the pit, hoping the Government troops holed in the wards on the first floor would last out long enough for her to make it. As she bobbed and weaved she could feel things whizzing past her in the chaotic air, dust spit up at her knees as ricocheting bullets ploughed into the ground and dampnesses of different provenances touched her here, there and everywhere. And as the hospital's final wing disappeared in a fireball which blossomed, like a monstrous chrysanthemum into the night sky, Lucy rolled into the pit.

Gobbing out some of whatever now shallowly filled its depths, she pressed herself against the windward side of the pit, thus protecting herself from the latest drizzle of debris which plipped and plopped its bits and bobs of this and that into whatever it was that washed around at its bottom. Sitting up to her waist in it, Lucy held her breath until the explosion's roar subsided into a cackling murmur, then started panting, then swallowed, sniffed, squeezed her eyes tight shut, opened them again and pulled her mouth into a taut rictus until her jaw muscles ached and she could begin to feel the stress dissipate. She did this several times, hardly even noticing the sounds of battle from either the township, the camp or the encompassing jungle, until she nearly jumped out of her skin when a voice next to her said, 'Hey, Yankee. Cigarette?'

She turned into the shadows on either side of her until she finally saw him. Lit dimly by the distant flames reflected off the opposite wall of the pit, she saw he was an elderly Yahoo with grizzled hair, wearing a tattered business suit and speaking English with hardly any accent. She swallowed hard before answering, in a harsh whisper.

'I'm English actually. And I don't smoke.' She said this in Yahoo. The old Yahoo shuffled slightly towards her, making ripples in the whatever-it-was. But he was only leaning over in order to get a battered and damp packet of Marlboro from his jacket pocket. When he spoke again, again he spoke in English.

'I shouldn't really be smoking at my age, but who cares? All my doctors are probably dead now anyway.' As laboriously as before, he took out a Zippo and lit the bent cigarette jutting from his prognathous jaws.

'Kofi Annan gave me this, you know,' he said, holding up the lighter before pocketing it again.

For a while they sat in silence, him smoking, her glancing occasionally at his dim profile. Beyond the pit the battle sounded as if it was moving away from them. As her eyes adjusted to the surrounding gloom, she could make out that whatever filled the bottom of the pit was purple and had bits floating in it.

'So.' The Yahoo blew out a last gasp of smoke and tossed the fag end into the middle of the pool. 'Where d'you learn Yahoo?'

'I was at SOAS. Um . . . The School of Oriental and African Studies. In London.'

'I know it. I was at the LSE. Years before you, of

265

course. So what are you? Aid worker? Doctor? Tourist?'

He said the last word with the heavy irony typical of Yahoos. Lucy couldn't help smiling.

'I'm an anthropologist.'

'Really? There's a good job with prospects. Don't suppose you were expecting any of this, were you?'

'I, um . . .'

'My apologies for the current state of my country, for which I must take my share of the blame.' He lit another cigarette, leaving her the opportunity to ask the question he was begging from her. But Lucy wasn't going to insult a Yahoo by getting straight to the point.

'I think I will have one of your cigarettes after all, thank you.' They shuffled closer towards each other until his packet was within reach. She heard something clattering on the other side of him, something he was dragging along with him.

They smoked in silence, Lucy hating it but knowing she couldn't show it.

'So you learned Yahoo at SOAS? Who taught you? Not a native speaker, I should imagine.'

'No, you're right. I was under Professor Sykes-Wolsey, the cousin of . . .'

'I know. A nice man. I liked him a lot. You probably read my book while you were there, as it's one of the few Yahoo texts available. My further apologies for our late arrival in the community of the literate, by the way.'

'I probably did. Part of my thesis was preparing a dictionary of Yahoo terms for . . .' But then Lucy bit her tongue. She didn't know this Yahoo, and they could be notoriously sensitive, on this subject more than any other. However, the Yahoo finished the sentence for her.

'The horse. Yes, I read that. Very perceptive. A gold mine for someone of your calling, I should imagine, wouldn't you, Lucy? You don't mind me . . . ?'

'Not at all. But you have the advantage on me. You are . . . ?'

'You would have read my translation of *Gulliver's Travels*, I think. Into Yahoo, obviously.' In the gloom Lucy's eyes widened. 'Not a bestseller in the domestic market, I regret. Probably because of the sensitivities you were attempting to observe a moment ago. Don't worry, I have no such squeamishness in addressing the darker periods of our history. After all, we drove out the quaddies a century and a half ago, thanks to your British imperialism. Another cigarette?'

'No. Thank you. I don't really smoke, actually.' In the pause that followed while he fumbled once more for his lighter, Lucy smiled to herself. She knew this Yahoo only too well, and was amused that even he used the euphemisms: 'quaddies', 'neds', 'dobbins', 'naggies', 'hoofers'. These were, of course, approximations of the Yahoo words, but they all served to avoid the name itself, the ultimate taboo.

'Yes,' the Yahoo went on, 'I always liked a flutter when I was living in London. The 3.15 at Haydock Park.' He chortled to himself, then drew on the cigarette again. 'Always lost, of course. The ironies won't be lost on you though, I'm sure.'

'No, of course. But . . .'

'Please, not yet. We've still got a little time left, and it would be bad manners to conclude our conversation so soon by cutting straight to the end. As you know, we Yahoos had a lot of lost time to make up for in the art of conversation. Now, where was I?' The Yahoo grunted as he shifted his position, then gave out a small gasp of pain. Lucy pretended to ignore it, to save him embarrassment.

'Yes, British imperialism. What a wonderful thing that was. All those beautiful uniforms, those splendid guns

267

and ships! Perhaps, with hindsight, our independence movement was a little premature, don't you think? We did well from the British: you educated us, you gave us useful work to do, and if you oppressed and slaughtered us towards the end, you only did it a little bit, I'm sure. And who can blame you, when we were being so ungrateful? But it was all your fault, don't you see? Sending smart boys like me to the LSE to get our silly Yahoo heads filled with all that British nonsense about fair play and democracy and freedom . . .'

'And Stalinism, Professor . . .'

'Social democracy, Lucy. We have always been meticulously democratic, as you know. We were clearly richer than we had been . . . before, but you taught us not to be satisfied to be your servants.' He grunted and gasped again, but went on, 'Your servants, as I said. Your employees, but with no fringe benefits, if you like. We knew, in the end, that we'd be better off without you, don't you see?'

'Of course, Professor. I don't disagree with you. I was just . . .'

'And we were better off, in our own little way. We built better schools and better hospitals. Our infant mortality plummeted just as our literacy rate soared. We were probably even happy, don't you know, and hardly ambitious at all.'

'And yet . . .'

'Precisely. Perhaps we are too stupid after all, too silly and Yahooish to be able to see that there's no room for silly little unambitious countries like ours any more. Incidentally, I imagine that you've been on your travels through the island just like me. Did you see how magnificently the Nike factory burned? Heavens! It was like your Guy Fawkes night!'

Lucy peered at where the Yahoo was sitting, and saw

268

a darker liquid staining the purple pool from somewhere on his right side. He grinned at her when he saw where she was looking.

'Don't worry, Lucy. Not much longer to go.' He looked up into the sky above them. 'Was that a raindrop I felt? What a shame. It will quite ruin the battle.'

'Are you . . . ?'

'Please, let's not talk about it, except to say my own side got me in my own side. Hmmm? And who can blame them? After all, given our problems, what else could I do? We were naive, and though hardly ambitious, all those hospitals and schools cost money which in the end we didn't have. You know the story as well as I do. That's obviously why you're here, sitting in this old cesspool with me for our little chat. Anthropologist? I don't really think so, do you?'

Lucy stared at him, and all he did was smile back in that infuriating Yahoo way. She wanted to scream at him, and struggled to control her fury.

'But you asked them back! You invited the fucking Houyhnhnms back here!' She ignored his instinctive flinch at the unspeakable word. 'Didn't you realise? You translated *Gulliver*, for Christ's sake! You knew what they were like! Don't you remember trying to find the Yahoo words to describe how they used the pelts of Yahoo babies to make Gulliver's boat? How could you do it? How could you do it?' By now she really was screaming.

'I know, I know. But they have a certain expertise, Lucy. We really were in a terrible mess. Our deficit financing was all gone to pot. It seems what you English taught me all those years ago about economics wasn't the whole truth. Or at least not an enduring truth. They said they would sort everything out. As the leader of my people what else could I do? After all . . .'

But Lucy was now sick of him. As the rain began to

fall more heavily, she lunged at him. He tried to swing the AK47 round from his side, but she grabbed it from his trembling hands before he could fire and swung it hard into his mischievous, ironic, low-browed face and then hammered it into the wound at his side. He tried to say one last thing, then his deep-set eyes glazed over and he fell sideways with a dull splash into the pool of blood, shit and bodies.

Beyond the pit the rain, now torrential, was putting out the fires from the recent attack, but between the sizzling she could hear, in the distance, another noise: the screaming of babies, intermingled with soft cracking sounds. Part of the children's ward must have survived the rocket attack. Standing on the Yahoo's body and still clutching the gun, she pulled herself out of the pit into the darkness, and started running back towards the hospital, firing wildly towards the noise of whinnying and the clip-clop of bloodstained hooves.

Snatches

Snatches

Alternatively, Lucy sneezed, relaxing her grip for an instant and letting the serpent in. Her lover, whose name was John, swerved slightly to the left as the baboon came howling from the edge of the trees. The settlement between the Neanderthals and the encroaching Cro-Magnons, agreed amicably, broke down drunkenly at the feast which followed the protracted negotiations, and the first club of the coming genocide crashed down onto a differently shaped skull. The spear hurled the first eighty-ninth of the ultimate distance it would travel by one of the first tyrant God Kings of Babylon from the howdah on his war hippopotamus continued on its trajectory towards the heart of the last unicorn, who, on dying, dissolved immediately, eluding the fossil record and a more enduring shame.

Although maybe the hominid fossil the Leakeys found was a boy, thus ruining my best gag.

Christ before Pilate got off on a technicality, denying his followers both a convincing narrative mythos and a World-beating corporate logo. His death soon thereafter under the wheels of a runaway ox cart was mourned by eleven of the original twelve disciples and his mother and girlfriend, who didn't let on that she was thinking of chucking him anyway. Judas Iscariot went into olive-oil futures. On his resurrection Christ returned to Nazareth and resumed his career as a carpenter, forgetting all that love and peace stuff. The Roman Empire remained pagan, and fell. Mohammed, blessings be upon his name, with no hegemoniacal Christians to react against, prospered as a camel dealer. Eliot, Jesus, Mike, Maria, Consuela, John and Suzi went home after work on 11 September 2001, only one of them bothering to sacrifice a small capon or gerbil at the family altar that evening.

Alternatively, he lost on appeal, and things transpired along lines more or less familiar in one reading of History, although Crespolini stubbed his toe on entering Saint Lucian's.

Although possibly when Saint Lucy jumped from Simeon Stylites's pillar, halfway down she was caught in the talons of a passing pterodactyl, thereafter escaping from its nest full of hungry fledglings to live a full and happy life in the hills with talking animals.

Cortés arrived on time, and things followed on accordingly.

Although following the Fall of Vienna in the late seventeenth century of the Christian calendar, 300 or so years later Ireland would strain under the rule of a brutal pasha and all expressions of nationalist fervour were ruthlessly extirpated by janissaries from Ulster.

So you couldn't eat caviar in Vienna, because Vienna no longer existed.

Although the Contessa was, in fact, a vegetarian.

And Trotsky won.

Although Hitler won too.

And Stalin lived to be 397 years old.

Evelyn Waugh's first marriage was long and happy.

Stephens was born a cat.

Seumas Black was born in Bournemouth, and went home with Stephanie for Christmas.

Professor Sykes-Wolsey was born an octopus, like all his family hitherto, including his great-uncle Julian Sykes-Wolsey and another relative who ended up badly, being eaten by a sperm whale instead of being blown to bits. Julian Sykes-Wolsey's decapod poetry was beautiful, but necessarily unknowable to the race of men, so Seumas, if he'd been around in yet another possible scenario, had no hangover, nor one from the night before, and so was less hasty in choosing the manuscript, and nothing much changed.

Cynthia was transferred instead to gene-map the souls of fish in Wendover.

Or a previously young but still short novelist balanced precariously in a laundry basket to wank furiously into someone else's bathroom sink at a party in West London, forgetting to lock the door.

But Candide was merely a fictional character.

While Trotsky lived to a ripe old age, breeding rabbits for food in his backyard in the suburbs of Mexico City, occasionally venturing out for a drink in a midtown bar with Luis Buñuel, in this version of events still and always an exile from Franco's Spain and fascist Europe in general, both of which eventualities may or may not have been a direct result of the political shenanigans of the Contessa and her paymasters in Moscow. They were usually joined by Jack Kerouac, who only drank water.

Or Colin stuck with computers. Or stayed with his wife. Or left her. Or she left him. Or he crashed the car on the way home from the pub, or on the way to the pub. At the end of the day, who knows and who cares?

Although it is a matter of historical record that the humorous writer and civil servant Brian O'Nolan, or Flann O'Brien, or Myles na gCopaleen, was once observed advancing hand over hand in a southerly direction along the supportive railings of Merion Square in Dublin, repeating over and over to himself the comforting mantra, 'Fuck the fucking fuckers.'

But the bodies piled up or, if you're unlucky, the fragments of bodies, blasted to bits, burnt alive, beaten to death, brutalised, barbarised, bludgeoned, and the blood soaked the soil into an uninhabitable marsh, coughing damp clouds of carrion stink into the agitated air, heavy with carbon, and in the tangle of the timelines, the following will happen, being predetermined and unalterable.

On the Arabian Front

Mark ducked into the tent with his head bent down against the sandstorm raging outside, then unwrapped the scarf from round his mouth and nose. Joan and Kevin were already in there, and the beer already open.

'Christ,' Mark yelled, against the sound of the wind and the sand and grit hammering against the canvas walls. 'That was a close-run thing.'

'You got it, though?' Joan asked, snapping open a beer for him.

'Just about, though Christ knows what it'll look like back home.'

'How was he?'

'Pissed, of course, but magnificent.'

Kevin and Joan laughed snuffingly, as Kevin went about the business of loading up the bong. Mark asked about the weather, and Kevin said the latest he'd heard was that the ice sheets had reached Oslo.

Joan changed the subject. 'Is he coming back here?'

'Think so, after he's had a natter with Colonel bloody Bogey.' Mark squatted down on the floor of the tent, took the beer and drained the bottle in one long pull. He exhaled with damp satisfaction. 'Got another?'

Joan was just passing him his second bottle when the tent flap lifted again and two startlingly good-looking middle-aged men ducked in, pursued by the detritus of the desert. The man in civilian dress staggered slightly as he carefully stepped over the camera equipment in order to reach his camp bed and the bottle of whisky underneath. Once he'd sat down he twisted off the top of the bottle, glugged down several large mouthfuls, shouted, 'We happy few!', burped and passed out where he sat.

The middle-aged man in uniform, now squatting between Mark and Joan, waggled his bushy eyebrows as he took the bong from Kevin and inhaled and then exhaled deeply before speaking.

'Everyone here okay?'

'Come off it, Bogey,' Joan snorted. 'What do you think? What the fuck's going on?'

Bogey smiled and shrugged. 'Search me, Joan, I'm just the head of Media and Intelligence for this theatre of war. You're the fucking journos. Isn't it your job to tell me?'

'I'm a teckie, mate,' Mark insisted, waving his finger rather unsteadily between the Colonel's face and his own. 'I know fuck all.' The others ignored him.

'Bollocks, Bogey,' Kevin snapped. 'We've been stuck here five days now. When are we going to start moving upcountry where the action is? Ed over there,' he gestured at the now snoring star TV war correspondent, 'has been filing crap since we took that last shithole from the Fundies, just lots of colour and backing our boys' bollocks.'

'I understand Ed is very fond of our boys,' Bogey smiled, squatting down again after prising the whisky bottle out of Ed's unconscious hands. 'He takes a personal interest in many of the troops, as you know.'

'What about our girls, eh?' Joan sneered. 'And none of which gets us any closer to knowing what the fuck's going on!'

'Now, now, Joan, you know perfectly well I wouldn't stonewall you.' Bogey kept on smiling despite the nasty face Joan had pulled. 'We stopped doing that after the switch. We're all on the same side now, for Christ's sake.'

'We're not *on* the same side, Bogey. We *are* the same side.'

'Yes, of course. You forget I'm duration. I remember how things used to be before we switched. Old Ed'd remember that. It was our job never to tell you buggers a thing except when we wanted to, and sometimes I still find it not quite decent the way we do it now.'

'"Not quite decent", eh, you wanker?' Kevin's Geordie accent had given way to Bogey's Sandhurst drawl effortlessly, and then gone back again just as smoothly. 'What's not quite decent is the fact that even now we're meant to be running the show we still haven't got a fucking clue what's going on.' Kevin grunted gratefully as Bogey passed him the bong.

The tent flap opened again and they all cringed for a second as the latest figure entered in a swirl of red sand. They ignored him as he made a business of taking off his scarf, goggles and balaclava, until he joined the circle and accepted, first a beer, and then the whisky bottle, which Mark was now nursing. The others nodded at him, and Mark said, 'Did you get through?'

'Yep. Satellite kept up long enough for the main evening. It'll make fantastic TV, all this fucking sand, I don't think. So what's up?'

Bogey bridled. 'I was about to ask you that, Peter. The old man said you were chief ops wallah this week, for Christ's sake.'

Peter grinned. 'Come on, Bogey! Only kidding. The second Foot brigade launched an assault on that Fundy position the other side of whatsitville half an hour ago. If you wankers were even remotely professional you'd be watching the video feeds right now.' Peter leaned back looking smug, drained the whisky bottle and took the bong from Kevin. Everyone else scrabbled down in front of a small monitor nestling among the pile of equipment.

281

On the tiny screen they saw the standard interactive split screen as the camera corps followed each unit to different parts of the action. Mark and Joan wrestled playfully for the remote until Joan got it and the feed from camera seven filled the screen.

'Seven's Beverley, isn't it?' Bogey asked. Everyone waved at him to shut up as they concentrated on the fuzzy images before them. Despite the red sand filling in the air, they could clearly see the backs of Britforce troops advancing through a gun emplacement, as the camera panned from side to side to show the corpses of the Fundy defenders. Then Beverley started running, the image became increasingly jerky, and they strained to hear her breathless commentary.

'What's she saying?' asked Mark.

'Fuck!' Kevin pressed an earpiece closer into his ear. 'Fuck me! They've got a Fundy general!' Everyone in the tent cheered, except Ed, who snored, and then they stared more intently at the screen.

'Look! Look, it's a Yank.'

'So it bloody well is. Good work, boys! And girls, of course.'

'Don't forget the lovely camera-work, Bogey!' Mark admonished the colonel, who shrugged jovially in apology.

'Who's that? Come on, Bev, get a close-up!'

As if acting on orders, the camera closed in on the faces of two frightened-looking men, their hands raised, and held at bayonet point by a squad of about five soldiers, each with a camera attached to his or her helmet, and each of them swaying slightly. In the tent everyone was now peering at the screen almost in disbelief.

'Bloody hell. Isn't that . . . ?' Bogey whistled through his teeth.

'You bet! It's that bastard anchor from Fox.'

'And who's the Fundy general?'

'Whatsisname, um . . . Oh, fuck. He's one of the worst, you know.'

'This is amazing. Come on, Bev, get the bastards praying!'

'Joan, go to split screen,' Kevin yelled, pressing his finger into his ear again. Joan pressed a button on the remote control and all over the screen were scenes of victory, as Fundy troops, in either their helmets or their headscarves, were shown surrendering before the assault of the Britforce troops.

'Quick,' yelled Mark, 'go to five. That's Ken.'

And now the screen was filled with an impromptu press conference, the sound of shells exploding, sending horizontal bolts of static across the screen. Two men, tied to chairs and to each other, were having microphones thrust aggressively in their faces. In the tent they listened to the questions the journalist troops were yelling at their captives. Kevin slapped his palm against his forehead. 'What? Peter! Who the fuck's in charge down there? They've let that twat from the *Telegraph* ask the first question!'

Peter shrugged. 'Sound man. Led the assault. One of our finest.' But everyone was shushing him so they could hear the captives' answer. The fat American, his face smeared with blood, was showering the Britforce troops with obscenities, accusing them of treachery, drunkenness, atheism and everything else he could think of until a BBC lance corporal clubbed him into silence with the butt of his rifle. The Saudi the slumped Yank was tied to at first refused to answer the barrage of questions, and then invoked the shared god of the parties to the Fundamentalist Alliance to bring calamity down on the perfidious Brits and their Euroscum secularist partners. A female soldier reporter from the *Daily Mail* slapped the prisoner into silence and started forcing a bottle of Malibu down his throat. In the tent they were all punching the air and whooping with joy. Mark opened more beer and Bogey pinched another bottle of whisky from beneath Ed's bed. Then Kevin, his finger in his ear once more, motioned them for silence.

'Hey, everyone. We've got a live feed from the PM, channel twelve.' Joan instantly clicked the set over, and there stood the Trubshawist Prime Minister of Great Britain in the House of Commons, looking formidable and triumphant. Everyone in the tent indicated to everyone else that they should shut up, and they all concentrated on that familiar, drooping red face with that wayward fringe and those saggy, baggy, watery eyes, as he began to speak.

'Madam Speaker, I can announce tonight to the House that our forces and those of our many allies have broken through the Fundamentalist Alliance's lines on several parts of the Arabian front.' The cheers from the MPs drowned out what he had to say next, the Prime Minister being one of those orators who surfed through applause in case he forgot what he was saying, but the cheers only redoubled as he took a swig from his hip flask, went a vivid green and threw up over the despatch box. Even his former colleagues in the rump of the Labour Party cheered, while the huge number of Trubshawists, all clearly blind drunk, bellowed till they fell. In the tent in the desert on the Arabian front in what must have been the thirtieth year or something of this unending war with its constantly shifting alliances, the origins of which no one on the British side could quite remember, and even if the oil in the region had all run out a decade ago, they were laughing and cheering so much they almost didn't hear the signal to scramble.

'Hey,' slurred Mark, 'that'sh ush!' And, stopping only to pick up their weapons, cameras and recording equipment, they stumbled out into the sandstorm to join their comrades, equally pissed up and itching for a scrap.

News from Nowhere

The doves flew up into the bright blue May Day morning sky with a noise like tearing silk and Ned, John and Lucy thought they might burst with pride as they led the Lewisham Pioneers Brigade into Freedom Square, their hoes and pitchforks sloped against their muscular young shoulders. From the huge crowd wave upon wave of cheers greeted them, echoing off the gables of the high houses on all sides, the sound bouncing back on itself and swirling round the giant maypole and the white, black, yellow and brown boys skipping this way and that, each holding the end of a bright ribbon which trailed up to the top of the pole, 200 feet above their heads. Closer in towards its base, little girls bedecked Landseer's stern, antique lions with flowers of every type and colour. From the platform in front of the People's Arthouse the Moot elders raised their fists in clenched salute as the Lewisham Brigade marched past, and the crowd cheered louder than ever as Lucy, Ned, John and their comrades returned the salute, then wheeled left past the band of sackbut players and harpists (whose art they all aspired to), before leading the parade out of the square towards Moot Meadow.

The cheering never abated all the way down Whitehall, and from the open, leaded windows of the half-timbered People's Hostels tiny children, old women in wimples and craggy veterans of the Liberation threw more and more flowers down on the heads of the young people below, all looking so splendid in their freshly laundered smocks and gleaming gaiters.

And now the cheering grew even louder, and John, Lucy and Ned, like their fellows behind them, looked round to see in the distance the tiny figure of Old William in his suit of armour acknowledging the salute from the platform as he rode through Freedom Square on his beautiful piebald shire horse. Lucy waved the bunch of daffodils and bluebells she'd caught and shouted something in Ned's ear. He smiled and shouted back, and she kissed him on the lips with joy. This year they actually knew the fellow playing Old William. He was a miller from Deptford who often ate at their own feasthouse at the bottom of Hilly Fields when he came to collect grain from the common store in Old Lewisham Church.

Lucy shouted something else in Ned's ear, but this time, smiling, he shook his head. It was so noisy he couldn't hear her, so she yelled again.

'His beard, silly!' she bellowed again, and he nodded, and they both laughed. It was true. His beard was, well, rather stringy, but on a day like today nobody cared, and Ned and Lucy kissed again and on they marched, past the small allotments and their pretty little sheds and Wendy houses where (they'd been taught at school) in the Old Days had stood Downing Street, the Treasury and the Foreign Office. And finally they entered Moot Meadow, just as Old Big Ben struck eleven.

They were still feeling euphoric, and there was still so much left to do and see, but Ned, Lucy and John couldn't help feeling a small sense of anticlimax as they reached the middle of the Meadow, which marked the official end of the parade. Old men and women came and kissed them and gave them more flowers, but as there were thousands of people behind them they'd been told they shouldn't linger at this point, but instead move out through the field full of folk playing on the grass surrounding Westminster Abbey. And to this end, there were a hundred and one things to do. Stretching along Millbank were a thousand brightly coloured awnings, beneath which stalls provided refreshment of every kind, and the potboys and wenches tapping the mead, cider and ale barrels were already handing out tankards by the dozen to the happy crowd. And down Victory Street there were jugglers, fire-eaters, clowns and minstrels, archery butts, face-painters, poets, blacksmiths and hundreds of looms, freely available to all, where even now people were weaving beautiful tapestries as they bellowed out epic poetry. Everywhere the scents of blossom, new-mown grass, cooking and patchouli oil mingled in the clean, bright air.

The three friends looked around them, then back at each other, grinning so hard it almost hurt, feeling spoiled for choice. A gaggle of roaring children ran past them, their hair plaited and braided with beads, waving the crayon brass rubbings they'd just made in the Abbey. Outside its great doors, an endless succession of haywains was delivering food to the common store held in the nave. Watching them, John suddenly ran off towards the Abbey, returning after a couple of minutes with a crock of lentils for each of them and, held precariously under his arm, several bottles of ale. Thus provisioned, they walked off towards St James's Park, stopping short to sit down and lean against the base of one of the statues which once marked the Meadow's ancient boundaries.

Ned got a clay pipe from out of his smock pocket and filled it with coltsfoot and home-grown hemp from a moleskin pouch, and for a while they just smoked, passing the pipe from one to another, ate and drank in happy silence, watching as more and more people paraded into the Meadow, the clock of Old Big Ben ticking off the minutes towards noon. Beneath it, hung from the walls of Westminster Hall, three enormous tapestries of Morris, Marx and Ruskin flapped gently in the warm spring breeze and John, sniffing after another swig of ale, finally spoke.

'Why'd they keep that place, you think?'

'What's that?' Lucy answered, her mouth half full of lentils.

'That old dump. That Houses of Parleyment.'

'Well,' answered Ned, and then paused. 'Well, it's a nice old building, innit? Like they kept the Abbey and places. Dun't marrer what it once was, do it?'

'Spose.'

Above them birds sang sweet songs on the air.

'But why then do the elders still use it, you think?'

'They don't, silly!' said Lucy. 'All that old rubbish, it's crèches an stuff now, innit? They moot in the Old Hall. That's genuine Middle Ages, that is. I been there when our Brigade got to moot about the harvest last year and we wannid to dig up some old place, whassit?'

'That arthouse,' said Ned. 'I remember. They'm talked and talked about all that old rubbish in there, and Old Ben he just gets up and says bollocks to it, let's knock it down and plant barley!'

'Yeah! Right. That Old Ben, eh?' And each of them chuckled as they thought about Red Ben, the grizzled Lewisham firebrand who was always grumbling about how the Revolution had been betrayed, but was full enough of old stories for no one ever to mind him much.

'"You youngsters . . ."' John started, imitating the old man.

'"When I was your age we was levelling Birmingham!"', all three of them chorused, and all laughed so much they started rolling on the grass until they were so breathless they had to stop. John, still chuckling, pulled himself to his feet and ran off to get some more ale, while Lucy and Ned sat back again against the base of the statue, kissing for a while in a long, soft, lingering way. Out of the corner of her eye Lucy saw John returning, so they drew apart from each other and took the stone bottles from John when he reached them. John sat down the other side of Lucy, then leaned forward, looked behind him and then up at the statue. He turned to his friends.

'Who's this old bugger, then?'

Ned groaned and Lucy rolled her eyes, slapping John playfully with a daffodil. 'You dozy sod! Was you asleep all our schooldays?'

John smiled sheepishly, and turned behind him again. 'Trubshawe,' he read from the granite. 'Sounds familiar. Wasn't he that drunk or summut?'

'You know, you daft fucker! He weren't just a drunk. He wrote that book, innit, and then like Old Karl after he died all the old folks applied his teachings,' she now sounded as if she was remembering something once learned by rote, 'in the wider sphere of politics and economics. "Learn, recognise, forget, then learn again." That's what he said, innit. An' we was always told he was all right cos he was half right. You got to forget, but you also got to remember, that's what they said after, and that's how we won the Revolution. An' it was cos of him the Yanks and the Mullahs invaded. Well, not him, but his teachings.'

'I remember. He had a dog, innit?'

'Oh, I loved that old dog of his,' Lucy cooed. 'You remember those poems we used to learn about his old doggie, and how the Yanks and the Mullahs kicked it to death and it was still alive all those years after its master had died, just pining away? It was so sad. Shuddup, you two,' she suddenly shouted as her friends laughed at her. She was a sensitive as well as an intelligent girl, and while the events of a century before meant practically nothing to them, she was still very conscious of the Wars of Liberation against the occupying forces of the Fundamentalist Alliance, and the subsequent Morrisian Revolution which had liberated England once and for all.

They sat in silence once more and drank their warm ale. The second bottle had made Ned unusually reflective, or perhaps it was just the comedown after the excitement of earlier that morning. 'Why they leave us alone now, you suppose? The Yanks and Mullahs an' all?'

'Spose we ain't got nothing they want no more,' Lucy answered, running the grass between her legs through her fingers. 'Since we post-industrialised all we got is our farms and our art, and then they was too busy fightin' each other an' killin' an' all.'

'I heard they all got sick and died,' said John. 'They all waiting for Old God to save 'em and got fuck all, so their people killed the leaders and now they're like us and jest get on with life and being happy.'

'That'd be nice,' Lucy smiled. 'That'd be real nice if it were so. I hope it's true.'

Ned turned to look at her, saw that slightly sad, wistful look of hers he loved so much, and nuzzled her hair and licked her ear, while she tucked the side of her head against his face. John glanced at them, smiled, and then saw some of the group of tillers from Blackheath they travelled up west with in the distance, coming towards them.

'Hey, you two, it's Jane and Lizzie and that lot.' He waved his arm as the five Blackheath girls ran over to them.

'Hello, you lot! Innit great, eh? We'm saw Old William

right close up on his nag! Ooh, I cheered so much I'm hoarse!' Lucy stood up to kiss each of the girls, as did John and Ned.

'So what you wanna do now? Becky says they'm spittin' a hog on the Embankment, biggest old bastard you'm ever did see. Fancy it?'

'No no no,' squealed a younger boy who'd run up to join them. Lucy recognised him as a bird scarer from Islington they'd gone hop picking with the previous summer, and gave him a hug which he wriggled free from, embarrassed at the attentions of someone not only as important as Lucy, but also so beautiful. 'Gerroff, Luce!' he giggled. 'No listen, they found another pile of that shit! You know, that Moddy shit we heard about. All hidden away by some enemies, it was, in one of their big houses. I just heard they having a bonfire over Haymarket, right where the Old Boys burned all that stuff from the Traitor Gallery! It's happening right now! Come on, all that formaldehyde stuff goes up like buggery!' And waving at them to follow him, the boy ran off across the fields towards the Haymarket. The Blackheath girls shrugged and giggled.

'Yeah. Why not, innit? You lot coming?'

Lucy, Ned and John looked at each other, shrugging and non-committal, when they saw, beyond the group of girls, an older woman in a beautiful damask dress, her long auburn hair tied with ribbons and wild flowers.

Lucy looked round at Jane and Lizzie and the rest of them, and smiled apologetically. 'Sorry. Maybe later. We got . . .' She nodded towards the woman, and the girls, glancing round, immediately understood and, suddenly subdued, made their farewells and wandered off in search of fresh excitement.

* * *

293

The new Ministry of Beauty building had been considered by some of the scribes in the chronicles as excessively modern, and had given rise to widespread and sometimes acrimonious debate. For her part, Lucy liked it, and had given Ned a playful whack in bed one morning when he'd pretended to have no opinion on it at all. And while it wasn't necessarily to John's taste, as they now walked over to it with Old Christabel, he couldn't help but admire its gleaming white battlements, buttresses, steeples and spires. They raised their fists in salute to the yeoman with his shield and broadsword standing by the dovecote at the main entrance, and stepped across the mosaic floor to the reception desk, where Old Amos, another veteran of the Levelling of Birmingham, was whittling away at a piece of wood with his old, horn-handled knife.

Old Christabel dipped a quill into an ornate brass inkwell to sign her agents in, and then ushered them upstairs to her office.

'Please, comrades, sit down.' Lucy, Ned and John sat down on the benches and cushions she'd gestured towards as she lit a number of beeswax candles around the room. Although the sun shone brightly outside along the Embankment, behind the People's Hostels in Whitehall where the Ministry had been built, its small, high, stained-glass windows allowed in little natural light. This had been one of the causes of controversy over its design, many people arguing that such a deliberate exclusion of natural light was a dangerous echo of the catastrophic mores of the bad old days of fossil dependency. What hadn't been said in response, but which hardly needed saying anyway, was that some of the business conducted in the Ministry was best conducted in darkness, and it was best for everyone if the light of day were never to shine in on it. Everyone knew that, and found it generally more comfortable not to dwell on it too deeply, or for too long.

Old Christabel now sat down in her own oak chair, and smiled at the three of them.

'I was very proud of you three today. A lovely parade, innit. Done yourselves proud. However,' and she smiled to soften the blow, 'even today our work carries on. We've had a lot of successes recently, and I think you've heard about the Haymarket bonfires, but the terrorist threat is always there. We don't need to know everything about it, and I wasn't given this job by the Moot to frighten our people with fairy tales about things that might never happen. But I trust you three, and I trust you not to go gossiping in the feasthouses about things folk don't need to know, innit.'

The three friends nodded, and smiled. They'd all been trained by Old Christabel, and forgave her her occasional moments of pomposity. After all, the threat, as they all knew, was very real indeed. She stood up and handed them a parchment each, which they strained to read in the candlelight.

'That's the information we've been able to get out of that Yank spy we caught in the Bohemian embassy last month. What the Yanks call their government has told us through the . . . channels we keep open to them that they have no knowledge of this woman or any of her contacts on that list. I don't know if that's true or not, but I do know that the Yanks are getting a pounding from our Mexican comrades on the Texan front, and our allies are reporting tremendous victories everywhere from Mesopotamia to Siam. Some of these you will have read about in the chronicles, even though much of this news comes in quicker than our scribes can write. That is not a criticism of the post-technological path we have chosen, and anyway most of our people prefer to consider beautiful things, rather than the ugliness the world is still being forced to endure because of the reactionary forces of the Fundamentalist Fossilists. Which brings me to why I've had to interrupt your special day.' She smiled an apology, and Lucy, Ned and John smiled back as she handed them another parchment.

'The Yank spy has also been trafficking in ugliness. We know that there is still a market for this . . . this stuff, despite all we've achieved in the time since the Revolution. That is why you and I are still needed, however regrettable some people, myself included, think that may be. It's ironic in a way that we have successfully post-industrialised, post-technologised and post-bureaucratised, and yet more or less the only part of the state yet to wither away is the part of it required to thwart the ambitions of counter-revolutionaries who would without hesitation imprison us once more in the dungeons of governments and Fossilist Capitalism, along with all the ugliness that's part and parcel of those horrible things. That's why we're here, Lucy, Ned, John.'

Old Christabel stopped speaking for a moment, and they slowly realised that she was crying. Lucy stood up, went over to her, put her arms around her and kissed her gently on the cheek, while Ned and John stroked her beautiful hair and hummed comfortingly at her. Eventually she controlled herself, kissed them all and continued, although still with some difficulty.

'I'm sorry, I'm sorry. But if you knew some of the things . . . But no, that's not for you to worry about, and you've got work to do. He's a dealer. His address is on the parchment. Try and bring him back alive. And you'd better take these with you.'

Lucy, Ned and John left the building through a low arch on its river frontage, leading straight to the jetty sticking into the clear, blue river, where they were helped aboard a barge by one of the Ministry boatmen. The three of them knew better than to discuss their mission with anyone, so they filled their time as they were rowed upriver to Hammersmith watching the bank pass by, spotting salmon and kingfishers, or picking up occasional snatches of continuing May Day revelry above the sound of the splashing oars and the birdsong. Once ashore, however, they ducked into the Dove and, over a pint of scrumpy each, discussed tactics.

The address they were looking for was a short walk from the river, beyond the meadows and market gardens that stretched from beneath the ruins of the Hammersmith Flyover Heroes' Memorial, where getting on for a hundred years before the beginnings of the Uprising were marked by the successful ambush of a joint American–Islamist patrol. The three friends felt a tingle of emotion as they passed under it, and then skirted the crowds still celebrating May Day, despite the approaching dusk and curfew. There was still enough light to make out the row of pretty little cottages where their quarry lay, in the last house of all. There were sounds of loud and happy laughter coming from each dwelling, their rose-hemmed windows lit brightly by the rushlights and candles burning inside, but nonetheless Lucy put her finger to her lips, and when they reached the last house, its windows dark, its interior apparently silent, they all started moving with deliberate and silent slowness, like cats. Lucy very gently lifted the wooden catch on the red painted door and tiptoed into the hall, Ned and John following her and drawing long objects from their smocks in the gloom.

Instead of the noise of revelry, here they heard something else, quite unfamiliar. It sounded like music and speech, but muffled strangely, as if half strangled and overlaid with a strange hissing. And beneath that they could feel rather than hear a very rumbling hum. Lucy gave a thumbs-up sign to her friends and, again with exaggerated slowness and care, lifted the catch to the door from behind which the noises emanated.

At first he didn't even notice them, which was just as well as all three instinctively gagged on the heavy, acrid smell filling the room even before they saw the box, its front glowing with a stuttering white light as tiny figures moved jerkily around inside, or the simple generator next to it and, next to that, the can of illicit petrol.

Lucy motioned Ned to one side of the seated man and John to the other, in order to grab him in the way they'd been trained, when too late she realised his attitude had changed, that she was being reflected in the front of the box against one of the passing patches of grey darkness. She froze, as did Ned and John, while the image in the box kept moving, and the man turned in his seat with surprising speed, pulling out an American-made zap gun.

Before he could fire, John threw his short combat hoe, which caught the man on the wrist and sent the zap gun flying onto the bare wooden floorboards. Lucy and Ned jumped on the man and held him down while they tied him up in thick strips of cowhide. Thus constrained, he was the first to speak.

'So, the Ministry of Beauty's finally caught up with me, eh? You clodhoppers took your time, didn't you?' He was fat, white, clean-shaven and exuded a malevolence they rarely came across. John, who'd specialised in this area, thought he detected a Yank accent, though it may have been French. Lucy took a step forward.

'You'm Fossilist prick. We'm got you fair and square, and we'm gonna stop what you do innit!'

'Really? And what, precisely, do I do, you yokel bitch?

I provide a service of a kind you dippy treehuggers won't and can't. I cater to those people who still remember what art should really be about – about challenging the power and authority, even one as dumb-assed and pitiful as yours! Not everyone wants to weave fucking tapestries, you know!'

The man was now raving at them, so Lucy slapped his face hard while Ned and John started sorting through his treasure trove of contraband. Ned quickly took in the titles on the stack of matchwood video boxes, each containing scuffed plastic American videotapes which were even illegal there, while John rifled through the pile of banned art books on surrealism, abstract expressionism, cubism, conceptualism and post-conceptualism and all the other uglinesses that had almost destroyed the world for ever. The fat man's eyes darted from Ned to John and back to Lucy, and he smiled slowly and vilely.

'You shut it, fatty!' Lucy hissed. 'We'm don't need no shit from you about givin' folks what they wants. That's what Yanks do, and they'm all mad and Godified. We'm gives folks what they need, you fucker, and they don't need you!' Never taking her eyes off him, she bent down and picked up the zap gun. 'So, you'm gonna zap us with this ere Yank shitstick, eh, piggy?'

'Too right I was. And there's more like me, prepared to make a stand for freedom against your filthy regime! And it's not just loonies like you'd like to make out. I got clients, girly, powerful clients you'd never believe. You know Old Barry the so-called Moot Elder? I've dealt him surrealist objets trouvés that'd make your big brown eyes water! I'm just looking through this copy of this movie to check it's kosher for guess who? Lord High-and-Mighty Moot Master, you dumb Paki tart!'

John bridled, despite all the times he'd been told never

to let a suspect try to rattle him with the forbidden words of the old times, and he tensed himself, gripping his retrieved combat hoe behind his back harder, but he let Lucy do the talking.

'Go fuck yerself, you'm Yank-lovin' arsewipe. Spose you'm think you all big and powerful like the Yanks cos when you'm caught you talk hatewords, innit. Like we'm shocked, big boy. You'm call me what you like, fatso, cos we'm got you and we'm gonna get you'm clients you callem. Cos we don't need you'm ugly Fossilist Consumey stuff. We'm free from all that shit now, like we'm free from fighting and exploitation and Godities shit like you'm Yanks love and drove you all crazy cos you had everything and thought you had to kill everyone else to make em like you!' And now seeing a crucifix hanging beside a Nash print on the wall, she pulled it down, spat on it and then ground it beneath her clog.

Ned's eyes passed quickly from Lucy, to John and back to the man, who stared sullenly at the smashed cross on the ground. Behind him John could see old, tattered reproductions of paintings and photographs of bizarre, nightmarish scenes, meaningless, garish patterns or sickening installations that had neither beauty nor meaning, and, thanks to all he'd ever been taught for as long as he'd lived his short, happy life, he began to feel an uncontrollable rage and disgust welling up inside him. The man must have noticed this, because he now turned to Ned and spat.

'What is it, nigger? Don't like anything that challenges your cooned-up utopia? You wait! You wait till the Yanks get back here, you just wait till we get our atom bombs back, till we reconnect with the Internet! Then you'll be . . .'

Lucy slapped him again. 'The Internet? Don't give me

300

you'm babyish fairy tales! You'm . . .' But John wasn't prepared to listen to any more of this, or any more of the old hatewords thrown at his best friends and comrades. He rushed forward with a yell, but not before the man had coughed a throat laser into his mouth and bitten onto the trigger. Lucy saw what was happening, and kicked him backwards in the stomach, but the beam shot from his mouth in a blinding light, instantly dissolving John's arm. And although what happened next happened so quickly it could hardly be seen, it also happened with an intense slowness of motion, of a kind unfamiliar to any of them, apart from the fat man watching his illegal videos, except in dreams just before waking or once a year when they received a pipe full of skunk to celebrate Morris's birthday.

The razor-sharp edge of Ned's combat hoe smashed through the bridge of the prisoner's nose, then swung on as Ned shouted, 'Racy Moddy mumfucker!', and sliced across his popping eyeball, the welling horizontal line of blood bisecting the criminal's eye like a thin cloud passing before a bloodshot harvest moon, and thereafter splashing some old, old Thames & Hudson books on the Bauhaus and Henry Moore, and the fat man slumped with a sigh. On the battered, forbidden TV set, the scratched-up, ancient tape of *Les Enfants du Paradis* continued to play, poisonously.

THE PROMISED PLANET

The Promised Planet

'So what do you think's the worst decision the human race has ever made?'

'What?'

'You know. Was it agriculture? Bipedalism? The adoption by the Roman Empire of Christianity as its official religion? Or what about the joint stock company? Or the Industrial Revolution? Or monotheism? That's a good one. Personally, I think space travel's right up there with the serious, serious mistakes. I mean! Just look around us!'

'Shut up, can't you? We're getting close.'

'You never have an opinion about anything, that's your problem. What's for dinner? I don't mind. What shall we do tonight? What do *you* want to do? It's always up to someone else as far as you're concerned.'

'That's not true.'

'Oh really? Name me one time you've ever expressed your own opinion on anything.'

'I volunteered for tonight's run. Like you.'

'You didn't volunteer. You're no more capable of independent thought than these fucking rocks! You just did it to get on the right side of the committee.'

'So what about you?'

'Oh, I *like* it out here. Gives one a chance to get to know one's workmates, doesn't it? A nice opportunity to chew the fat, talk over old times, discuss higher things. So, what was the human race's worst decision?'

'You.'

'That's nice. Come on, be serious.'

'I don't know. It doesn't make any difference anyway what I think. What any of us think.'

'Doesn't it? Doesn't it really? So what about nationalism? That's a nice abstract subject. Give us your thoughts on that.'

'Will you just shut up. We're nearly at the . . .'

'Quick! Get down!'

'Fuck me, that was close. I hate it when they do that. You all right?'

'Yeah. Fine. Er, thanks.'

'Think nothing of it. You should really keep on your toes, though. If I hadn't been here you'd have been toast. You should concentrate more. Perhaps the oxygen levels in your suit are playing up. Do you want me to have a look?'

'No, I'm fine. Let's get on.'

'Okay. Hey, mind yourself with that probe, you could have had my eye out if I wasn't wearing this helmet. Oh look, the second moon's rising. Hey, do you think they actually *enjoy* doing that?'

'Doing what?'

'What do you think doing what? What that one just did.'

'Enjoy? I shouldn't think so. We don't know enough about them to know what they think. Or even if they think.'

'You reckon? I suppose you may be right. Although I think there's more to them than we like to imagine. You see that herd over there in the distance. No, over there, beyond the geyser. For God's sake, take my viewfinder. That's right, there.'

'What about them?'

'Well, look at them. They're not doing anything, are

they? But only as far as we know. They might be up to all sorts of things.'

'Like trying to kill us, as usual.'

'Or *not* trying to kill us. Have you considered that? Maybe they're trying to *communicate* with us.'

'What? Like that? Funny way of saying hello.'

'It's just a for instance. My point is that ever since we arrived we've never even tried to find anything out about them. Just built the settlement and tried to keep them out.'

'But they're just animals. Aliens. Whatever. There's nothing to find out.'

'Isn't there? What if they're smarter than we think? Or more sensitive, or artistic?'

'Artistic? What are you talking about?'

'It's just another example. We never bothered to find out. As far as they're concerned we just came out of the blue and built this fence in the middle of their grazing lands . . .'

'Grazing? There's nothing to graze.'

'Who knows? We don't even know what they eat. They don't eat *us*. They might be territorial. This track to the solar enclave, it might be their migratory path, you know? As I said, we just don't know.'

'You talk too much.'

'That's another thing. Can they talk? That noise they always make before they explode . . .'

'Trying to kill us . . .'

'Whatever. How do we know that isn't language? Eh?'

'Don't be stupid. We know they're just animals. If that. One of the scientific workers . . .'

'Oh, science is it now? That was another fundamental error.'

'What? Why?'

'Now you're trying to change the subject again! The

fact remains that they were here first, and we've stolen their planet. Or part of it, anyway.'

'Rubbish. This is our place. This is where we belong. This is the promised planet. Even you know that.'

'Oh yes. The promised planet. Not very promising, is it?'

'That doesn't matter.'

'Doesn't it?'

'Of course not. You've seen the computer models. Everyone has. And this is the place we've been searching for for all these centuries. So it doesn't matter what was here before. We were, ultimately, and this is where we'll stay.'

'Very eloquent, I'm sure. So tell me, who promised us this shithole?'

'Oh, come on.'

'No, I've forgotten in all the excitement of trying to survive from one day to the next in this poisonous dump, where we can't breathe the atmosphere, can't grow anything in the toxic soil, rely entirely for sustenance on incredibly complicated processes converting the meagre stellar power from that stinking purple star we're orbiting, so I'm just wondering what kind of joker promises his chosen people such a fucking awful home.'

'He did. You know that.'

'Oh yes. Him. I remember him. I remember when we finally met him eighteen planets back and he'd forgotten who we were.'

'He was old.'

'He was senile, more like. You know, I wanted to ask him, Why choose us? Why not choose some other poor bastards instead? It must have occurred to you, even to you.'

'Never. It's our destiny.'

'Oh yeah. Destiny. That's one of those great words,

isn't it? Answers all questions with a great big fuck-off. Like homeland. What do we need a homeland for? Why can't we be satisfied with a home?'

'Because it's not safe. We've seen that throughout our history. We're never safe except when we have our own place.'

'But we're not safe here! No one's ever *safe*. For fuck's sake! We had Alpha Centauri, Tau Ceti 5, Betelgeuse 7, and apparently we weren't safe on any of them. And before that, back on Terra, we had New York! We had Dublin!'

'Yes, and we also had Berlin and Budapest and Vienna, and were we safe there? You know we weren't.'

'That was first time round. Things change. Things changed, after Israel. And what about Israel? We were meant to be safe there, except we were never safe, and the only safety we could guarantee came courtesy of the Yank Fossilists whose antics sank the fucking place! They never thought about that, did they? We were quite happy to take their weapons and fight their oil wars, but didn't think about the thirty-metre rise in sea level that came along with their bloody oil.'

'I know. That's why we finally went off planet, after the revelation.'

'Oh yeah. The revelation. Brilliant.'

'Look, what's your problem?'

'What's my problem? What's my problem? Can't you *see* what my problem is? My problem is having to wear a radiation anti-pressure grav-suit every time I want to go out for a smoke, having to walk miles every day through a dark, dangerous wilderness, in constant danger of being blown up by those things out there, to collect that foul gunk which is the only thing that stops us all starving to death, and the rest of the time having to breathe your recycled farts and drink your third-hand piss, under a stinking dome under constant threat of implosion because this planet is basically fucking uninhabitable, that's what my problem is.'

'Your type just complains about everything.'

'Listen. We had everything. We're good-looking, we're funny, we're clever, we had jokes, we had *cooking*. Remember cooking? Of course not, because you can't cook that shit here, and all because . . .'

But as she spoke she saw her begin to change shape, and only just managed to pull out her blaster before she was on her. She staggered back from the crater created by the grav-suit's explosion, badly shaken. She'd never guessed she'd be a Medusian shape-shifting thought-parasite too, like so many of the others. She pressed a button on the chest of her suit, and breathed deeply inside her helmet as the endorphin dose surged through her biosystem, and then trudged on, carefully keeping to the middle of the track and as far from the parallel vulcanite fences as she could, while the cyanide winds blew unceasingly across the rocky purple plain and in the distance large, explosive, pangolin-like creatures shifted around despondently.

Squid

Obviously Crespolini shared many of Lucy's genes, and also some of Colin's, Stephens's, Cynthia's, Stalin's and Seumas's, as well as his Italian namesake's. He shared few of their defining qualities, however, apart from eye-coloration from one ancestor, or length of nose from another. It didn't detain him, and nor did his forebears' obsessions, with art, politics, religion, love or death. Apart, that is, from love, and across the interstellar darkness he sensed the subsonic chirrupings of his girlfriend, whose name could be translated as Lucy if we had the power to do such things, and with a flick of his tentacles and a muscular spasm evacuating his body sac, he propelled himself through the emptiness of space towards the object of his love, ceaselessly but consciously calculating his modulating density in base thirty-five.

Eternity

Trotsky'd said he was going on ahead to check with the caterers, leaving Stalin alone and naked on the platform. Well, not exactly alone. Although this place was, to all intents and purposes, the small branch-line provincial Russian railway station he'd always secretly imagined Heaven to be like, it teemed with a multitude of countless billions of souls, while at the same time, thanks to their ethereal insubstantiality, being practically empty. Stalin looked down the line in both directions as the tracks tapered away into the perspective void, wondering what he was meant to do now.

A short distance away, a figure dressed in the braided uniform of a Tsarist railway official was leaning against a sign, written in French, announcing that it was forbidden to remain for any length of time next to the sign. It was also reading a newspaper whose pages were completely blank. Stalin approached the figure, but before he could say anything it put a bony finger to its scarlet lips and wordlessly pointed down the platform to another figure, identically dressed, leaning against an identical sign and reading an identically blank paper.

Stalin snarled to himself, turned to go down the platform, but found his way blocked by the composer Prokofiev, who'd predeceased him by an hour.

'Well, that's made my day, it really has,' Prokofiev said. 'I was feeling quite depressed until I saw it was you.'

Stalin glowered at him. 'Can I help you, um . . .'

'No, no, not at all. I was just saying hello, you ignorant piece of Georgian shit. Well, see you around!'

'Not if I see you first,' Stalin muttered under whatever he now had instead of breath as Prokofiev drifted away down the platform. And then he thought, 'Who's in charge here? I can't be expected to just hang around all day like this!'

And just as he was thinking this another uniformed figure tapped him on the shoulder, put its finger to its lips and pointed down the platform, where another figure repeated the performance, as did another, and yet another, until, having walked what seemed like miles for what must have been most of the morning, he found himself back where he started, which he recognised because it was next to the ticket office. He rolled his eyes in frustration, when a smaller creature, not unlike a lemur in appearance and dressed as a porter, pulled at his arm and gestured towards some iron gates which opened to reveal an ancient, tiny elevator. A short demon, dressed as a bellhop, looked up at him.

'Josif Vissarionovich! All right, then? Hop in, we're off!' Before Stalin knew it, he was crammed inside the lift, his nose pressed up against the now closed iron gates, with the demon standing just beside him and hundreds of thousands of other spirits pressed up behind him. 'All aboard for the skylark!' the demon bellowed, and pulled a rusty lever which screeched the lift's descent.

Stalin tried to elbow his way back a fraction to get his nose away from the hard metal, and succeeded enough (although the impalpability of ectoplasm proved to be exasperatingly palpable) to be able to turn his head a fraction. He peered narrowly over his pockmarked shoulder at the other occupants of the lift closest to him. Many, he knew, must have been his own victims, and

314

he chuckled at the thought that they turned out to have been guilty after all. Right behind him, slouching, stood a morose-looking child-murderer who'd been picked up for sabotaging a jam factory and had been beaten to death by his fellow inmates somewhere in Siberia last night. He looked up and half smiled.

'Nice to meet you,' he mumbled, then looked back at the floor. Next to him an SS officer who'd just died of malaria in Paraguay nodded at Stalin, and behind him a minor commissar, gone before due to a combination of emphysema and grief on hearing the news of Stalin's own demise, rather forwardly winked at the personage who'd inspired him to be quite so zealous and callous. And behind him stood rank upon rank of sinners, all of whom looked just plain bored, as if they couldn't care less. Stalin turned back to the iron gate, grinding his teeth.

Something wasn't right here. It was beyond all doubt where they were heading, which was to eternal torment. Trotsky had already told him that, but none of the rest of them seemed in the slightest bit bothered. Why weren't they howling in anguish? Screaming in terror? Tearing their hair? Gnashing their fucking teeth, for Christ's sake?

'You are,' the demon observed with a grin. Stalin ignored him, but also made an effort to stop grinding and pushed his face further into the wall and out of sight.

Somewhere behind him an American industrialist cleared his throat and apologised to a Peruvian Monsignor whose foot he'd trodden on. Further back an alcoholic Inuit woman sneezed, spraying a thin aerosol of snot over a Malayan gangster, a Norwegian collaborator, a Swiss banker, a German carpenter, an Algerian civil servant, a Nigerian masseuse, a Welsh farmer, an

Israeli greengrocer, an Uzbeki shepherdess, a Japanese hydrologist, a Canadian herbalist, five French hairdressers, an Ethiopian poet and thousands of others. She apologised curtly, and several hundred of them forgave her in subdued tones. Stalin rolled his eyes in growing disbelief.

What the fuck was the matter with these people? They didn't even seem to be possessed of despairing resignation, and his eyes widened as the implications of his observations began to sink in. No, that couldn't be right. They just don't realise what they're all in for, that's all. Yes, that must be it. Ignorant bastards, Stalin thought with a relieved smile.

'Oh no, mate,' the demon drawled. 'They know all right. The only tosser round 'ere 'oo 'asn't sussed it is you, yer dozy cunt.'

'Shut up,' Stalin snapped tetchily, although this did nothing to put his mind at rest.

The lift continued its descent, occasionally jerking as it gathered speed, while inside the stale air was growing perceptibly warmer. Stalin glanced quickly over his shoulder again at the legions of the indifferent. This was all wrong! Unless . . . Unless he'd got it wrong, unless he'd made a terrible, unbelievable blunder. Unbidden, his own bons mots flashed through his mind. *Eliminate the individual, eliminate the problem. One death is a tragedy; a million deaths is merely a statistic.* He squeezed his eyes tight shut to drive these unhelpful thoughts into internal exile, but it didn't help. Of course he'd made it sound as if the deaths didn't matter, to appear to be just part of an inexorable, amoral murdering machine, but surely they'd all guessed that that was just part of the act? The fact that their lives didn't seem to matter made it all the more terrifying and terrible. Terror. That's what he wanted them to feel, and most of all terror at their own inconsequentiality in the face of the grinding, unstoppable mechanics of History. So of course every single death had mattered enormously, because they'd had it coming and it was what they'd deserved. Revolutions aren't about *power*, they're about *revenge*. All those patronising intellectual ponces in the Party, all those petty fucking peasants squirrelling away a few specks of grain just for themselves, all those stupid soldiers and workers and kulaks and artists and all the fucking rest of them. They obviously had to pay, because it was their fault. It was all their fault. All of it. Who else's could it be? That was obvious, and if they weren't punished, they'd never learn not to behave like that again. That was how he'd engineered men's souls. But the point wasn't just to punish them by terrorising them with the knowledge of their imminent deaths or those of their families or friends. *The point was to make them pay for ever.* He now knew that death is merely the business of an instant, and apart from a certain mawkishness that might result from separation from people you might like, was no big deal. It was what came next which really made the difference, and which he'd always been certain was going to be eternal torment for all those evil bastards who'd been complicit in making life so awful in the first place. But, from what he was seeing now, it seemed he'd been misinformed.

The lift rattled on down to Hell, and from the corner of his eye Stalin noticed a Nazi architect of the Holocaust, who'd been acquitted at Nuremberg and gone on to become a filing clerk in a pencil factory, stifle a yawn. By pure coincidence next to him stood the former British interrogating officer who'd fixed his evidence in return for certain favours defined as such by his political masters in Whitehall, one of whom, equally coincidentally, stood close by picking his teeth. They'd both been

317

killed in automobile accidents at almost exactly the same time, although far apart. Both looked half asleep. And now Stalin found he could look into the souls of everyone there, as could all of them, and see all their crimes and cruelties and callousness and murderous expedience masquerading as principle, and no one seemed to care except him.

'Gruesome, isn't it?' cackled the demon at his side. 'Got it yet?'

Stalin ignored the imp. His mind was now working fast. This wouldn't do, it wouldn't do at all. But he saw a way. He'd done it before, and he could do it again. As soon as they reached Hell he'd find out who was in charge, and ingratiate himself the way he'd done before. No, not ingratiate precisely, but make himself useful in certain ways, until he became invaluable, and then, after he'd bided his time, he'd make his move, just like before, and he'd be top dog after he'd got the rest of them out of the way. Then he could sort things out once and for all, no questions asked. They wouldn't know what'd hit them, all those complacent damned in Hell, but they'd find out, just like they would in Heaven after his victorious war against God, *when he brought them all back to life*. Yes. Yes! An eternity of living torment back on Earth, with no hope of salvation or damnation through death, just being alive and human for ever! That would teach them, teach them all! Stalin grinned manically to himself, his eyes darting around to see if anyone was watching, but if they were no one was interested. Then the lift started slowing down in its descent.

Inside it was now almost unbearably hot, although only Stalin was sweating by this stage. The iron gate in front of him was glowing red, and he thought he could hear something below, and suddenly remembered what Trotsky had said about a trial. Or was it a party? The noises grew louder, the sounds of shouting and laughter and breaking glass, and then he started to recognise individual voices. Shit! Trotsky'd said they were all waiting for him, all those Bolshevik bastards he'd got rid of. He tried to get a grip on himself. He'd dealt with them before, and he'd do it again, but now he could hear them singing, and wasn't that Gorky's voice, flat and out of tune as usual? And Yhezhov's, and Yagoda's, and Kalinin's, and Rykov's, and . . . shit, he was certain that was Vladimir Ilyich's. No. No. He had to stay cool. He could deal with this. He could deal with this like he'd done before. He'd sort it out, get his way, deal with them, deal with it all.

Then the lift juddered to a halt, and the glowing gates clanked open to reveal a dark, desolate subterranean cavern, with no sign of anyone there except, squatting naked on a low pile of clinker, Adolf Hitler stroking Stephens the dog.

Stalin spun round, but the lift was now completely empty of anyone except the smirking demon who touched his fiery, rimless cap and curtsied. Confused, Stalin stepped gingerly into Hell.

Hitler looked up.

'Hey, Joe,' the Nazi drawled lifelessly, sounding infinitely bored and depressed. 'If I'd known you were coming I'd have baked you a cake.'

Purgatoria

Back in Limbo Prokofiev was bored too, but not that depressed. Everyone was bored, but it wasn't so bad, and there were occasional excitements. They'd all enjoyed it when Kennedy turned up, his head empty and open at the back, and then proceeded to spend the next few years of eternity sodomising every GI who arrived following a premature death in Vietnam. But after a while that got boring too, and mostly the accumulating dead drifted around, engaging in idle gossip or telling stories or reading the blank newspapers or falling in love or eating ambrosia and getting pissed on nectar. Yes, it was boring, but it wasn't so bad, all in all. Although Professor Sykes-Wolsey never, ever stopped sighing.

Inferno

And deep, deep down in Hell Stalin held his head in his hands, weeping uncontrollably. They were all sat in a circle in one of the deepest pits, and Lucy stroked the back of Stalin's head to comfort him. On all sides tyrants, despots, mass murderers, dictators, genocidalists, ideologues, racists, kings, prime ministers, priests, strategists, conquistadors, capitalists, commissars, popes, rapists, agronomists, scientists, mineralogists, film moguls, thoughtless waiters, teachers, generals, professors, bureaucrats, publishers, industrialists, editors, typists, artists, actors, emperors and tribal elders tutted their sympathy. Even some of the attending demons looked sniffy. Then Lucy tapped her vulcanite pencil against her clipboard with just the tiniest hint of impatience, and stroked a serpentine wisp of hair from her low forehead before speaking.

'Yes, yes, Joe, we all share your pain. Now come on . . .'

And Trubshawe, damned to eternity as a dog, howled to high and empty Heaven.

Provenance and Acknowledgements

What you've just read now reads, I hope, as if it has a deliberate if flimsy narrative cohesion. It was, however, written over a period of three decades. First versions of 'The Apotheosis of Saint Lucy', 'New Mexico' and 'The Dilemma of Don Juan de Escalante' were written, rather precociously, when I was at school; I wrote 'The Last Train from Madrid' eking out a single bottle of Imperial Eagle lager while waiting seven hours for a train in a bar in Barcelona station in 1978; 'Joe' and a very early version of 'Sod' were written when I was at university, the latter inspired by an incident when I was walking down King's Parade one day and felt a coin slithering down the inside of my trouser leg, and for some reason or other I immediately assumed that I'd started sweating money. That version was originally published in *Aaaargh*, a self-financed student rag, in 1981. Rather shamefully, the central thesis of 'Ape' formed one of my answers in Part I of the Cambridge English tripos, with inevitable results. After that, I stuck to drawing cartoons and gave up on the fiction, except for a few occasions in the mid-eighties when I was invited by the authors Christopher Priest and Lisa Tuttle to their annual Halloween party, where each guest was enjoined to bring along a scary story. Naturally, all the professional writers never bothered, while the gushing amateurs spent weeks drafting and redrafting. That's where 'Family' and 'Best Friends' first saw the light of day.

Then I gave up fiction completely until a couple of years ago, when ideas started coming into my head which, all in all, would never find elbow room in a cartoon. Thus this book, where I've dredged up stuff from long ago and cobbled it together with some new stories and, in two cases, transliterated previously published material. 'Men of Steel' originally appeared in cartoon form in the *Guardian* in 1992, and 'Joe's Last Dreams', or most of it, was first published in the 'As I Please' column in *Tribune*. My thanks to both those papers for continuing to grant me a berth in my day job.

Thanks are also due to the following, in no particular order: my late parents, for everything; my old English teachers, John Steane and Andrew Wilson, for early encouragement; Chris Priest, Lisa Tuttle and Caradoc King, for ditto; my dear friend, the late Giles Gordon, that prince of agents, who had faith in this book; Francis Wheen for fixing me up with David Miller, my new agent, and Miller for flogging with such despatch what I thought was unfloggable; Dan Franklin at Jonathan Cape for having the grace and insight to have it flogged to him; Anne Beech, Rab MacWilliam and Nick Webb for helping me on my way, and likewise Sean Magee, Jonathan Meades and Will Self; the late Dr Robert Buttimore; Charlie Adley; the late Jon Lewin; Philip Saunders; Mark Seddon, Joan Smith, Kevin Maguire, Peter Oborne and Bob Marshall-Andrews QC, for providing some thinly disguised characters; all the other real people either named or unnamed depicted herein, for being such deserving targets; Joyce Bridgeman, who continues to save me from penury by sending out the invoices; Colm Tóibín and Antony Farrell, for services to inspiration; Michael Foot and the late Jill Craigie, for more general inspiration; and finally, inevitably and eternally, thanks to my wife Anna and our children, Fred and Rose, who admitted to liking *bits* of this book, which is as much as anyone can decently hope for.

Martin Rowson
Lewisham, spring 2005